In the image of Man, copyright Mark Long, 2018

First edition, November 2018.

Published by Orchid Imprint. www.orchidimprint.com

For permission requests, please contact PermissionsRequest@orchidimprint.com.

For more information about this book, please see www.InTheImageOfMan.com

For more information about the author, please see www.MarkLongAuthor.co.uk

The characters in this book are fictional and are not intended to represent any real-world person. Where there are real people in any job described, the depictions are not intended to represent the real-world individual. Any supernatural beings depicted may or not exist and are invited to contact the author.

Orchid Imprint

ISBN: 978-1-9993044-09

Chapter 1

The asteroid tumbled in space, end over end and twisting on its axis. Microwave pulses bounced off, reflecting from the complex angles of the surface as it neared the planet. The pulses came from a trio of missiles curving up from the Earth to meet it. The asteroid was accelerating, its path curving as the gravity of the blue green world distorted space. The missiles were angled to meet the mass of rock. The 56,000 ton mass gained velocity with every second that passed and each metre as it fell towards the planet.

One of the nuclear tipped rockets pulled slightly ahead of the others as the gap between the makeshift weapons and the tumbling rock narrowed. There was a blinding flash, soundless in the vacuum of space.

The billions below gasped a breath and held it as their TV screens went dark.

Chapter 2

Six months earlier.

It was a rainy night, not a good time to be standing in a lay-by on the A34 trying to hitch a ride. Jason cursed himself for asking to be let out here but the driver of the Volvo had been singing along to Radio Two and you had to draw the line somewhere. Also, driving gloves. In Jason's opinion, you could tell a lot about a man that wore driving gloves. After the festival, it was too much even in exchange for a ride and he left while he still remembered what proper music sounded like.

He pulled his windbreaker hood forward to cover more of his face and stuck his thumb out again. He fumbled to light his last joint one handed, the wind and rain making it nearly impossible.

The driver of the truck saw the hitchhiker in the high beams of the truck ahead and thought that he looked like a half-drowned puppy. You always saw them at festival time. He certainly had nothing against hippies. He had been one, back in the day and still had a soft spot for them. He had thumbed his way back from a happening more than once back in the innocence of youth and he knew how it felt to be passed by every damn car. He wasn't supposed to have passengers but sod it. The system couldn't be smashed but sometimes you had to stick it to the man. He indicated left and hit the brakes. It was going to be a bit tight but he could help.

There was a slick of diesel and water over the right side of the road and the trailer slewed to the left. The driver tried to compensate but the load of washing machines weighed more than the cab and by the time the correction took effect, the road surface had changed. The load went sideways, half on the road and half into the lay-by, grass whipping at the underside.

Jason looked at the side of the truck coming at him without understanding, his mind frozen with the suddenness of it. The spray of water coming from the tires, the dirty red of the sides, the oddly cheerful Rupert the Bear crucified on the front, the metal bar that was suddenly in his face. Time slowed in his last moments and his mind flashed back the few years to his childhood and his own toy bear. He never had trusted that smug bastard.

His head snapped back, his spinal cord severed. He flew back, hitting the concrete barrier solidly. Jason died without ever realising that he was hurt, his last emotion being surprise, the scrawled graffiti telling him to "PEACE OUT!" unseen. He would have appreciated it had he known. The lorry jack-knifed to a stop, the cab and truck mirroring him, both necks broken.

It was an end. It was also a beginning.

Three days later, the sun was shining and the road dry. The marks of tyres were a scribble on the road surface and the mud was still raw where it had been churned up. Jason's father, mother and sister stood near the spot where he had died and wept quietly. Tears fell from the faces of the family and made dark spots on the scuffed ground. It seemed such an ordinary place, too ordinary for something so awful to have happened.

Jason's family put together a makeshift shrine out of ribbons, CDs of his favourite bands, a graduation photo and an old (and distinctly not Rupert-like) teddy bear. It wasn't much to mark a life but they wanted to believe that it made a difference. It was an undirected belief, unaddressed to any god. It stayed with the shrine. Something, a nameless thing watched, at first without understanding or awareness. It was still watching long after the tears had dried from the road.

Chapter 3

The spirit floated nameless and unaware. It was not the spirit of Jason. That had gone to wherever such spirits go. This was an older thing, a being that had come into existence with the atoms of the world. It had been at the heart of stars, in vast dust clouds and now by a roadside. It had experienced such things but not known them because it had been without thought. It felt the pull of the belief pooled around the relics of a life lost too soon and it was drawn to it. It drank of the belief and became aware of itself. It drank a little more and became aware of its surroundings.

People went by in cars, trucks and sometimes motorcycles, all moving too fast for the spirit to understand them except as things that believed. Some of the minds were sharp but most were dull, idling while their hands guided their vehicle. The spirit slowly feasted on the belief, gaining sentience and ability as it depleted the pool. It became aware of its hunger and its limits. It needed belief if it was to remain itself and not return to being one the countless billions of spirits that existed without knowing. It would need belief and those things in the cars had some. The spirit rationed itself, taking no more from the pool than it needed. There was very little left by this point.

Mr Ray Charles was a vending machine repair man. He was aware of the famous Ray Charles and considered the coincidence of names to be one of the few interesting things about himself. He would often introduce himself as "Ray Charles, no relation," but it increasingly got him baffled looks as younger people tended not to be familiar with the American soul singing legend. He was driving along with Radio Four droning on in the background when the car started juddering. It was a rather battered silver Vauxhall Cavalier that the company supplied so that he could ensure that the supply of chocolate bars, crisps and slightly tired sandwiches could continue to be vended at ludicrous prices to people with no time to get better food. Mr Charles sighed and pulled into the lay-by, his tire bumping and flapping as he did so. A stray bolt from a truck had gone through the tread.

Mr Charles did what any practical man would. He swore and got out of the car to look at the tires. The front nearside would never be the same again. Being a prudent pipe-smoking kind of fellow, he carried a spare tyre, a jack, one of those odd spanners and a warning triangle in the boot of the car. He also carried tools and spare parts for vending machines, but that need not concern us here. The triangle was set up and the tools and spare tyre methodically brought to the appropriate place on the car. Mr Charles liked things to be done properly.

It was the swearing that brought the spirit to the scene. These things have power in the world of spirits. Hatred of a god is as much a belief as a prayer and while Mr Charles' curse was a very minor one (Mrs. Charles having strong views on immoderate language), it was better than nothing to a hungry spirit. He watched as Mr Charles took off his jacket, retucked his shirt, pulled off the hubcap and loosened the bolts of the wheel. He watched again as the car was lifted on the jack and the wheel removed. All of this was utterly new to the spirit but he was an attentive audience. Mr Charles was a sensible man so he put the four bolts from the wheel in the dish of the hubcap so that they wouldn't get lost. It was a fine and sensible plan right up until the moment where he stepped on it catapulting the bolts into the long grass by the side of the road. Another curse arrived as a bonus.

The spirit watched all this with fascination but with limited understanding. The process of changing the tyre was as new an experience as the proximity to a person. The mind of Mr Ray Charles shaped the spirit in new ways, its nature as malleable as fresh clay. If Mr Charles had been a different person, subsequent events would have gone in a very different direction, but Ray was a fundamentally decent person and the hungry spirit was fed well.

Mr Charles scrabbled in the grass, the sun gleaming off his bald spot, carefully trying to avoid grass stains on his blue suit, and managed to find three of the bolts fairly quickly but the fourth was more elusive. Time was ticking on and Mr Charles had a schedule to keep. "Oh for God's sake, where is the damned thing?" he cried. That was close to a prayer and the difference between a god and a spirit is only one of belief.

The spirit exulted for a moment because he had never had anyone ask anything of him before. The feeling was one of authority and importance. Clearly, the spirit needed to answer this prayer. Burning bushes were not an option as they would have taken far more power than he had. Besides, there was only scrubby (and slightly damp) grass on the side of the road. Displays of lightning would have been even harder and creating a new wheel bolt out of raw belief was out of the question. Damnation of the bolt was relatively easy, but he wasn't going to get any belief out of that and it was also pointless since there was no soul in the steel. The best that he could do was to reveal the location of the hidden bolt. Drawing the last of the power from the shrine, he created his first miracle, bending two blades of grass a tiny distance, rather less than a centimetre. It wasn't much but it let the sun through to glint on the oily metal. Once, twice, and then Mr Charles saw the little flicker of light. He scooped up the bolt with a triumphant cry of "And Bob's your Uncle!" The nameless spirit became known as Bob, even if only to himself.

Fresh, directed belief is very different to belief that is left hanging around to be claimed. It was intoxicating and powerful. At once, Bob decided that he would go with his worshipper and hope that he would get some more belief as he went along. The pool of belief was empty now and there was nothing here for him. Bob was gaining in intelligence as he grew in power and it seemed reasonable that there would be more belief where there were more people. He was also truly grateful in his way to Mr Charles. It wasn't every day that you got a first believer.

Bob had experienced a lot of the world but he couldn't be said to remember it because memory implies understanding and thought. Until he happened upon the roadside shrine, Bob had been nameless and thoughtless. If he recalled sensations then he could now make some sense out of them but the world seemed a new and strange place. He followed his believer into workplaces and campuses and saw many people. Of course, the people ignored Bob because they couldn't see him but also because they pretty much ignored Mr Charles. Bob wondered if people needed to be believed in as well. If so, his believer was out of luck. The only people who ever paid much attention to Mr Charles were a voice on the phone called Tracy and Mr Charles' wife, Anne. Neither of those could really be said to believe in him (beyond the obvious fact of his existence) even if they talked to him.

Naturally, Bob followed Mr Charles home and came to learn a little about the people around him. Anne believed a great deal, much of it about television, but she also believed in another god with an intensity that made Bob quite jealous. She would sometimes read a book about her god and tell Mr Charles that he should do a particular thing or not do another thing. Mr Charles would just smile and change the subject but this worried Bob. Why should some other god have his believer?

Bob was pretty hungry when he found the second person to believe in him. He had followed Mr Charles to an office in Slough. People worked in little cubicles with low walls and most of them looked much the same – both the people and the desks. There was one that stood out because of the amount of clutter. There were shamrocks, tiny plastic trolls with vibrantly bright nylon hair and even a rabbit's foot dyed green. There was a computer buried in there as well, the grey plastic unchanged by the brightness around it.

Because Bob was curious, he had watched and learned from a lot of what Mr Charles did and tried to help him with a few more small miracles. These didn't seem to work as well as the first one with the bolts. He knew that Mr Charles was supposed to fix the machines and it was a simple enough thing to separate two bits of a stuck mechanism, but rather than making Mr Charles happier, it seemed to cause problems and frustration. It was quite a while before Bob understood that the machines were not supposed to work before Mr Charles had a chance to fix them. Bob now knew more about vending machines than any god in the universe. Anne had said that her god was all knowing and all seeing but that seemed like bragging to Bob. Bob had become, in a very small way, the god of vending machine repair. It didn't look as if there was much future for a god in a field that no-one was much interested in especially with only one believer who wasn't all that pious. Bob could exist with a single believer but it was a starvation diet. If he lost Mr Charles, he would stop being.

Bob was mulling this over when the person who worked at the desk adorned with troll dolls and animal parts came back from lunch. It was a woman in her early thirties with pale skin and reddish hair. She sat in front of the desk and her shoulders slumped. She looked worried and that was of interest to Bob. He knew in a general kind of way that worried people prayed more. Considering the situation some more, Bob realised that all the offices that they visited had a lot of computers and not many vending machines. It could be a step in the right direction to become the god of computers. They were mechanisms and Bob understood the vending machines pretty well now. He reasoned that it couldn't be that hard. He would still visit his first believer of course, but it was only natural for a god to have many worshippers. Distance didn't mean anything to Bob so he could go back any time that he wanted, and he decided that he would spend some time with this human as well. Perhaps the animal parts were for a sacrifice.

At first, Bob just watched and listened. He learned quickly and couldn't forget things. Words began to make more sense to him; Mr Charles didn't speak much when working because he was normally alone and he rarely spoke when he was at home. In part, this was because his wife was speaking but it was often because the television was on and one of Anne's beliefs was that no-one should speak at these times. This didn't help Bob since there was no mind behind the words. As a result, Bob hadn't had a great deal of meaningful speech to listen to, but here everyone talked all the time. Everything that the people in this place did seemed to revolve around the computers or the phones. That was how he learned the name of the woman who worked there; she told an angry customer that her name was Mary Callahan and Bob realised that this was why those same words were on a plastic sign attached to the cubicle wall and the plastic card hanging around her neck. A little practice had taught him the relationship between sounds and written words although the spelling often made very little sense.

It took a little while to work out what was going on in the office but it clearly had something to do with people being paid for having had an accident. Bob decided to look into the computer a little more deeply. At first, he was completely lost but there were clues here and there. Electricity was very different to the sort of power that he had but he could sense it all the same. It was flying around at tremendous speed in all directions inside the computer. Some of it was moving in a regular pattern and other signals flashed by in different shapes all the time. If he concentrated, he could make out numbers (well, highs and lows) on the wires but they didn't seem to mean anything. Bob didn't speak English, of course. He didn't even know what language was until he had been awakened. What he could do was understand the thoughts of worshippers (or more often, potential worshippers) and that gave meaning to the sounds. The computers didn't seem to have any thoughts at all but they seemed important. People in the office spent all day attending to them, typing on them, reading them and sometimes swearing at them. Anything that mattered to people was potentially a source of vital belief so he wanted to understand. He tried looking into Mary's mind but a person's mind is a rather hazy thing unless they are deliberately thinking about the thing that you want to know about. When she spoke, he could find the meaning but there was a haze of thoughts in the background.

Bob decided to go with personal experience. He had learned about vending machines from a vending machine repairman. Perhaps he could learn about computers from a computer repairman. Unless computers were a lot more reliable than vending machines, there had to be one somewhere in the building. He left Mary for a while and went looking around. It was interesting in a way and he managed to snack on some really heartfelt cursing coming from a younger man some distance down the hall. As Bob listened, he realised that the man was angry because his computer wasn't working. That was perfect as he would be bound to call a repairman. Bob would have thanked his lucky stars except that, as a budding god, a godling if you will, he didn't believe in anything like that. He was a little disappointed that the repairman wouldn't be there until the next day but at least he got a little more cursing to keep him going. It was at about this time that Mr Charles left to go on to his next job. Bob kept him in the back of his mind.

Since there was nothing to do but wait, Bob went back to watching Mary. She filled in forms and answered the short letters that he had heard the others call Email. Most of them seemed to be about very unimportant things but at least he could understand them more or less. After a while, people started to leave the office and Bob followed Mary when she went out to the car park. Her car was a lot like the place where she worked, in that there was clutter everywhere. There was a cross and a star and a little gold medallion hanging from the mirror and Bob became even more sure that Mary wanted to believe in something. Even the most minor godling can recognise religious symbols even if they don't recognise the god that they belong to.

When Mary got home, she fed her cat. Bob didn't much care about animals as they didn't believe except in the vaguest possible way and that belief, especially with cats, is mainly in themselves. The way that the cat behaved made him think that it believed that it was at least a little divine. Mary called the cat Bast and that was a word that jogged a memory in Bob. It had been a hot, sandy place and there had been many gods and many worshippers. None of them had worshipped Bob, of course. There was little to remember as none of it had made any sense at the time. After Mary fed the cat, she turned on the television and watched a program called Eastenders. Bob had never seen a mind so focussed on a television programme before, not even when Anne had been watching Antiques Roadshow. If only he could get Mary to believe in him with the same intensity, he would be much less hungry.

As soon as the program finished, Mary suddenly started rushing around the flat, trying to do two or three things at once. She was making a meal and straightening cushions as if her very life depended on it. Her thoughts were hard to make out because she didn't think about one thing for more than a moment before rushing on to something else. When the meal was in the oven, she rushed to the bathroom and had quite a leisurely bath. As soon as she was out of the bath, she started rushing around again. This time, her thoughts were easier to read, in part because Bob was learning how her mind worked. She was expecting a visit from her boyfriend, Max.

When Max arrived, Bob got a bad feeling about him. It wasn't jealousy because Bob had no interest in the physical aspects of Mary, but what Max thought and what Max said were very different. This was a new experience for Bob since Mr Charles was essentially a fairly simple man. All the while that he was talking to Mary, his mind kept darting back to an image of another girl. Bob knew that it was the duty of a god to protect his worshippers; that was part of the deal. He just didn't have any clear idea of how to protect Mary against something like this. He didn't know for sure but he didn't think that Mary wanted to share Max in the way that she did. Bob watched them eat and talk as he thought about his responsibilities and whether there was any way that he could carry them out. He couldn't make the rains fall or, at best, not more than a handful of drops and he certainly couldn't stop an earthquake. He was, after all, still just a minor spirit with a hunger to be more. He watched them as they went into the bedroom and undressed. They mated and that all seemed quite normal to Bob. He had seen very much the same in his billions of years of existence. It was only then that it occurred to him that Mr Charles and Anne had never mated while he had been there. He was still wondering about that when Mary started calling "Oh God!", over and over. It would have been a shame to let the belief go to waste when he was so hungry and Bob thought only of eating for a while.

After Max and Mary fell asleep, Bob watched them for a little while. Snoring wasn't very interesting and they hadn't started to dream yet. He decided to check on Mr Charles and do his duty. It wasn't as if there was much that he could do but he had to try. He was a little stronger from Mary's heartfelt cries and the boundaries between himself and the universe were a little clearer. Travelling from one place to another took only a thought. Gods couldn't be everywhere at once but they could move around so quickly that it was hard to tell the difference. Mr Charles' house was on a quiet street well away from the city centre and within the one-way system, but that didn't matter to Bob who could just appear anywhere that there was a worshipper. All seemed very normal there with things much as they had been on the other nights when he had watched. The couple were also in bed but Anne was reading her book and Mr Charles was working on some kind of puzzle in the newspaper. There didn't seem to be much for Bob to do until Mr Charles dropped his pen which promptly rolled under the bed. Mr Charles tutted (Anne had some very strong views on swearing so that was strictly limited to the car) and got out of bed to fish for the pen. Bob seized his chance! He could help his worshipper and maybe he would have more faith. Bob used his fresh strength to pass another miracle and tapped the side of the pen so that it rolled out, stopping against a pyjama clad knee. Mr Charles' expression was quizzical (much as it had been when he was working on the puzzle) and he softly said "Thank you." Anne looked over and asked him what he was thanking her for. Mr Charles smiled, "Nothing, dear. Just talking to myself." Bob felt a small but precious jolt of belief.

In the morning, Mary went back to work and Bob rode with her. Max had left early to get back to his flat to change for work but his thoughts had been on meeting someone called Sharon as she parked her car in the same place as he did. Bob went with Mary as she carried out the rituals of the morning, the first coffee, the changing of the voice mail message and the routine greetings to her co-workers. He had noticed that Mary was much given to small rituals and he found that encouraging. That morning, she had weighed herself before and after her shower. He knew that she had been disappointed by the result and knew from her mind that she had expected to get the same result after her shower but she weighed herself twice just the same.

Throughout the day, Bob kept visiting the young man with computer trouble. He seemed to be spending the morning alternatively gossiping with colleagues about football and calling up something that he called the "No help at all line" to complain that no-one had arrived yet. Bob was there when the engineer finally arrived. He had expected an older man rather like Mr Charles but this was a gawky youngster barely out of his teens and still graced with a face full of acne. Bob concentrated very hard on what the newcomer said. Most of it would have been quite incomprehensible to someone without the ability to read minds as it contained strings of letters that meant something to the engineer but nothing at all to the people that he was talking to.

Whatever the problem with the computer was, the repairman fixed it with a few clicks of the mouse. The lecture on the importance of using the online help took considerably longer. Bob found this difficult to follow because the repairman was not really listening to what he was saying. Half formed thoughts of Goblins and Orcs were behind the recitation but Bob managed to understand enough to be useful. That was apparently more than the insurance claims officer (he had learned the title from Mary) had been able to do. "So, what was wrong with the damned thing this time?", he asked. The repairman sighed and explained in great detail and many words, very few of which made any sense to Bob or the insurance claims officer. Computers seemed much more complicated than vending machines and more popular. After all, there were computers on every desk but only three vending machines on the entire floor. They seemed important and Bob decided that he should try to learn more about them.

When Mary went to lunch, Bob stayed at her workstation. While much of the computer repairman's speech had been nonsense, Bob had understood the part about the checking online help. A small series of rather strenuous miracles brought up the online help and the definition of ASCII. It seemed that the pulses made up numbers and words. Bob had experience of simple circuitry in the vending machines but this was far more complex and interesting. He read on. Pressing the keys was a great deal of effort (for a very small godling) and Bob wondered if it would be possible to just move the energy around. He had learned to do this with the vending machines. He tried and found that it was simple enough to stop the energy or to let it flow. The only difficulty was that he had to concentrate on what he was doing because everything happened so fast

Bob was still trying to make some sense of what the computer was doing when Mary returned. Bob popped out and saw that the screen had changed to blue with white writing. Mary seemed annoyed by this and turned the computer off and then on again. Bob decided to experiment on someone else's computer next time to avoid upsetting his believer. He understood that Mary wasn't, strictly speaking, a believer but she very much wanted to believe in something and Bob was determined to be that something.

Bob stayed in the office when Mary left and read more, fascinated. There was so much to learn and these machines allowed him to learn much more rapidly than watching people in real life or on the television. For the first time, Bob felt a hunger for more than belief, a pleasure that was not the absence of want. He discovered that each computer connected to many others and he could search for information from other places. He had seen Mary doing that but he hadn't understood what she had been doing at the time. He wanted to understand the world but the content of the computer didn't seem to be much help unless you were strangely fascinated with car accidents. He needed to understand people if he was to get them to believe in him and those computers wouldn't help him. Bob decided to do some research on gods. If he wanted to be a popular god then he had best know what people wanted from their deities. He started a search. "Results 1 - 10 of about 31,400,000 for gods." It certainly seemed that people were interested in gods! Bob was sure that had to be a good thing. Most of the information seemed to be about gods who had been popular for a while such as Jupiter and Minerva or Odin and Thor. He knew the names without knowing how he knew them. Bob didn't feel ready to compete with the big boys so he had best avoid their temples. He searched for temples of the main gods. There were 1,900,000 references to temples to Thor. Bob wondered if Thor could really have that many temples. He looked a bit more closely and then realised that all the references were to temples long gone. He checked for temples of Zeus and Minerva and Odin but it was the same for all of them. Everything was ruined and half forgotten. If those gods were still around at all then they were hanging on by their spiritual fingertips. Bob wondered if these people believed in anything so he searched for "belief". There were a great many references to belief but they mostly seemed to be about "God" – not "a God" or "The God named such-and-such". Could there be one god that had pushed all the others out of the way? Bob knew that he had to learn more about that god. He started to read but most of it didn't make any sense to him. People talked about the god as if he was only one and yet they were talking about very different gods. This made no sense at all. Bob knew the way that belief had to work even though he had only been aware for a few weeks.

Such things are intrinsic to the nature of even the least of gods. People believed in gods. The gods did things for the people in return. This god would have to be doing some impressive miracles to be able to get that many believers.

Bob decided to check on Mary again. He didn't know what he would do when he had many believers but he would be certain to look after the two that he had or nearly had. It only took a moment to find Mary in her living room. She was sitting at the table in a dining chair and trying to write a letter. The page was blank and Bob could see that she was crying. Religion was supposed to make people happy, thought Bob. He tried to see in to her mind but it was too jumbled to understand. He caught a glimpse of Max and a great feeling of loneliness but nothing that made much sense. As he watched, a teardrop rolled down Mary's face and splashed on to the paper. She wiped it away with a sob, leaving a damp trail. Bob didn't know how to cheer up a human but he could do something about the tears. He caught the next teardrop and held it in the air. A second followed and a third and soon Bob was struggling to hold them all at once. There was nothing he could do but put them together into a big drop until he could get rid of them. Soon, there was a single fat drop that wobbled and caught the light. The reflection caught Mary's attention and she tried to focus with red rimmed eyes on the little ball of tears.

Bob suddenly felt very self-conscious but he didn't know what to do other than hold the tears. Mary watched the light reflected through the ball with a strange mixture of expressions. She was no longer crying but she still looked sad and now puzzled. She reached out a hand to catch the tears but Bob moved the ball back. Mary rubbed her eyes and slowly shook her head.

"I can see it but I don't believe it. Oh god, what is happening?" That was a prayer of sorts but how could Bob reply? He could hear her thoughts but he had no idea how to make her hear him. Maybe he could give her a sign. Slowly and a little clumsily, Bob shaped the tears into a small smile shape.

Mary watched and her position was tense, her expression intent. "Is there someone there?" Bob made the ball bounce up and down like a nodding head.

"Where are you?"

Bob had no idea how to answer that one with a few tears. He was still thinking when the next question came. "Who is it?" At least this was a question that he could answer. Slowly he formed three watery letters: "BOB."

Mary looked, her eyes still wet with tears. "I am going mad. Sweet mother of God, I am crazy." Bob didn't have a mother; he had always just been, so he didn't know what he could say to that. "Are you real?"

Bob formed the word "YES." He hoped that she didn't ask anything that needed a long answer.

"Are you a ghost?"

"NO."

"Then what are you?", Mary asked.

Bob formed more words in the air. The tears were evaporating fast. "I", "AM", "YOUR"... Could Bob claim to be her god? She would certainly expect more in the way of miracles than Bob could provide. Was lying to his believer acceptable? Bob thought that it was better not to take the chance and finished with the word "FRIEND" in very small letters.

"But why are you here?"

There was very little of the tears left. Bob spelled out "I NEED YOU TO BELIEVE IN ME." one word at a time.

"Believe in you?"

The word "YES." formed and faded in front of Mary.

Mary went to bed without any more tears. She kept looking around the room as if she expected to see something there, but Bob was no more visible than he usually was. Just before she closed her eyes, she whispered "Goodnight, Bob." Bob felt content, pleased by the small devotion. He popped over to see Mr and Mrs. Charles but they were sound asleep. Mr Charles was dreaming about vending machines but he resisted the temptation to see what Anne was dreaming. She wasn't a believer, after all. Since Bob's little flock seemed quite safe, he returned to the office to do a bit more research. He needed to know how gods could have mothers. He wondered if he should consider himself an orphan.

It was quite light before Bob finished his research. He had learned a great many things about what humans believed but a lot of it seemed to make very little sense. It didn't seem to make much more sense to a lot of the humans, but some of them were very emphatic that they and they alone had the truth about religion. The Christians and the Jews and the Muslims all seemed to believe in more or less the same god, but none of them could agree (even among themselves) on who the god was or what he wanted. Some of the pictures had been interesting though. The ones he could find were of an old human in white robes with a full beard. Bob wondered if Zeus was still in business after all. Anyway, he would have to find out more about that later since people were coming in to the office and they would notice him using the computer.

Bob moved over to Mary's desk and waited. He could have gone straight to Mary, of course, but he wanted to think things over. It was a while before Mary turned up but Bob found the time useful. She seemed in an awful hurry to reach her desk and her supervisor looked at her angrily and then down at his watch. Bob quickly passed a miracle and the minute hand jumped back. The supervisor looked surprised but just shook his head before walking off in the direction of the coffee vending machine so recently serviced by Mr Charles.

Mary quickly unlocked her PC and put on her telephone headset. Since Mary was busy catching up all morning, Bob shifted between her and Mr Charles just to make sure that they were both alright. Mr Charles was in a classroom listening to someone explaining in very, very simple terms what customer service was. Bob managed to catch quite a lot of what was on the course since the instructor seemed to assume that his audience were somehow mentally defective.

Mary got a quick lunch from the vending machine. She sat down at her desk and opened up the notepad on her PC. She looked at the blank page for a few moments and started typing:

"Last night, I met Bob. Well, I thought that I did. I don't know what Bob is or who he is or…" She hit the backspace over and over to delete the text. "Damn it, Bob, who are you? This is crazy."

Bob wondered what to say. He let himself flow in to the keyboard until he was just under her fingers. Carefully, he let his essence control the circuits. "i am bob."

Mary just stared at the screen for a moment surprising herself that all she could think was 'why doesn't he use punctuation or upper case?'. She typed "Are you a hacker? Is this some kind of joke?"

"maybe i am a hacker. this isnt a joke. serious."

"Is that you, Max? You could get in to all kinds of trouble hacking in to the office.", typed Mary.

Bob typed back, "not max. i am bob. i want to help you. i need you."

"Is that someone from the IT department? You know this is harassment?"

"sorry sorry not from it. we spoke yesterday, words in tears. please help me."

Mary's expression softened, becoming thoughtful. "How did you do that?"

Bob had no idea how he had done that. Miracles happened when he wanted them although he had to admit that they were very tiny miracles. "you wanted to believe. need you to believe."

"Believe in what? Believe in you?"

Bob was pleased that she was getting the idea. "yes, believe in me."

Mary typed back. "Why should I believe in you? I don't even know who you are."

"but i believe in you."

"Am I going mad?", typed Mary.

"no. please help."

"How can I help you? I don't even know where you are.", typed Mary.

"i need you to believe in me. can you show me that you do?"

"How?", typed Mary.

"could i have a sacrifice please?"

Mary typed quickly now. "If you are thinking goats and pentagrams then you can stop that right now, Mister!"

"no goats. please, can you sacrifice your e9 to me?"

Mary frowned. "My e9?"

"your e9 from the vendamatic."

She looked down at her desk. "The chocolate bar?"

"yes."

"How do you sacrifice milk chocolate?", she asked

"break it and think of me."

"Can I still eat it afterwards?", she asked.

"yes."

Feeling very foolish, Mary reached down and snapped the chocolate in two. Bob had his first sacrifice and the smell of milk chocolate wafted up to the heavens.

That night, all the traffic lights were green on Mary's trip home.

Chapter 3a

The rock moved through space, tumbling slowly end over end. It didn't have a name or even a number. It was a rock like millions of others. It was, in short, unremarkable in every way.

Chapter 4

In the morning, Bob went with Mr Charles and watched how he talked with people. The course had been very definite about how you should communicate with customers and the trainer had spoken with an almost reverential tone when talking about them. Bob wasn't quite sure if this was a religious belief but it made sense to be sure. However, Mr Charles seemed to talk to his customers in exactly the same way as he always had. Bob wondered about the "added value of a smile" that had been discussed on the course. The customers mainly seemed to want Mr Charles to fix the machine and to go away once this was done. Since Mr Charles wanted the exact same thing, everything went rather well.

Bob knew that it was important to know what people wanted because it related very closely to what he wanted. Bob wanted belief, as much of it as possible. He had to give people a reason for believing in him in a very specific way. He was coming to understand more about people and those who might become believers and it wasn't enough that they believed in him in the same way that they had faith in the existence of the toaster. That was a passive belief. They had to actively believe and that meant that Bob had to stay in their lives and help them.

At lunch time, Mr Charles stopped off at a motorway service station and had a Ploughman's cheese sandwich and tried to do the crossword. Bob had noticed that the sandwich was always cheese and the crossword was always uncompleted even though there was an unshakeable faith within Mr Charles that he was good at the puzzles. That suggested that beliefs were not always rational.

Since the crossword never made sense to Bob, he went to watch Mary who was surfing the web for beauty tips. That didn't make a lot more sense, but Mary was good company and so Bob learned about the importance of cleaning the skin and then covering it with creams until it needed cleaning again. Just before Bob was going to leave, Mary opened up the notepad on her PC and typed "Bob?"

Bob persuaded some electrons to jump the gap on the circuit board, spelling out "yes?" It was much easier than pressing the keys.

Mary smiled and whispered, "Just checking."

Bob went back to Mr Charles and rode with him while he drove to his next appointment. He knew that cars were dangerous from what he had seen on television and he wondered why humans made things that exploded all the time. Of course, Bob didn't know what he could do if his first worshipper exploded but he liked to be there just in case. The afternoon was spent in more offices fixing vending machines. Bob spent the time wondering what Mr Charles needed to make him happy. There didn't seem to be anything very much that Mr Charles wanted from life and as long as there was work for him to do and not too many training courses then it was enough for him that every day was much like the last. Bob almost wished that Mary was as easy to please, but not quite. He had also worked out that happy people don't have much need for gods.

That evening, Mary went out to a bar with some of the people that she worked with. Bob tried to spend some time with her, but the bar was too noisy for him. The music didn't bother him but all of the people who were there seemed to have lost all their barriers. Their surface thoughts rang out incoherently and what people said didn't match what they were thinking. People drank, smoked, danced, shouted and didn't really understand each other all evening, so Bob went back to Mary's office to look on the internet for information on bars. It didn't make any more sense on the web.

McGillian's was a pub on the high street, a link in a corporate chain of almost identical bars. The music was too loud and the air was thick with the scent of fried foods and stale cigarettes. On a Friday night, it would be packed until closing time but it was always a bit dead midweek. The other workers at QuikQuote were generally young, fed up with their jobs and happy to bitch about it to each other over a few pints of lager or glasses of house wine. The sessions were informally referred to as the Wine Whine by the girls. Mary sipped from her glass and looked over to where her supervisor, Darren Johnson was holding court, surrounded by the usual crowd of shift leaders and the would be upwardly mobile. They always laughed too loud at his jokes and then complained about him afterwards. Mary had no interest in promotion and she, along with most people that she knew, would sooner be doing something other than handle insurance reports with the always present chance of abusive customers. On the plus side, they did tend to break the monotony. One of the shift leaders came to the bar next to Mary, an empty bottle of lager in his hand. "Simon", she thought. She nodded and took another sip, trying not to make a face. The wine had warmed up enough to taste.

"Mary! Not joining us?", asked Simon.

"Maybe later.", replied Mary, her smile polite rather than warm.

"And 'maybe' means yes, right?", Simon leered.

"It means 'maybe'. It seems like there are more than enough people over there for now.", replied Mary.

"You want to loosen up a bit, have some fun. I mean, it is all team building, right?", said Simon. Mary noticed that his eyes were meeting her cleavage and resisted the urge to adjust her neckline. She recalled that many of her female co-workers referred to him as "Slime-on" due to his wandering eyes and, if rumour were to be believed, hands.

"I am doing just fine, thanks. I am enjoying my drink and maybe I will come over later." Years of customer service helped her to keep her tone level. She noticed that the music had changed from EMF's Unbelievable to Radiohead's Creep. She couldn't have said it better and she had no intention of falling for his dubious charms. The words "cheap" and "tart" applied well to the wine, not to her.

Simon cocked his head to one side. "Didn't think that I would see you tonight. It is mostly us singles out. You still seeing that Max? He knows how to party, that guy. Shame he isn't here, eh?"

Mary bit back her initial and probably career limiting reply before wondering why. It was not like Simon could fire her or anything, but he was pretty tight with Darren. "I didn't know that you knew him. He is busy tonight, so I thought that I would come for a nice quiet drink. Well, we all make mistakes, don't we?" She wondered if Simon was too drunk to get the hint.

"Yeah, well, I don't know him, but I see him in clubs and such.", replied Simon.

Mary nodded, wishing that Simon would go back to his sucking up.

"You don't go clubbing very much though, do you?", asked Simon, his tone arch.

"I am beginning to wish that I had a club right now", said Mary, her tone flat.

Simon grinned at her and scooped the fresh bottle of beer off the counter before heading back to the table with the other cronies. Mary went to take a drink but found that her glass was already empty. She scowled at it and ordered another wine, this one large. It was going to be a long evening.

#

Bob was a god. He knew this. He didn't know how he knew this, but he knew it just as he knew that he was not the only god. There should be others, he was sure. He started to feel very alone. That was new, a feeling that had only become possible as he became aware. He remembered places that he had seen, but not comprehended. Rock, star, dust - but those were things he had merely witnessed, not experienced. He was becoming more; a thinking being. He had barely existed until new creatures came to be that wanted and needed and feared. There had been so much fear in the small scurrying things, anger in them when they competed. That wasn't belief but it was something, in the same way that starlight is not the noonday sun.

The first gods had been those of fire, lightning and wind; forces of nature that the first people knew to be a danger. That had been the fuel to their fear, a certainty that had sustained the first gods. The world had changed and people forgot what once they believed. As time passed, the people had learned to control the things that scared them and their beliefs had changed as they did. Bob knew this at his core, knew that there was power in terror but that power didn't call to him. Bob was spun from a different thread, formed by it in ways that he could not define, yet it bound him absolutely. Bob remembered how he felt witnessing Max's contempt towards Mary and Bob had not enjoyed that feeling. There was power in it but it was utterly alien to the belief that formed the core of him. It was not for him. If he was to ask humanity for its faith, he would have to give them something in return, neither master nor servant. That felt right to him. That felt good. He wished that he had other gods to learn from but only saw the nameless and mindless sparks around him. He would need to learn more and find where the other gods had gone.

Bob was still researching when he felt a… Bob didn't have a word for it but it was an awareness that he was wanted, that his attention was being drawn. He checked Mr Charles first but he was sound asleep. That meant that it had to be Mary. When he got to her house, he found her lying on the bed, dressed in an oversized T-shirt and looking around owlishly. "Bob? Come out, come out wherever you are."

Bob wondered how to reply. He could understand Mary's thoughts, more or less, but she didn't seem to be able to hear anything that he sent back. Her mind also seemed a little blurred like the other people at the bar. He would have sighed if he had been able to but he didn't have lungs or lips or… well, any number of things. He knew from his reading on the web that gods were supposed to be all powerful but in practice they couldn't do a great many of the things that humans took for granted. Bob looked around and saw that there was a glass of water on the cabinet by the bed. That would do very nicely. He formed a watery "Hello" in the air.

Mary smiled and giggled. "I wish that I knew how you do that. It is a very good trick." Her words were slurred and lagged behind her thoughts by a split second.

Bob didn't know how he did the trick with the water. It just seemed to be something that gods could do. Parting of the waters, walking on water and turning water into wine were all apparently famous god tricks. "I just can.", he spelled, one word at a time.

"How do you know when I want to talk with you anyway? Men aren't usually very good at communicating. No, that isn't fair. Men are crap at communicating."

Bob thought about this. He got the feeling that he was only getting half the conversation but it was hard to know what Mary was thinking. It had to be the alcohol, he reasoned. Anyway, Mary was expecting an answer. "I listen to what you say."

Mary laughed but didn't sound happy. "Well, that will be a first. Are you sure that you are an imaginary invisible *boy* hacker and not an imaginary invisible *girl* hacker?"

That wasn't an easy question to answer. Bob wasn't at all sure that he was either of those things so he replied "No, not sure."

Mary giggled again and asked "Can you see me?"

Bob replied, "Yes."

"Have you ever watched me undress?" Mary stared archly at a point about two feet to the left of where Bob considered himself to be.

"Yes.", replied Bob. He was pleased to have an easy question for a change.

Mary tugged down her T-shirt, making quite sure it covered her. "I think that makes you a boy then. Do you think that I am pretty?"

The question didn't really apply to Bob since the things that he liked about humans had very little to do with what they looked like. He loved Mary in the same way that a plant loves the sun. It was not a conscious decision. That didn't have anything to do with how she looked and didn't help him to answer her question. Lacking a better answer, he looked in to her rather foggy mind and gave the answer that he knew that she wanted. "Yes, very pretty, Mary."

"Sweet talker. So, Mr Bob, if I am so pretty, where is Max tonight? Can you tell me that?"

Ah, that was something that Bob could manage. He could and would help his worshipper just as she had asked.

The next morning was one of the quieter ones. Bob was well aware that people had holy days when they were supposed to worship various gods. Muslims had Fridays and the Jews had Saturdays and the Christians had Sundays, although they all were supposed to have the same god as Bob understood it. Maybe the different days were arranged to give their god a certain amount of belief per day rather than giving it all at once. Perhaps there was a rota of who provided the necessary faith. Oddly enough, each of the groups had their own different temples although there didn't seem to be much difference beyond the architecture. A priest told the worshippers what their god wanted although Bob had no idea how the priest knew what that would be. There didn't seem to be any divine communication that Bob could see and these things are fairly obvious for godlings. There had been one time when he thought that he may have found another god; it was a Sunday and he was following some people that seemed to worship in a large shop full of plumbing supplies, tools and kitchens that didn't seem to cook food when a huge voice filled the place. However, it was talking about discounts on gas powered barbecues and it only took a moment to trace the voice to a middle aged and very definitely mortal person sitting at a microphone. Bob went to Mary and watched while she slept.

It was quite late when Mary woke and it was a slow process. She groaned without opening her eyes and sat up slowly, clutching her head with her eyes still tight shut. She reached out one hand to the bedside cabinet and felt for her contact lens case for a moment before finding it. "Thank God for that, at least I remembered." Bob had watched her remove her contact lenses before but had never reminded her. He would from here on. He watched as Mary went about the rituals that marked the start of the day but he didn't follow her into the shower. He wasn't sure why she had reacted that way to the thought of being watched undressing but if she wanted him not to watch then he would do his best. Mary looked around as she undressed, a look of doubt on her face. She didn't usually have weird dreams after a few drinks but it had been a heavy night after the encounter with Simon.

Instead, Bob looked around the house for a way of leaving a message for Mary. He found the pen and paper from where Mary had been trying to write a letter a few days ago. There were small raised areas where tears had fallen on the paper. He tried to lift the pen, but it was heavy so he sneaked a little ink out of the nib and shaped it in to letters and words on the paper, answering her question from the night before. She may have forgotten but Bob remembered. Having helped Mary, Bob went to spend some time with Mr Charles.

Mr Charles was already out of the house when Bob found him. Finding a believer wasn't a case of looking around an area until he found the person. Instead, places were defined by where there was belief that he could tap into, each person being a small spring of strength and well-being. It was more like going to the believer and then locating the things around them. Bob didn't have a physical location, just a place where his attention was focussed. By feeling where a person linked to him was, he was effectively with them. Mr Charles was walking around a supermarket with a list of rather cryptic instructions that he would peer at with a pained expression. Slowly, he filled the basket with all sorts of things, many of which seemed utterly useless to Bob. He was struggling to decipher "Brilpds" when Bob felt what would have to be called a prayer had it not been filled with fury rather than supplication. He hurried back to Mary.

"What does this mean? How did you get in to my house and how dare you... how DARE you! I... you accuse Max of being with some girl and you know how good he is to me." Mary's words were lost in the tears that fell from her red rimmed eyes.

Bob listened to the words and the thoughts behind them and they didn't quite match. Mary wanted the words that she said to be true but she didn't believe them. She was trying to make herself believe but Bob understood belief well enough to know that it didn't work that way. He gathered a few tears up to shape in to words.

"And don't you dare do that trick with the tears again. You only do it when you want me to think that you are sweet."

Bob sighed, at least in his mind, and took a little more ink from the pen. "Is this better?" The letters strongly resembled twelve point Arial.

Mary squinted at the page. "Yes. No. How the hell are you doing that? Why can't you phone like anyone else?"

The ink spelled out, "I don't know how to use a phone." This was true and simpler than explaining that the dialling was easy but the speaking was hard.

Mary sniffed and said "It doesn't matter. Why did you write this? What did you hope to gain? Are you jealous of how happy we are?"

Bob wondered about that. Was he a jealous god? He wanted Mary's belief and he didn't want her to leave but that wasn't really the same thing. Instead, he decided to try being reasonable even if Mary wasn't. "I was answering your question. You wanted to know where Max was last night. He was at the club until 1:27 when he went to flat fourteen of Coniston house where he slept in the bed of Alice Johnson. Wasn't that what you wanted to know?"

"And they slept together? You are telling me that Max slept with another girl?"

Bob wrote, "Yes. After they mated, they slept. Is there anything else that I can help you with, Mary?"

Mary grabbed the paper, wadded it in to a ball and hurled it at the wall. "Bastards, the lot of you.", she shouted and ran out of the room.

All the next day, Mary ignored Bob. She didn't stop believing in him, but she concentrated on not thinking about him with an intensity that was close to prayer. When Mary wasn't thinking about not thinking about Bob, she was thinking about Max which made her cry and that led her to thinking about why thinking about Max made her cry and that led her back to Bob. As a result, she was putting much more effort into thoughts about Bob than she did when she was talking to him. Bob left her notes and tried everything that he could think of to cheer her up, but nothing seemed to make a difference. Even when he typed on her PC at work, she would just close down the application and pointedly ignore the words that she had seen.

Bob wished that he could talk to other people who could help him to understand why she was upset, but somehow this didn't seem like something that Mr Charles could be much use with. Mr Charles seemed to have enough troubles keeping his wife happy and he didn't even know Mary. As the week carried on, Bob decided that his best bet was to watch people and see if he could understand them better. Because he liked being close to a believer and because he thought Mr Charles to be a very superior sort of person (he did, after all, believe in Bob's existence even if he didn't know quite what Bob was), he spent time with Mr Charles and his wife. There was a quiet love there, worn smooth by the years. One of the things that Mr Charles did to keep Anne happy was to take her out to dinner once a week and this was their customary day. There was something almost ritualistic about the way that this was done. It was always on a Thursday night, always at 7 pm precisely and always the same restaurant. They would always have the same thing each week: chicken in white sauce and vegetables for her and roast beef, roast potatoes, roast parsnips and buttered swede, all drowned in gravy for him. They would talk about things that didn't matter very much and eat their food without thinking about it much. Bob was no expert on how people interacted but this seemed to be enough for them. This Thursday was no exception except that Mr Charles seemed to be paying even less attention than usual to the conversation.

After several vague replies, Anne took Mr Charles to task about it. "Ray, have you heard a word that I said?"

"Sorry, dear", he replied, "Something about the road works, wasn't it?"

"Do try to keep up, Ray. Honestly, sometimes I think that you are incapable of doing more than one thing at a time. Now listen as I try again." Anne launched into a complicated story of why one of her colleagues should have been promoted rather than another of them that Bob didn't follow at all. Mr Charles seemed to be having no more success and it was all rather confusing since he didn't know any of the people involved. It didn't help that his attention kept being drawn to a rather worrying pain in his chest and, now that he thought about it, radiating down his right arm. He winced and tried to burp without success.

"Manners, Ray! Have you got indigestion again? It is your own fault, you know. You eat all the wrong foods and you never take any exercise. It is no wonder that-". Anne was interrupted by Mr Charles slipping sideways from the chair, still trying to smile at her as he headed for the floor.

Bob didn't panic because he couldn't. Gods, even small ones, do not have adrenal glands or anything very like them. Bob looked down and tried to work out what he could do. People were starting to gather around and make suggestions that contradicted each other and, all the while, Mr Charles was slowly fading away. Bob tried listening to his thoughts to see if there was any clue in there as to what was wrong with him but the thoughts were jumbled and fragmentary. Images of children in old fashioned clothes butted up against images of a funeral with a younger Mr Charles. The last image before Mr Charles' mind shut down was from a television program and showed doctors using some machine with metal paddles and wires. Bob recognised the show; it was one that Mary watched sometimes. Bob had watched it with her and knew the names of the main characters and had seen them work the machine. There didn't seem to be anything like that around here and there seemed to be less and less of Mr Charles although his body was still there. Bob went inside, trying to understand what was wrong, flowing through the flesh and blood of his believer as he had with the insides of the computer. There was his heart and it was struggling. He wished that he knew more about medicine or how to perform healing miracles but nothing had prepared him for this. He wished that he could talk to a doctor but it could take days to explain who he was and what he wanted to know. Mr Charles didn't have days. If only... but why not? Bob jumped back to Mary's office and started up the browser. Slowly, the browser loaded and Bob was sending it key presses before it was ready. The search was quicker but Bob knew that he had very little time. A search for heart attacks led him to Cardioversion. There was information about drugs which Bob didn't have and times and voltages. He was pretty sure that he couldn't manage 200 volts and certainly not for five milliseconds but he would have to do what he could.

Things hadn't changed a great deal in the restaurant which surprised Bob. He knew that he had only been away for twelve seconds but somehow he had expected the humans to have done more. Bob was just diving towards Mr Charles' chest when he heard Mary calling him. He wanted to go, but she would just have to wait. There was no time.

Inside Mr Charles, very little was happening. The cells were alive and there was still some busyness especially in the digestive system. but it seemed rather pointless and disorganised. Bob headed for Mr Charles' heart which wasn't even trying to beat now. It quivered, but there was no blood flowing through it. Because Bob didn't have enough power, he would have to get as close as he could to the muscles and deliver what he could there. He felt for the nerves and found them, still giving faltering commands. It was the muscles that seemed lifeless and tired. Bob traced the systems of the heart, trying to understand and apply what little he knew. There wasn't enough oxygen and no blood was coming in to the heart's muscles to feed it. He followed the artery up and there it was. A clot had formed and that had stopped fresh blood from getting in. The clot was dark, sticky and thick, quite blocking the pipe. It was too big for Bob to move. He would try all the same because of what he owed Mr Charles but all he had were small miracles and this would be something a bit more complicated than shaping some ink. Bob tried to grab the edges of the clot to move it but it just shredded away in a cloud of dark red. He tried again but there was no solid core to hold and more of the mass of cells tore away. Bob was about to go back to the computer to look for something that would help when he realised that he had broken up some of the clot already. He tried again, pulling it away, a little at a time and as quickly as he could manage. He could feel the body around him dying a little at a time and knew that he must hurry. It took seconds more to clear the blood vessel but at last the job was done.

Bob waited for the heart to start again and counted slowly in the way that humans did. One. Two. Three. Four. Nothing. The heart wasn't beating. Mr Charles was dying and Bob didn't know what to do. He jumped back to the office and searched for more information, anything that would help him understand a heart. The computer had never seemed so slow before. Bob raced through link after link before he found the diagram that he needed. Back in the restaurant, someone was taking Mr Charles' tie off and feeling for a pulse but Bob didn't stop for him. He dived in to his believer's chest and started pulling on the walls of the heart in sequence. The blood was thick and heavy but he had to keep his believer, his only true believer. The blood that came in was barely better than what had left but Bob carried on, spending his own strength to pump blood through the man. After a few beats, the blood was redder, fresher and the muscles began to wake up. Another beat and the muscles were helping Bob and the next beat came before Bob was ready. Other parts of Mr Charles body started to work again as fresh red blood got to them. Bob pulled back out of the man's body as Mr Charles' chest was rising and realised how weak he was. He had spent almost all of his strength to keep his believer alive and he was nearly as feeble as he had been when he had drifted nameless and unaware. Only the knowledge that he was needed kept him from drifting. Bob floated above the figure on the floor and tried to remember why it was important. The man coughed weakly and then more strongly as if choking. Colour flooded back in to his cheeks as he gasped air. He tried to sit up, but turned suddenly, vomiting on the floor. The people around him looked confused or disgusted or simply embarrassed but slowly the realisation came. This man was alive. A murmur went up… "Thank God for that."… "It's a miracle."… "Close squeak that." A rather quiet and deeply mortified voice came up from the floor. "Would someone pass me a napkin please?"

Mr Charles was looking remarkably well all things considered when the ambulance crew arrived. Bob was feeling stronger from the moment of belief that had accompanied his first believer's recovery, but he was still more tired than he had ever been since his awareness began. He watched as Mr Charles was taken out to the ambulance and driven away and Bob then went to answer the calls that he had been ignoring for the past few minutes. He disappeared from the restaurant car park and arrived in Mary's flat.

A book passed through the space where Bob had chosen to arrive. Max was there, standing in the doorway and that was the direction that the book had been headed. Mary was still crying, her mascara running down her face. A single tear drop had fallen on to her blouse and Bob realised that she was wearing her smartest clothes. Her face was flushed and her voice was tear roughened as she shouted at Max. "God, you bastard! How could you be so stupid as to think I would believe you now?" Bob wasn't sure what he had done to deserve this but then realised that she wasn't talking to him.

Max was backing away as if he were faced by a wildcat that he had taken for a sleeping moggy. "But Babe, you know that I love you. I have never even-". Another book punctuated his sentence for him.

"Number fourteen." Mary glared, her face clashing horribly with her hair.

Max looked puzzled. "The bus?"

"I heard that she was more of a bike.", replied Mary.

"That was a cheap shot, even for you, Mary." Max suddenly seemed calmer, his position more definite.

"Well, what is she like then? How would you put it?", asked Mary.

Max paused for a second and then smiled without warmth. "Well, how about thinner, younger, prettier and much more adventurous in bed?"

Mary froze in place for a moment and then started looking around frantically. The lamp was plugged in, there were no books left near her and the chair was too heavy. By the time she selected the can of furniture polish, Max was just closing the front door, robbing her of a target.

She cried for a long time afterwards, half curled on the sofa. Bob could only watch and listen to her sobs. He had mended one broken heart today but had no idea where to start with this one. There were tears enough for a dozen messages but he didn't have the strength to shape them or the words to say. After too long, he heard a loud sniff and his name.

"Bob?"

He looked around for a pen. He was so tired and even ink would have been a challenge. There didn't seem to be anything that could be written on nearby. Those things were all piled up near the back wall or the door where they had been thrown.

"I wish you were here, Bob.", she continued, still crying through the words.

Bob concentrated and brushed the back of her hand with no more pressure than a breeze.

Mary shivered, unsure what she had felt. "Is that you, Bob?"

Bob touched her hand again, even weaker now.

Mary wiped her eyes with one hand but fresh tears wet them again. "Stay with me, Bob. Please, don't go."

Bob touched her hand once more and it was lighter than a feather, barely enough to feel. He stayed there until she cried herself to sleep and beyond, watching the new dawn slowly fill the room. He studied her face, tear-stained and blue with run mascara. Bob felt her need for love and wanted to help. He could love her, he had to love her but was that what she needed? The last time he had done what she wanted, it had hurt her so much.

Chapter 5

The alarm didn't wake Mary; it was beside the bed and she was curled up on the sofa. Bob wondered if he should wake her up, but he thought that she must be tired. Could it make that much difference if she missed a morning answering questions about insurance policies? He decided that it was better to let her sleep. He also wanted to check on Mr Charles and he knew that Mary would not miss him if she was still sleeping. He would know the instant that she woke. He had watched her sleep and was beginning to recognise the things that made her Mary. The things that were uniquely her were not obvious to anyone that didn't see people as wonderful points of light in a dark world.

Mr Charles was sitting up in a hospital bed looking quite well but a little embarrassed. Bob wondered if that was because Mr Charles was dressed in a blue and white backless gown rather than the slightly tired suits that he normally wore on weekdays. A nurse was trying to explain why he couldn't have a fried breakfast even though Mr Charles was explaining in the politest of tones that he always started the day in traditional English style. In the end, Matron was called and Mr Charles agreed that maybe it would be best to wait until he had seen the consultant.

Bob still felt weak but he was concerned about Mr Charles. The small god slid into the chest of his first believer and watched the blood flowing through him and the dance of nerve signals. There were still parts of the blood vessels that were half filled with a greasy gunge, slowing the blood. He had read about this during his frantic research the previous night. Carefully, as economically as he could manage, Bob broke a tiny portion of the congealed cholesterol away, letting it swirl into the rushing blood. As the flow improved, the blood started doing some of the work for him. As he cleaned out the blood vessels, Bob became aware that he was being watched, a new experience for someone that had always been invisible. He widened his attention and noticed that Mr Charles had his hand over his heart, but he was smiling. It didn't seem possible that Mr Charles could know what was happening, but his hand stayed over where Bob was at work. When there was no more work to be done, Bob pulled back, tired but sustained by the quiet belief. After a moment, Mr Charles said "Thank you." although there was no-one standing near. Bob wondered how to reply. The only electronics near enough didn't have a display. For want of a better option, Bob stretched out the thin brown powder that lurked at the bottom of the NHS mug into the word "Welcome" followed by "I", "am" and finally "Bob". Mr Charles' smile broadened but he didn't say anything else. There didn't seem to be anything that needed saying and he felt tired but happy.

A little while later, a nurse picked up the empty cup and took it for washing. Mr Charles didn't mind; he was enjoying a late morning nap.

Since his first worshipper seemed to have a lot of humans around him and no current need of anything more than a bacon sandwich, Bob decided that it was safe to go back to Mary.

She was still sleeping on the couch, twitching fitfully. Bob had seen humans dream before, but it was one of the many things that he didn't understand. When Bob had been looking on the internet for more information on gods, he had learned that some of the humans thought that all of the world was part of a dream in the mind of God. Bob never dreamed and didn't think that gods could sleep but, all the same, it seemed sensible to learn as much as he could. Slowly and carefully, Bob entered Mary's dream, slipping into her mind without making a ripple.

Bob watched Mary watch Mary, herself and outside herself as sometimes happened in dreams. She was rushing along a corridor that was made up of half seen doors, notice boards with posters covered in jumbled letters and walls apparently painted with curdled milk. The version of Mary in the dream was smaller and younger; a hasty sketch that didn't look like her but which somehow captured who she was. There were children in the corridor and they were all talking but the sounds didn't quite form words. They all seemed bigger than Mary although Bob knew that she was of average height and they didn't seem to be older than the dream version of her as far as he could tell. Without having walked there, Mary was suddenly in front of a brown wooden office door and the corridor had grown huge and empty. There was a knock from the other side and it opened to reveal a giant of a man. Bob got the impression of a teacher and a name, Mr Hodgkiss, but this was the idea of a man sketched from memory. His face was all moustache, nostrils and wildly staring eyes. His voice sounded like a car crash, but words somehow arrived in Mary's mind. "Have you been a BAD Girl, Mary? To the Nuns! You will be punished", he roared wordlessly. Silently, Mary turned and walked with eyes downcast through the space left by the watching nuns that now lined the corridor. The door which suddenly had always been at the end of the corridor opened without being touched and Mary stepped through into the changing room with the familiar battered lockers lining the wall and the smell of wet towels. Mary, now back to her current age, was wearing a gym slip, singlet and plimsolls; she was hugging herself as if freezing. She called out in a little girl voice that was somehow still her own. "Bob?" A figure darted its head around a corner and Bob a ponytail and a beanie hat worn at a jaunty angle. Before he could make sense of that, the bell for the end of class started ringing and girls started streaming in. The ringing got louder and the dream began to break up, scattering into fragments. Bob tried to orient himself and leave Mary's mind as she woke up, but he was still tangled in her thoughts as she fell from the sofa and hit the floor front first. The pain jolted her awake and threw Bob out, stunned from the new and very unpleasant sensation. Mary scrambled to her feet and Bob saw her scoop up the ringing phone and raise it to her head.

"Max, you bastard! Burn in hell forever, you... oh... sorry. Yes, but... Sorry, Sir. It... I am... are you sure? Well, yes... oh, damn. I am so sorry. I can be there in 30 minutes maximum. I promise. Goodbye, Sir."

Mary rushed to the bedroom and changed into fresh underwear then showered and changed into more fresh underwear before dressing in a tearing hurry. She grabbed her key, her bag and for some reason, the television remote. She arrived in the office no more than 40 minutes later. Her boss was waiting for her and Bob was reminded of the teacher in the dream for a moment. He wondered if QuikQuote Insurance services kept nuns somewhere in the building. Mary's supervisor marched her over to his cubicle and the purely nominal privacy that it offered and started explaining the disciplinary procedure as laid down by Human Resources. Mary seemed to be sinking deeper into the chair as she was lectured, aware of her colleagues pretending not to listen to the conversation.

Bob listened, but it all seemed very dull and pointless even if the supervisor was enjoying it to a remarkable degree. To him, it seemed a very disrespectful way to treat his worshipper and Bob found himself wondering if he was allowed to choose those who believed in him. He certainly wouldn't have chosen to include this self-important idiot. Bob realised that he didn't even know the supervisor's name. Mary was bound to know it and there was a good chance that it was close to the top of her mind. Bob looked into Mary's head, trying to find the man's name. It was getting easier and harder to read Mary's thoughts these days. While Bob could see surface thoughts with much greater clarity than before, all the other half-thoughts and recollections made it hard to pick up what Mary was thinking except when she was talking. Mary seemed very confused and her thoughts were jumping around. She kept thinking about the fight with Max last night, Sister Mary Eunice (whoever she might be) and wishing that she could resign and worrying that she might be fired and that she really should have brushed her teeth before she left for work. Several of these thoughts were happening at the same time. After a few seconds, Bob decided that it was unlikely that the supervisor was really called Mr Gitface and decided to look around the cubicle.

The desk was just the same as any of the workstations at QuikQuote but it was much less cluttered than Mary's. Apart from the PC, there was a photo of the supervisor standing on what looked like a big hill holding up one thumb and smiling at the camera and a book called "Being the Best – 5 minute exercises in excellence." Bob decided to look through the computer which was normally more interesting. According to his Email, the man was called Darren Johnson (Manpower) and he spent a lot of his time sending emails to women that he had met on the internet. Bob didn't think that Darren was a busy executive who often travelled the world, but if the women accepted it then maybe it was true. Bob was still looking through the mails when Darren turned back to the computer.

"…so, if you work the rest of the day, we will call it an unpaid holiday and we won't need to get HR involved. I think that you will find that I have been generous.", said Darren.

Bob watched as the supervisor opened up the web page that controlled holiday allocation. He was already in the computer so it didn't take much more effort to understand what was going to happen next. Bob decided to pre-empt it.

"Right. So…", Darren paused. The screen was blinking an error at him, reporting that the day was already booked as vacation and so he could not add unpaid holiday for the day. He cleared the error and checked who had authorised the holiday. His own name was listed in the box labelled "Approving manager". The screen showed that he had approved it 6 weeks ago to the minute. Slowly, he turned crimson. Bob noticed that this was not all bad as it tended to hide his acne. He looked at Mary and there was something cold in his gaze that clashed with the heat of his anger. "And why exactly did you not tell me that you had booked holiday? Do you want to make me look like a fool? Do you think that I have so much free time that I want to waste it checking if you are supposed to be in the office?"

Mary looked back at him. She had always sat through his tantrums before but she felt tired. As far as she was concerned in that instant, half of the world were idiots and all of them had Y chromosomes. She closed her eyes for a moment, looking down into her lap before speaking. "You called me in here when I was on holiday because you are too stupid to read the roster… and you want to make it my fault? You… you… utter waste of human skin. You call me up and bring me all the way in to town and… You know, you men never think about… Damn it, you bastard! You are all the same." Tears started to run down Mary's cheeks. "You stupid, stupid idiot. It could have been so much, I mean…" Mary shook her head as if trying to get water out of her ears. Her voice was stronger when she spoke again. "This job is terrible. All day long, I have to try to convince people to take out insurance with rotten companies that I know won't pay unless they are forced to over a barrel and all the while, I am watched by you and clones of you who would love to be dictators but haven't got the charisma to… You know, now I think of it, I don't need this hassle and I don't need you and I don't need Max, not that you have a clue who Max is because you never so much as asked how I was like any proper human being would, but no, not for you. Anyway, I don't need you and I don't need this job and it is over. Do you hear me?" Mary was leaning forward over the desk and her face was close to Darren. Bob noticed that her tears were falling on his mouse-mat. "I Quit. Now, right now. I never want to see you again." Mary's dignity slowly crumbled as her words were drowned in tears. She sank back into her chair and there was a terrible silence from the cubicles around them. Mary cried for all the might-have-beens and the never-will-bes and she cried for herself. Darren just looked on, wondering which bit of the two week training course that had made him a manager was supposed to help him with this.

Chapter 6

Mary woke up in her own bed with the alarm ringing. She had tried tuning it to a local radio station but she was not naturally cheerful in the mornings and so the chirpy and vapid DJ did not improve her morning mood. A simple irritating beep would serve very nicely, thank you. She showered and dressed, just like she did every day. She was all ready for work but she had no work to go to. QuikQuote hadn't really given an explanation as to why she shouldn't go into the office but the letter was there on the table just the same. She was suspended until further notice without pay although she would be paid for the time while she was on holiday. Mary didn't know how long her holiday was booked for or how it came to be booked. She suspected Bob but that didn't seem likely. How could he have known to change the records? She wished that she had asked her supervisor but it was too late for that.

Because she was dressed and felt that she should leave the house, Mary wandered down to the newsagents and bought the local paper. She wasn't sure which day was best for jobs, but she loathed the idea of going back to QuikQuote and dealing with her supervisor and her co-workers after the all too public tantrum. She went over the adverts while eating breakfast. They seemed full of odd abbreviations like CCDL and EXP and she found it hard to keep her mind from wandering to the disastrous fight with Max and the almost-as-bad falling out with her supervisor. She wiped at her eyes, muttering to herself about small print and kept looking. She didn't fancy any of the jobs very much but she couldn't say that selling insurance had exactly appealed. The delivery driver jobs didn't say that they were for men only, but they did require "good strength" and in one case, a willingness to grow a beard. Mary wondered if that advert was breaking the sex discrimination rules. She might be willing to grow a beard for the right salary even if she wasn't actually capable of doing so. It wasn't something that had come up in careers guidance at school. She had always been distrustful of careers advisers. If they were so good, why did they all have such a crap job?

The sales jobs were all the same; fantastic salaries, if you could sell masses of something completely unsellable. That left factory jobs which wouldn't pay her rent, office jobs which required experience that Mary didn't have and one advert that required phone skills for "one-to-one telephone services delivered from the comfort of your own home." Things didn't seem that desperate just yet although the offer might seem more appealing as the rent came due.

The rest of the day was spent nominally looking for work on the teletext service but actually watching daytime TV. While talking to dull and possibly insane members of the public had at times seemed to tax her patience, repeats of the Jerry Springer show and Tricia seemed to actively reduce her IQ. Even if she didn't need the money, she would need to find work if her brain was not to turn into cottage cheese.

She decided that the personal phone service job would be taken only when she actually started drooling or starving. The work might seem more acceptable then. She had an early night with a good book and felt rather smug for not thinking about Max at all.

Bob watched Mary while she slept. He had been with her all day but hadn't known what to say. It was always confusing to him when what people said and did was different to what they thought and felt.

Mary went out after breakfast to get more papers and milk and spent the day looking at adverts for jobs and trying to work out when she had changed schools so that she could write a CV. Bob had left before she had woken up; of course, there was no way that Mary could tell that he had been there at all.

Mr Charles was out of bed and spent much of the day wandering through hospital corridors wearing a backless hospital gown, a tartan dressing gown and an embarrassed expression. For some reason, he had to wait outside of a lot of offices even though he had arrived late from the previous one. Bob watched him as he walked on treadmills and answered a lot of questions about his diet and "lifestyle". This last term rather confused Bob since he had looked at the lifestyle section in some of the magazines that Mary read and, as far as he knew, Mr Charles had never had a makeover or rearranged his house to make it harmonious.

Mrs. Anne Charles seemed to be in charge of everything in the house where they lived including Mr Charles himself. After several hours of examinations and much tutting, Bob's first believer was presented with a list of things that he could eat and of the sorts of exercise that he should take. His smile was rather forced as he read the list and he attacked his vegetable casserole with less enthusiasm than he might. Bob had spent part of the night carefully cleaning the fatty white gunk out of Mr Charles' arteries, just to be sure. The doctors seemed quite worried about it and since Bob only had two believers, he didn't want to risk losing one.

By midweek, Mary had decided not to get up at the usual time since there was nowhere to go and no-one wanted to see her. As if by some unspoken rule of nature, the delivery men were there bright and early. Mary opened the door to them in an old and rather wrinkled T-shirt and fluffy slippers, looking more than half asleep and altogether puzzled. The van was parked illegally next to her car with its hazard warning lights blinking. She stared at the logo on the side, trying to remember what to say. A man in baggy trousers and a polo shirt was standing on her doorstep carrying a large cardboard box.

"Hello?", she hazarded.

"Mary Callahan? Morning, love. Got your system right here, don't know a thing about them myself but I hear that these are very good indeed. Can we come in? Only this isn't getting any lighter and I have other places to be, if you would be so kind. Ah, thank you!" By this time, Mary found that she had opened the door and stepped back to let the man in.

"Nice place you got here, always thought that magnolia was a classic, myself. Wife doesn't like it but then she watches all those home improvement shows, doesn't she? I got one of those nice big plasmas, we get staff discount, you see. Anyway, I wanted it for the footie and she uses it to watch paint dry. I asks you! Right, just getting the monitor." With that, the delivery man moved off at a trot. Mary waited for him to return, determined to speak before she got buried in a blizzard of words.

She started just as he entered the hall. "Uh, I don't mean to be any trouble, but-"

"No trouble at all. I deliver these all the time. Mind you, not often out here, right on the edge of my patch this is and that struck me as strange, you know, because you were listed as first in the day and the computer normally plans my route so that all the nearby deliveries are first. Not that I mind, of course, better than being in the warehouse any day. I love being a driver, I do. Right, one more box and then I have some paperwork for you to sign."

Mary called after him to wait a moment but he called over his shoulder that he would be right back. He returned a few minutes later with a large flat package and a clipboard.

"Right you are, here we go. If you would just like to sign here, love?"

Mary took a deep breath, trying to calm herself. It didn't work. She took another. It didn't work either. She took a third and used it to shout. "Will you please shut up?" By this time, the delivery man had already stopped talking and looked more than a little hurt as a result. The ensuing silence was so profound that Mary felt embarrassed to break it but irritation won out. "I haven't ordered anything and I have no idea what you have just delivered or who it is for. I was asleep and I have had a very bad few days and I don't need this and I can't afford it."

The silence returned when she stopped speaking and stayed for a few seconds. Mutely, the delivery man raised one hand. Mary glared at him, "Be brief."

"Flat two, forty-seven, Corporation Road?", he asked. His voice was gentle, much like that used with a dog that might bite.

"Yes." Mary pointed at the number on the open door.

"Mary Callahan?", he said, cautiously.

Mary began to wonder if she had completely lost her mind without noticing. She looked at the man, still standing there with his hands full. "Let me see that clipboard", she said, taking it from the hand that was clamping it to the top of the box. The clipboard showed that the order was for a very expensive, top-of-the-line multimedia PC with everything, marked as paid. Mary was just trying to work out who had screwed up and how when she saw the special delivery instructions. "Tell Mary that Bob says hello." She paused for a few moments before turning back to the delivery man. "Where do I sign?"

Several hours later, the PC was set up on the sideboard, looking very new and out of place in the rather cluttered and slightly old fashioned flat. Mary looked at the large flat screen picturing rolling green fields stretching out in front of her and the blue sky with white clouds that looked absurdly cheerful. She sat there, hands over the keyboard, unsure of what to do. Eventually, she started the word processor so that she could write a proper CV. She was staring at the screen when words appeared.

"Hello Mary."

She blinked. She had several things that she wanted to say but she didn't know which to say first. She typed "Bob? This computer costs a lot of money."

Bob considered this for a moment. He wasn't sure what would constitute a lot of money. Much of what he knew of the world was based on what he had seen on television or in the internet. He had seen a number of emails that promised millions of dollars for quite trivial things such as helping a Nigerian lawyer move some funds. The computer seemed very cheap by comparison. He typed "It wasn't very much money. How are you feeling, Mary? I worry about you." Bob had come too close to losing one believer and wanted to be very sure not to lose Mary. He wasn't sure how literal a broken heart was.

Mary tapped back. "I am fine. What do you mean, not a lot of money? I can't afford to buy a computer, Bob. I don't have a job!"

The words formed silently on screen. "The computer hasn't cost you anything. There are thousands of jobs online. How is your heart, Mary?"

Mary typed, "Well, someone paid for the computer. They don't just give them away, do they? How am I going to find a new job online? Why can't men ever say what they mean?
55

Yes, of course I am upset about Max. I am swearing off men forever and that includes you, Mr oh-so-clever-hacker. Are you going to run away as well?"

Bob was struggling to follow the conversation. Bob had entered the credit card details in to the website and that apparently was paying. "I paid. You do tests so that you can find your ideal job. Please don't swear off me. I need you, Mary. You have to have faith in me."

Mary sighed. "How can I have faith in someone that I have never even seen? I never know when you are watching me. I have no idea where to find you. I don't even know your last name. Oh God, how do I know that you are not some weird stalker?" Mary looked at the computer as if it might explode.

After a pause, the words "Would it help if you could see me?" appeared on screen.

"YES!!!"

The hard disk chattered for a second and then the browser launched, showing a picture. The picture was of a man in his late twenties with a ponytail, a close fitting cloth hat and a rather sheepish smile.

Mary put her hand up to her mouth. "Oh my God" and then started typing. "You look just the way that I had imagined you!" This came as no surprise to Bob since he had based his appearance on her dream, creating the image one pixel at a time. He wondered if he should say that he could hear her perfectly well and that she didn't need to type but it seemed that it would cause more questions than it would answer and so he decided not to make a big thing of it. He could always hear any words that were intended for him.

Mary started to type again, "What is your last name and where do you live? You can't stop there."

Bob thought for a few milliseconds. To give himself a little time, he typed "I move around a lot for my work. I am never in one place long." Names were powerful things, Bob knew that. A name shaped a thing and he would have been a different god if he had a different name. He remembered the moment when Mr Charles named him; "And Bob's your Uncle." Would Bob Uncle sound strange? He couldn't remember anyone called Uncle in the personnel database of QuikQuote. He borrowed Mary's memory for a few seconds. It became easier to enter Mary's mind with practice. He saw a word that sounded right in some memory that she thought very old. He formed the words "My name is Bob Uncail."

Mary stared at the words for a moment. "Well, pleased to meet you Mr Uncail who knows things about my boyfriend, my ex-boyfriend, and who probably watches me through a telescope when I get ready for bed and who writes in tears and won't stay out of my dreams and... you do know that you are seriously weird, don't you?"

Bob knew that he was very different to Mary but he hardly had the experience to compare himself to other gods, even small ones. "What answer would you like, Mary?"

Mary typed hurriedly, fingers finding the wrong keys and having to backspace. "The truth, Bob. I want the truth. I have had more than enough liars in my life and God knows that I don't need another one. Don't you think that you are weird?"

Bob considered this. While he was thinking, he got Mary's new computer to look up the definition of weird.

weird   /adjective, -er, -est, noun

1. involving or suggesting the supernatural; unearthly or uncanny: a weird sound; weird lights.

2. fantastic; bizarre: a weird getup.

3. archaic. concerned with or controlling fate or destiny.

–noun Chiefly Scot. 4. fate; destiny.

5. fate (def. 6).

He was clearly supernatural. He wasn't fantastic though. He was perfectly real and no fantasy was involved. He had been around in one form or another since before man so he was certainly archaic. He hadn't been aware of what he was experiencing but he had been there, much like many of the people of the sixties. He didn't know anyone called Scot so that was no help at all. As for fate, he knew that he wasn't fate. That job was done by the Norns. So, two out of five was not all that weird. He typed "A bit weird, yes."

"And how am I supposed to get a job to pay for this expensive computer, geek boy?", replied Mary.

"You write your CV and then you post it online where thousands of potential employers are waiting." Bob was very sure of this as the website had been perfectly clear on this point, stating it over and over in large fonts.

Mary looked doubtful. "Are you sure about this?"

Bob was very sure. "Yes, Mary. It will be a chance to develop your potential. You do have faith in me, don't you?"

Mary sighed. "Bob, nothing much is working at the moment in my life, but I am glad that you are in it, crazy as that may sound. Yes, I have faith in you."

Bob typed a smiley emoticon. "Then everything will be alright. Do you have a CV?"

Mary had a CV in the drawer of her desk at work with a lot of other jobs that were not so very different to QuikQuote on it. "I was just about to write one."

Bob typed "Good." and while Mary typed out her CV, Bob thought of jobs that might be interesting for her to have.

The first requests for Mary to attend an interview arrived three days later. Mary was surprised to get interest from so many different types of organisations and thought that it was even more remarkable that they had sent the letters so quickly. She knew that she would have to discuss it with Bob when he was next online and wondered what he would say when she pointed to the pile of stiff white envelopes that she was yet to post. They all sat stamped and definitely unread by potential employers.

It was 6:15 pm and no seconds when BobUncail@yahoo.co.uk came online. Mary had been sitting at the PC, drinking a mug of tomato soup and watching the right hand corner of the screen intently. She had never seen Bob sign in before. He just seemed to be there and talking to her. She had meant to ask him one day, but with all the things that had been happening to her, she hadn't got around to it. Now she had seen the process, she was a little disappointed; somehow she had expected more without ever knowing what it was that she was looking for. The message window popped up before she could click on his name. She ignored his friendly greeting and started typing as if she disliked the keyboard.

"Don't you 'Hello Mary' me like butter wouldn't melt in your mouth. I know what you have been doing.", she typed.

Bob thought that was strange since he didn't think that Mary could have known what he had been doing - reading online newspapers from around the world. He had taken so long because there were all sorts of different languages to learn. He half remembered something about a tower in Babel but it was long ago and he had trouble understanding things from before his awakening. He was still trying to remember as he typed "That is nice. How are you, Mary?"

Mary's face was set without expression. Max had known to be very careful when she looked like that but Bob still had things to learn. "What? Are you mental? How can you sit there when it is all your fault?"

Bob was finding it very hard to understand Mary today. "I haven't been anywhere near there, Mary. How can it be my fault?" The tower was in Hillah, surely? He was pretty sure that he had been drifting around somewhere nearer to Berkshire than Babel.

Mary reached over to the coffee table, nearly falling off her chair as she scooped up the five envelopes that had arrived that morning. "And someone else applied in my name to be an advertising copywriter in London, a dental hygienist in Bristol, a sales assistant in a sex shop in Birmingham and a librarian here in Slough then? Or am I supposed to believe these people suddenly want me to come for an interview because they thought that I might be feeling a bit low and could use a lift?"

Bob wondered why the London School of Economics hadn't written. He had been quite certain that he had put Mary's name at the top of the list. "No, that was me, Mary. I don't think that they had heard of you before."

"And what made you think that I couldn't apply for a job myself? And what possible reason could you have for thinking that I wanted to move to Birmingham to sell sex toys?" Mary's hair looked even redder than usual for some reason.

Bob didn't know quite what he had done wrong here. "I thought that you wanted a new job. I was trying to help."

"Typical of a man to think that he knows best. You come along and you are buying PCs and applying for jobs for me and I don't know what else. Well, no more helping me, do you hear?", she typed.

The words "Yes, Mary." flashed on screen just as she unplugged the power cable from the back of the PC. She would have to send letters apologising to the companies in the morning.

Chapter 7

Mary didn't connect her computer to the internet while she typed the letters apologising for applying for the jobs that she hadn't applied for. Bob took this to mean that she didn't want to talk to him and didn't interrupt. She left the local interview until last. The library was only 20 minutes' walk from her house, just off the roundabout. Of course, there was no way that she could get a job as a librarian. She had barely been in a Library since she left school. Still, she could use the practice at interview technique and it was very local. Mary wondered if there was a crime anywhere in the statutes called "Wasting librarian time". She was fairly certain that there was not or all of her fourth year English class would have still been serving hard time or community service at the least. She gathered up the four envelopes for posting.

On the day of the interview, she dressed carefully in a black skirt, white blouse and a black jacket with shoulders that looked very eighties. She wasn't sure if librarians went in for power dressing and, looking in the mirror, she decided that "nun with attitude" was not a look that worked for her. A grey cardigan was too mousy but she rather fancied that she looked like a librarian while wearing it. The light blue jacket didn't really co-ordinate with white or black but those colours went with anything. Light blue didn't work with the shoes though. Mary looked through her shoe collection and realised that they were all trainers, sensible work shoes or "Night out" shoes, most of which had never been worn. Mary switched to a pair of high heels with thin straps and changed her jacket for a red one. If she was going to be assertive, she might as well go all the way.

Mary had been walking for nearly two minutes before she started to have doubts about the shoes, partially because of the look but mostly because of the way that they made her toes feel. Thoughts about shoes got her thinking about Max who had a strange fondness for strappy high heels but Mary pushed the idea out of the forefront of her brain. She breathed deeply and thought about the interview that she was about to do. She quickly decided that she would sooner think about Max than the interview and then chided herself for lack of self-respect. Instead, she looked at her watch and saw that she still had plenty of time which meant that she would have to wait, getting more nervous by the moment. To waste some time, she popped in to the chemists on the high street. She hoped that they had a good selection of corn plasters.

The chemist was part of a national chain and Mary could have been in any large town in England from what she could see. For some reason, the familiarity of the place calmed her down as she wandered towards the footcare section. It seemed only a few moments before she was leaving the store, corn plasters strategically placed and smelling of free perfume courtesy of a sample bottle. Mary checked her watch again and realised that she would be late unless she hurried. Even with the best that Hansaplast could offer, she winced as she picked up her pace.

Slough Library was exactly where it had been when last she visited, back in the days of GCSE exams and boy bands, stuck on a roundabout between Tesco and the bus station. Not much had changed since then. The posters advertising adult literacy courses could have been relics of an earlier age. As she walked in, a memory from when she was sixteen popped into her mind of sharing a cigarette with Peony Jones after meeting her in the lobby. She hadn't really been a smoker then or since but she had wanted to fit in. She remembered how she worried that people would smell the smoke on her clothes when she went back in to the Library and she had doused herself in Avon perfume that she had nicked from her mum. It occurred to her that the scent sample that she was wearing was very similar. As for the Library, the walls were still painted the same as they had been years ago, not quite chocolate and not quite cream colours - and it took Mary a moment to realise that it was now and not then. She found herself standing in the lobby in front of the double doors, dressed for an interview, strappy shoes and all.

Inside, things had changed since Mary was last there. It still held books but they competed for space with computers and a CD Library. Signs on the wall were in English, what might have been Polish and a mixture of languages that Mary didn't recognise but could have been Arabic or Hindi from the oddly flowing lines.

The counter of the librarian's area was still there, but it looked smaller and more worn than it had. She realised that she didn't know where she was supposed to go. "Well, there is a metaphor for my life.", she thought. She pulled the folded letter from her inside jacket pocket and read it again. It said that the interview was with Ms Mooney and the time and day but didn't give any indication as to where to find her or what her first name was. It didn't even say that the interview was at the Library. Her resolve started to crumble and she looked back at the door and Slough beyond it. It could hardly be called an appealing town but compared to an interview that she was unqualified for in a location that she didn't know, it was a haven of warmth and light. She was just turning when she heard a loud beep from the computer on the librarian's desk. A woman of around Mary's age hurried from the stacks of books on the returns trolley to the computer and started moving the mouse, frowning. The computer beeped again, more loudly and the librarian's lips formed silent words. Mary walked over, as much to have something else to think about than anything else and arrived just as the machine beeped still more loudly.

"Damned thing! It never works right.", said the librarian. She spoke quietly but with emphasis as if she would have liked to raise her voice. She looked up and Mary saw that she wore her job like a costume with a grey skirt and a cardigan buttoned tight. Her face looked familiar, jogging a memory in Mary.

"Peony?", she asked. The librarian looked puzzled.

"No, she isn't here. Were you supposed to meet her?" The woman looked blankly at Mary and then grimaced as the beep rang out again.

Mary felt more wrong-footed than ever. "Uh, no, that is to say, I don't think so. Well, I don't know actually. I am looking for... no, her name was Jones and... I am sorry. What do you mean, do you know Peony Jones?"

The librarian kept looking and Mary found herself willing the woman to blink. As the moments stretched on, the librarian said, "Well yes, she is my sister. Are you looking for her?"

Mary blushed and wished that she hadn't started the conversation. "Oh no, I haven't seen her in years. You just reminded me of her."

The librarian finally blinked. "Well, we do look alike. You don't know anything about computers, do you? This thing isn't supposed to make any noise and it has been bleeping on and off all morning." She leaned back and made a vague motion towards the keyboard. Mary reached for the mouse and the cursor moved smoothly to the volume control at the bottom right hand corner and the little loudspeaker icon was suddenly crossed with a red line, rather surprisingly as Mary hadn't any intention of doing that. The librarian peered at the screen. "That is odd. I have been trying to get it to do that all morning. Oh well, thank you." With that, the librarian looked up and smiled broadly in a rather empty way, the warmth leached out of it by repetition.

Mary made herself smile back and the seconds felt like minutes. Each waited for the other to speak. They both started at the same moment. "I wonder if...", "Can I help?" They both tailed off.

Mary started again. "I am here for a job interview."

The librarian looked at her, tilting her head to one side. "Well, you are late then."

For a moment, Mary felt as if she were at school, visiting after classes again. She had so wanted to be a rebel in those days. She smiled brightly and asked, "Is there a fine? Or is that just for books?"

The only reader in the Library looked up with irritation at the sound of the usually silent librarian laughing.

Ten minutes later, Mary was sat in a small office in an oversized but rather worn swivel chair, looking across a desk at Claire Mooney, the librarian and the two untouched cups of instant coffee sitting on the desk. It took a moment for Mary to work out what was wrong with the scene. Her chair was larger and more imposing than the simple standard issue plastic chair that her interviewer was sitting in. She glanced around the room to make sure that she hadn't misunderstood where she was supposed to sit but the office layout was perfectly normal except for the reversed chairs. There were also two monitors on the council issue desk, one facing the door and one facing the librarian. She was tapping at the keys, clearly looking for something.

The librarian looked up. "I am terribly sorry, but we seem to have mislaid your application form. I know we reviewed it and liked it, but I can't find the blessed thing. There is no good way of applying the Dewey Decimal system to paperwork, I am afraid. Would you mind terribly if we filled a fresh one out as we talk? I will ask the questions and write it out if you like."

Mary smiled and tried not to look nervous. "So, we had best start with the basics.", continued the librarian. "Your full name and address please?" Mary felt on safe ground here and recited her address and details of her schools and previous employment. She had all of the details straight from having written a CV only a day or so before and everything was still fresh in her mind, not that she needed help to know where she lived, thank you very much. The next question surprised her though. "What colour were the chairs in the school Library, please?"

"Orange, plastic with backs that bent when you put weight on them." It seemed a strange question.

"And the English teacher's name?"

"Hallet, had terrible dandruff and chewed gum all the time.", replied Mary.

The librarian tilted her head. "He didn't keep popping out for smoke breaks?"

"No, I never saw him smoke while I was at school. Did you go to Westgate as well?"

Mooney nodded. "I guess that he gave up. Good for him. So, none of your work experience involved libraries. Have you dealt with the public very often?"

Mary explained that she had talked to members of the public in all of her jobs and tried not to cringe at the memory of the training that she had been given. QuikQuote seemed to be trying to make all of the customer service representatives sound exactly alike, as impersonally friendly as an advert and interchangeable.

"Do you speak any Polish, Hindi or Urdu?"

"A little Gaelic.", Mary replied. In truth, this was limited to what she had learned from her Uncle and that was mostly swearing. She hoped that she wouldn't be asked to demonstrate. "Do I need those languages?"

The librarian looked up from the form. "The council thinks so, but I don't think it really matters. We haven't been very successful at attracting non-English speakers to a large building mostly full of books in English. What can you tell me about Lovecraft?"

Mary wondered if "More joy of sex" was in the self-improvement section. She paused and was wondering how to reply when words appeared on the second monitor. "WHICH ONE?" She read them out loud in her confusion.

Mooney smiled. "Yes, good answer! The horror writer, not the romance writer."

The screen started to fill with information about Howard Phillips Lovecraft. Mary would have to have serious words with Bob when she got home but she was hardly in a position to refuse the help. She felt that she would have given a better interview if she was more skilled at reading from a teleprompter.

After the questions, Claire Mooney explained how the team that worked in the Slough Library was organised. Names and job titles blurred while Mary tried to remember them all. An organisational chart started to appear on the monitor. When the librarian paused, Mary jumped in to ask a question just as her careers adviser had told her to back in school. "So, if I got the job, would I be working for you?"

The librarian looked at Mary oddly. "Can you keep a secret? I have to tell someone and you will be the first, other than my husband." Mary nodded, not entirely sure if Ms Mooney were altogether right in the head.

"Well, I had a letter this morning." The librarian paused as if uncertain how to go on.

"Yes?", volunteered Mary.

"Yes. Um, I seem to have won rather a lot of money on the premium bonds and I was thinking of taking a career break." Mooney smiled with a faraway expression on her face. "I mean, what are the odds of the computers choosing me out of all those millions?"

Mary didn't have to think very hard about that. "Better than you might imagine." The smiley face that appeared on the screen confirmed her suspicions.

Chapter 8

Mr Charles was released from hospital at eleven o'clock on an unseasonably grey and cool morning. He turned his face up to the sky and closed his eyes just as if it had been a radiant spring day. The hospital had told him not to drive until he felt perfectly well again. He did feel well, better than he had for years but he couldn't have driven home anyway. The car had been at the restaurant and his wife didn't drive. She could drive, of course; she was very clear on that. She had passed her test and never had an accident but it had been a good ten years since she had been behind the wheel and Mr Charles felt too keenly alive to want to travel in a car with Anne as a driver. A taxi would do just fine for today and the fare wasn't all that much. Mr Charles smiled as he realised that he hadn't paid for the meal that they had so dramatically failed to finish. That would more than cover the cost of the taxi ride.

Anne was waiting at the door and opened it as soon as the car pulled up. She looked a little anxious, an expression that really didn't seem to suit her. Mr Charles didn't hurry as he walked along the path to the door. He took a moment to see the slightly untended front garden and to feel the paving slabs under his feet. He reached Anne as she hovered on the doorstep and held out his arms for an embrace. She hesitated as he moved closer so he swept her up in his arms and drew her close. It felt very good to be alive. He knew that many people might think his marriage to be loveless but he was content enough in his quiet way. Maybe he could make a few changes but he was looking forward to getting back to work and maybe a lecture or two from his wife. He reckoned that he owed her that much for giving her such a fright. They walked together into the kitchen and he sat at the table as she made a pot of tea. He took the cup gratefully and sipped. The flavour was not quite what he was expecting. He glanced at the counter and saw a freshly opened box of decaffeinated teabags. Well, that would be alright, he thought. Nothing would spoil his excellent mood and he would savour each moment.

The day developed like a perfect weekend though it was in fact a Monday, which made it all the more delicious. Anne fussed around him and while he appreciated the thought, he would be pleased to do a little more for himself after lying in a hospital bed reading books that seemed to have been chosen for their propensity to not over-stimulate the patients. It was only when Anne went to get the paper that he was able to relax a little. He vacuumed the living room carpet, more to be doing something than because there was any real need. He flicked through daytime TV but nothing caught his imagination. There was something that he wanted to do but he couldn't put his finger on exactly what it was. The idea was only taking shape by the time that they went to bed and Anne offered him a very chaste kiss for a woman who had been married to him for 21 years.

The next morning was bright and the sky was perfectly dotted with clouds like the desktop of a computer. Mr Charles dressed with a little more purpose than usual and called a taxi to take him to get the car. Anne wanted to go with him but he smiled and said that he would sooner that she went to work and stopped worrying about him. He waved her goodbye and then sat on the garden wall, waiting for the cab and experiencing the day. It was late but he tipped the driver anyway before walking through the car park looking for his Vauxhall. Even the presence of the wheel clamp didn't really stop his smile. He waited the hour until the restaurant opened for the late coffee and early lunch crowd and went in to talk to the staff. After 20 minutes of talking to the shift manager, a chap yet to see 30, the clamping firm had been called and the fee waived in exchange for a promise not to sue the restaurant chain or claim that the thickness of the gravy was in any way responsible for his collapse.

It felt good to be behind the wheel again. He had always rather enjoyed the solitary nature of his work and the time alone in the car, with the radio for company or with just his thoughts. He had planned just how he would do what he had decided upon and the route to take. The local DIY superstore had much of what he wanted and an arts and crafts supply shop had the rest. Satisfied, he stopped off at the supermarket and bought the low-fat and low-salt options that he judged most likely to taste like food and least likely to taste like the packaging that they came in. Although the consultant had recommended more fibre in his diet, cardboard would have been going too far in Ray's opinion. Mr Charles drove home and was already chopping onions before Anne came back.

Anne was still treating him as if he might break and she wasn't at all keen on him spending the evening in the spare room, especially when she saw the small saw, the lengths of wood and the rest of his shopping. He assured her that it would be alright and persuaded her to watch the television which she did with only the occasional call to check that he was still alive. He made good progress but didn't hurry his work; he wanted to do each thing just right. He was pleased by the amount that he got done before bed and more pleased still that he was able to persuade Anne that cuddling was not a threat to his health. Carpentry was not the only thing that couldn't be rushed.

The following morning, Mr Charles ate his breakfast of grapefruit and muesli with a studied acceptance if not actual signs of enjoyment and insisted on making a packed lunch for Anne. After she had left for work, he called the office and told them that he was feeling perfectly well, thank you very much, and would be back at work the next day. They expressed concern but Mr Charles was very sure. Something in his voice made it clear that he was more certain than he used to be. That done, he returned to his project in the spare room and Bob watched, curious and excited.

Arts and crafts had never been his strong suit but with a little care and a few revisions, his work was progressing in a generally satisfactory way. The main structure had been completed the day before and today was spent with doweling, Stanley knife, velvet, panel pins and, once where it wouldn't show, a little glue. When he was satisfied with the surround, he carefully mounted the beautifully white ceramic plate in the centre and laid out the pots of paint. This was the point at which he was no longer certain. He sat and thought until he heard Anne unlocking the front door. He put down the paintbrush, still unused, and went down to see his wife. He had missed her in his way.

The evening was very agreeable indeed by Mr Charles' standards. They had dinner and watched television. It wasn't really important that there was nothing much on. The point was not what was being watched but that they were watching it together. For some reason, everything seemed to have a touch of humour to it as if it were all some subtle game for Mr Charles. The quizzical looks that Anne kept throwing at him suggested that this was not a mutual feeling but that was alright. After all the decent programs (and Anne had no truck with the other kind) ended, they went up to bed. At the landing, Mr Charles asked Anne if she would like to see what he had been working on. He felt somehow shy as if he were a teenager asking Anne to a dance even though she had seen him in every situation possible including, very memorably, dying.

Anne looked at her husband. "Uh, yes, dear." Her tone was pleasant, even mild and it didn't seem to sit especially well with her as if she were still on best behaviour. Mr

Charles smiled a little indulgently and took her hand to lead her to the spare room. He turned on the light and stepped to one side to let her see what was on the table. He had done the best that he could and the overall effect was pleasing if perhaps not as tasteful as he had hoped. A frame was covered in black velvet, swagged at the top and sides. Within that was a smaller frame, gilded with great care if not great skill and filled with a burgundy satin. In the precise middle, measured with care, was the white plaque with two candle holders either side. The plaque was quite blank.

Anne said nothing for a moment before opening her mouth to speak. She paused, looking as if the word that she wanted was on the tip of her tongue. Finally, she said, "It is very nice, dear. It is a... um... well, a shrine."

"Yes.", replied Mr Charles, clearly pleased.

"In the middle, perhaps a Madonna?", Anne asked uncertainly.

Mr Charles considered the pop singer for a moment but shook his head. "No, dear, I don't think so. I want to put... well, I felt that someone was helping me back in the restaurant. I wanted to say thank you somehow."

Anne smiled. "You know I prayed for you while you were in hospital. The whole congregation did."

"I expect that he liked that. I sometimes wonder if he gets lonely." Mr Charles spoke slowly, uncertainly.

"Does God get lonely?", asked Anne.

Mr Charles thought about this. If he had been asked before, he would have dismissed the idea as silly. "I don't know. But I didn't mean... well, I just felt that someone was helping me. I wanted to thank him. I think that I should put a painting of him in the middle. It just seems right."

"You mean God or a guardian angel?", asked Anne.

Mr Charles smiled. "Well, something like that, yes." Mr Charles respected Anne's beliefs and didn't want to shock her but he felt that he owed Bob something.

"That's nice", said Anne, her tone not entirely certain.

Mr Charles nodded and put his arm around her waist. "Yes."

"Are you any good at painting, Ray?", she asked.

Mr Charles thought back to school. His best subject had been technical drawing. "We will have to see", he said and turned out the light.

Bob had been very interested in the construction of the shrine. The quiet belief that went in to it had been welcoming, filling him with a warm sense of strength and peace. He wondered if it had the same effect on Mr Charles. He had listened to the conversation between the couple, but felt that much had been said that he hadn't heard, as if the words unspoken were at least as important as what was said. Still, he wanted to help and he was sure that he could do this. Very slowly, the lid of one of the pots of paint started to unscrew.

The next morning was busy and a little chaotic as Mr Charles and Anne tried to get ready at the same time while trying to help each other and more often getting in each other's way. Almost by chance, they managed to get breakfast and out of the house only a few minutes later than they had planned and off to work. Anne had an unremarkable day doing obscure things with forms and Mr Charles spent most of the day catching up with paperwork and fixing some rather recalcitrant servomechanisms in the small workshop above the office. He wondered, as he so often had, why the workshop, which generally contained heavy things, was on top of the office which generally contained light things with the clear exception of Barry, the area manager. Mr Charles considered relaying the warnings that the doctors had given about poor diet to Barry but decided that it really wasn't any of his business.

The day passed much like other days and Anne and Ray were home within ten minutes of each other. It was after dinner (fish, green beans and boiled potatoes) when Mr Charles went back up to the shrine.

Anne raced upstairs when she heard the heavy thump that could only be a body hitting the floor. Mr Charles was laid out on the carpet, looking very pale. Anne burst into tears and tried frantically to think what to do while her tears dripped onto her husband's face. She was still crying when his eyes opened and tried to focus. Mr Charles wasn't quite sure what had happened but years of married life had given him certain instincts and he tried to comfort Anne.

"Don't worry, dear. It will be alright, whatever it is.. His voice sounded weak and a little slurred.

Anne looked down at him and suddenly seemed to want to run in several directions at once. "I have to call an ambulance. Your poor heart!" She rushed out before he could say another word.

Mr Charles carefully got to his feet and looked again. No, he had been right the first time. He heard Anne talking hurriedly into the phone downstairs and called "Don't worry, dear. No need to bother the ambulance again. I just fainted." It was only after she finished the call that she dashed upstairs, by now looking much less steady than her husband. He assured her that he was feeling much better and took her over to the shrine so that she could see. The image was almost as perfect as a photo. Mr Charles hadn't had a clear idea of what he had expected his personal god to look like but he wouldn't have guessed at the ponytail or the beanie hat. The name "Bob" in stylishly raked gold letters was also something of a surprise but it seemed to fit well enough to Mr Charles. Anne just stared for a good minute. Several times, she opened her mouth to speak but it clearly took some effort.

"When did you paint that, Ray?", she asked.

Mr Charles held up the perfectly clean and still wrapped paintbrush by way of an answer.

"A miracle of Bob, love.", said Ray. "He saved me in the restaurant."

Anne turned paler still, her mind racing to reconcile what she had seen and heard with what she had believed all her life.

When the ambulance arrived, it was to find Mr Charles trying to revive Anne who had fainted and that wasn't at all what the radio message had told them to expect. In the end, they decided that the safest option was to take both patients to Accident and Emergency and let them sort it out.

#

Father Keith Ryan was young to be a father to children let alone adults, a shepherd that had never been within a dozen yards of a sheep unless lamb shank counted. He felt sure that some of his congregation found it awkward bringing their problems to a man young enough to be their son, but he tried his best to help his flock. His frailties were ordinary human weaknesses and if he felt them more strongly than most, he tried all the harder because of it. He knew that he was a good man but worried that he was never quite good enough. As a result, he put up with a lot of foolishness that an older priest might not have tolerated. He was used to comforting those with wavering faith and felt well suited to the task; he had always had doubts of his own to overcome and the experience was useful. He had learned to tactfully persuade teenage girls that a life in the convent was probably not for them even if black was slimming and others that a kiss behind the bike shed was probably not a mortal sin. He knew that many girls had real problems but they rarely came to him for help. What his time in the priesthood had not equipped him for was Anne Charles. Her faith was a rock upon which doubts broke like a storm-tossed sea and she didn't need anything slimming, quite the reverse if he were to be uncharitable. He tried to picture her enjoying a kiss behind the bike shed but found himself quite unable, in part because of his vows but mainly because his imagination was simply not strong enough.

She sat across from him in the confessional. "So," he said, "let me be sure that I understand this. You want to confess your husband's sins? You wish to pay contrition for something that he has done but which you are wholly innocent of?"

"Yes, Father. He would not come but something will have to be done about it!"

Father Ryan tried to picture Ray. He couldn't be called devout but he had sometimes visited with his wife. He struggled with his memory and could recall little more than a well-padded man in his late forties with an expression of much practised tolerance. "And does your husband seek forgiveness, Anne?" He didn't think that Mrs Charles much liked being called by her first name but the feeling in the Church was that it built a relationship which was desirable, well, not to a level of desire and not that sort of relationship but all the same, a jolly good thing.

"He denies that it is a sin but he has made a graven image, Father. That is a mortal sin." Anne didn't sound like someone seeking greater intimacy.

"Idolatry? Not exactly an everyday sin, is it? Of course, it is problematic because it is only a sin if he worships the idol and not the thing that it represents. It makes a difference if it is flat like a painting or more of a statue as well. John of Damascus thought that it was a crucial point and the Church has felt that there is a place for such things as a way of directing the mind, but critics—"

"Father!", Anne interrupted, "we are talking about my husband, not Church theology. Are you going to help or not?"

Ryan paused, reminding himself that patience was a virtue if not carried too far. "Yes, Anne, I am here to help. Tell me more about this graven image. Has he perhaps taken up with Buddhism? It seems increasingly common in Berkshire for some reason."

"He has a shrine to someone called Bob in the spare room. You can't tell me that is right."

Ryan tried to find the right phrasing. "Anne, I think that you may be a little confused. Homosexuality is felt to be a sin by some but, that isn't idolatry. Even then, it is only really regarded as sinful if he... well, does something about it."

"Father Ryan, I have been married for 21 years this September. I think that I would know if my husband was, well, you know. No, he says that someone called Bob watches over him, like a guardian angel."

Ryan wondered for a moment if he was being tested in his faith but decided that not even God worked in such mysterious ways. "Well, technically, that isn't idolatry at all if he believes in this Bob and not in the shrine. Who are we to say that he doesn't have a guardian angel? The hosts of heaven are many and varied."

Anne pursed her lips, barely visible behind the mesh screen. "And do angels have ponytails and beanie hats?"

Ryan sighed. "A subject that few bible scholars have approached, I fear. Look, I don't think that this is getting us very far. Could he perhaps come in to see me? We could meet in a less formal setting if that would help."

"I tried, Father, but he won't come. He says that if God can be anywhere, there is no reason why he couldn't be in the spare room."

Ryan thought about this for a moment. "A hard point to refute, certainly."

"Honestly," said Anne, "you are no help at all."

"Possibly.", the priest conceded. "Has he had any life changing events recently? An illness or perhaps a death in the family?"

Anne considered. "Well, he had a heart attack on Thursday."

"Yes, well, that would certainly qualify. And how is he now? I am sorry to hear that he has been ill.", he added hurriedly.

"Right as rain except for being mad as a hatter. He has never been quite right if you ask me", Anne offered.

Ryan thought that the man must have the patience of a saint to have avoided the temptation of breaking the sixth commandment. "Well, Anne, this does seem to be my area. Would you mind if I visited you and Ray at home?"

"For an exorcism?", asked Anne, visions of unsuitable Hollywood movies coming to mind.

"For a chat. This isn't Hollywood."

Mary picked up the post that had arrived several hours earlier. There didn't seem a lot of point in getting up early when there was no work to go to. There were three letters and the first two were a waste of ink. When the message is "We don't want you to work here", everything else is polite noise. The third was from the Library and Mary was half way to the bin with it before she realised that it said something different:

"Dear Ms Callahan,

thank you for your recent application.

We are pleased to be able to offer you the post of Assistant Librarian at pay grade six at the main Library in Slough. We understand that you are currently available for work and so suggest that you attend from this coming Monday starting with an orientation day.

Please contact us to confirm that you will be available. We look forward to having you on our team.

Yours sincerely,

<indecipherable squiggle>

C Mooney, Head Librarian."

Mary read it twice then made a cup of tea before reading it again. She carefully stuck it to the fridge with a magnet in the shape of a grinning cat and went into the living room to turn on the computer. She watched as it went through its normal start-up and the desktop appeared. She started up the word processor and the word "CONGRATULATIONS!" seemed to type itself.

"Bob?", she typed.

"Hello Mary."

"You knew", she typed, "How did you know?"

"They use computers at the Library as well. There are computers in a lot of places and I can go anywhere on those", Bob replied.

Mary frowned. "You will get caught if you are not careful. Please, I have seen how they track hackers down and they get sent to prison. You are my only friend now."

"How could they catch me? I can run away faster than they can follow." Mary noticed that Bob typed very quickly. She supposed it must be from using a keyboard so much.

"I don't know but they must be able to. Have you ever seen *The Net* with Sandra Bullock?"

There was a pause. "No, I haven't. Do you think that I should?"

Mary typed back, "Well, maybe. I don't know. Just be careful, please."

"If you want me to.", Bob replied.

Mary frowned. "I don't know how to be a librarian, Bob. How can I possibly accept the job?"

"You will learn. It should be interesting and there will be many books. I haven't read enough books.", Bob typed.

"You know, I have no idea what you do when you are not talking to me. Do you have many friends, Bob?"

"Yes, I know. No, not many friends. You are my friend and that is good."

"You don't have a girlfriend, do you?", Mary asked.

Bob quickly searched the web in the background. Most of the references were to sex and apparently the best girlfriends were cheerleaders. There were many things that Bob didn't
82

understand about humans and this was one of them. Most religions seemed to have a lot to say about when people should have sex, but it didn't really matter to Bob as long as they were happy. "No, Mary, I don't have a girlfriend."

Mary smiled. "And I don't have a boyfriend. Maybe that is the best way. What do you think?"

Another thing that Bob often didn't understand was when people asked one question when they meant something quite different but he understood the question behind the one that she had asked. "I think that Max was a very bad boyfriend. He made you unhappy.", he replied.

"Would you make me unhappy?", asked Mary.

"No, I want to help.", replied Bob.

"My only friend is a cyberstalker who sends me computers and who I have never met face to face. Doesn't that seem odd to you?"

Bob thought about it. He didn't have much experience. "Maybe." There was a long pause. "Would you tell me about your cat, please?", typed Bob. He was curious about cats and the internet's obsession with them. They talked until it was time for Mary to get something to eat. She had carefully avoided the subject of words written in tears or self-spreading ink. She wasn't ready to deal with that just yet. Maybe she had imagined it. He was just a very odd computer geek. That was it.

Chapter 9

Mr Charles was glad to be back at work. One of the things that he especially liked was that a lot of his time was spent alone in the car with no-one to tell him what to do. He had a mobile phone but the office knew that he would do what his worksheet said and so he was normally left alone with the radio. There was something about Radio Four that he found immensely comforting as if the world were a little more like it had been and rather less like it really was. There were also the afternoon plays which were frequently interrupted as he reached his destination. He amused himself by thinking up alternative endings for those that he missed. It was, accordingly, with a relaxed feeling of undirected goodwill that he parked outside of his house. He took the toolbox out of the boot (no tools were left in the car overnight, just as the sticker on the rear window said) and headed for his gate. He paused for a moment, seeing the bicycle parked neatly under the window. Mr Charles closed his eyes for a moment and looked up unseeing at the sky. His smile returned. He would make the best of whatever was coming. He was alive, he was happily married despite everything and he would relish those things. He walked up the path and slid the key into the lock. He took off his jacket, parked the toolkit where it normally lived in the porch and went on in.

"Ray, we are in the kitchen." Ah, that was Anne's voice, a little stress on the word "we". He walked to the kitchen, trying to radiate calm, but not exactly certain how that was done. He looked preoccupied instead. The priest stood to greet him as he walked in.

"How are you, Ray? It has been a while since I have seen you.", said Father Ryan.

Mr Charles didn't much like being called Ray by anyone other than Anne, but he let it slide, holding out his hand to grasp Father Ryan's in a friendly shake. "I am wonderfully,

ecstatically, possibly miraculously alive. How are you?"
Nothing like cutting to the centre of the problem, he thought.

The priest smiled. "You look very well, I have to say. I
was sorry to hear that you have been ill. Interesting choice of
words, Ray. Isn't life always a miracle?"

"A fine question.", said Mr Charles. "More your area
than mine, perhaps. Now, if you had a broken vending
machine then I could offer an opinion." Mr Charles turned to
Anne and leaned in for a peck on the cheek which seemed to
fluster her. "Hello Anne. Did you have a good day?" Anne
smiled and busied herself making the tea with a quick "Yes,
dear." It was clear that she wanted Father Ryan to carry the
conversation.

"You know," said Ryan, picking up the thread, "that is an
interesting answer as well. Anne came to see me at
lunchtime and told me that you were taking more of an
interest in things spiritual. Maybe I should take up a little
vending machine repair on the side to even things up." Ryan
smiled at his own joke. Ray's smile didn't alter except
perhaps to become slightly more fixed.

"Why, yes, I have indeed. Would you like to see it? If I
know my Anne, she will have mentioned it." Mr Charles
laughed and felt instantly sorry when he saw his wife wince
slightly.

Ryan didn't notice Anne's discomfort. "Why yes, that
would be good. I didn't want to go in until you got back so I
have just been chatting with Anne. Your wife is a wonderful
woman."

"She amazes me daily. Today more than most, if I am to
be honest. Well, you had best come upstairs." Mr Charles led
the way to the spare room and opened the door. "Let me
light the candles so you can see it at its best." He kept
matches in the chest of drawers.

The priest didn't say anything for a moment. "It is... it is very well done, isn't it? All your own work, Anne tells me. The... uh, icon is very well painted. An unusual choice but clearly great artistry. I didn't know that you are so skilled with a brush."

Mr Charles straightened his back a little. "No, I can't claim that it is all my own work. The painting just appeared. As for the rest, well, I remembered a little of my lessons from school. You know, the woodwork teacher also taught RE and it only just struck me how nicely the two crafts fit together."

"Because he was able to make icons?", asked Ryan.

"No, because he followed a carpenter.", Ray replied.

"Um, yes, I suppose so.", agreed Ryan, "You say that the painting just appeared? Are you suggesting that Anne did it or perhaps some supernatural agency? It seems a little hard to credit."

Mr Charles looked at the painting. "It does, perhaps. If someone told me that a painting had just appeared then I would have thought them a little touched. However, it is here and it seems silly to ignore the evidence of my own eyes. Unless you have a better explanation, I think that we have to assume that this is the work of Bob."

"There was a saint Robert...", offered Ryan.

"Possibly not the same Bob unless he was ahead of his time with his understanding of CPR. The ponytail and hat don't seem to fit unless he was an exceptionally modern sort. Was he?"

Ryan thought for a moment. "No, I don't think so. He did something regarding a monastery, but I don't recall exactly what. To be honest, it can be a little daunting telling one saint from another. There are rather a lot of them, you see. Well, Ray, I think that I may have to ask the Bishop for guidance on this, if you don't mind."

Mr Charles clapped Ryan on the shoulder. "Why, do as you must. Should he wish to visit then he will be just as welcome as you are. Shall we go downstairs for tea? Anne seems to think it is the cure for all ills and I could certainly use a cup." Ryan followed Mr Charles back to the kitchen.

Anne had offered the priest another cup of tea, but he hadn't wanted to stay. He seemed rather troubled from the expression on his face, she thought, and very well he might be in her opinion. Mr Charles came back into the kitchen as soon as the front door closed.

"Did you mention that there was another cup in the pot, dear?", he asked.

Anne pushed the teapot towards him. "I hope that you were not rude to Father Ryan. Such a nice young man. It is a shame that he can't marry, I think.", said Anne.

"Certainly an experience that he will never have, dearest. You could always write to the Pope, I suppose, but the Church does seem a bit set in its ways."

"Ray! His Holiness has far more important things to do than read silly letters from the lay Church and it would hardly be respectful now. Fancy suggesting such nonsense!"

"Yes dear.", said Mr Charles. It was normally a safe option. He looked over the tea cup and saw that Anne's lips were set in a thin line. Perhaps it hadn't been the best choice of replies this time.

"So," she asked, "are you going to do what Father Ryan said and take down that silliness upstairs?"

Mr Charles smiled. "He didn't ask me to, dear. He seemed to think it quite interesting actually. He even mentioned that the Bishop might want to have a look at it. It would be a shame to deny him the chance, don't you think?"

"A Bishop coming to see a pagan shrine in my own house? I really don't know what my mother would think.", said Anne.

"Yes, it has been a while since you saw her, hasn't it? Perhaps you could visit next weekend.", said Mr Charles. Anne looked at her husband with an unreadable expression. "I will be quite alright dear. I can give you a lift to the train station." Anne looked unconvinced but said nothing. Mr Charles felt that it was a small victory.

It was four days before Ryan was able to secure an interview with his senior. Bishop Crossan was a dour Scot that many might have taken for a Calvinist until they heard his views. He liked to keep up with current thinking even if he often did not agree with the direction of the modern world. He had made time for the appointment in the late evening at his sprawling but run-down Victorian town house.

"Keith, do come in and sit down." he called from behind the large and cluttered desk. The office was clearly divided into two areas, one which resembled a lawyer's office and the other a cosy corner with comfortable chairs and a coffee table that was reserved for less formal discussions. It looked rather underused to Keith. He sat down on the carved wooden chair in front of the Bishop and wondered if the lack of a cushion had any significance.

"Your Excellency." said Ryan.

"We are all friends here, Keith. Servants of one master. Douglas will do well enough for now. Will you have a whisky? There is some sherry but I can't say that I much care for it, whatever tradition says." Bishop Crossan had kept much of his Glaswegian accent but time had softened it to a burr rather than a saw.

"Why, thank you, Douglas.", said Ryan and waited.

"Well, hop to it then! Cabinet behind you. Not too much water in mine. There is no ice. Ruins the flavour." Ryan scrambled to his feet and went to mix the drinks.

"So, Keith, you said you had something to discuss. Not a crisis of the faith, I hope. Always a worry with you younger ones, well, that and the temptations of the flesh. Keeping well away from those, I hope", continued the Bishop.

Father Ryan pushed down a blush. He had never found his vows of chastity to be much of a burden. "No, your Excellency, nothing like that."

"Good, good. Had to pack a chap off to be a prison chaplain only last week. Can't be having that, especially with all the media attention. Ach, if that is mine, do more than wet the bottom of the glass. It's hardly an Islay malt now."

Ryan returned with the drinks. His glass had perhaps a finger of the brown liquid while the Bishop had half a tumbler full. Douglas accepted it without comment and took a hearty mouthful. Ryan sipped his. The Bishop waited for the coughing to stop.

"So, what brings you here? I don't think that it was for a glass of Glenlivet." The Bishop pushed a carafe of water across the desk.

Ryan explained how Anne had visited the confessional and his subsequent visit to the shrine. Douglas Crossan slowly worked his way through the glass while listening. At the end, the Bishop stirred himself and looked directly at Ryan. His manner was clearly mellowed by the Scotch. "So, in essence, the husband of one of the parishioners has invented his own religion and you are concerned about it?"

Ryan sipped his drink and tried to hide a grimace. "Well, yes, Douglas. The miraculous element was what disturbed me the most. Perhaps it is a snare from the devil. Um... I know how silly that sounds. He could just be barmy but the painting was extraordinary."

The Bishop smiled thinly. "Ah yes, miracles are hardly two a penny around here, are they? The image of our lady seems much more likely to appear in the bread roll of some unfortunate in the slums of Rio de Janeiro than in a batch of Hovis bought at the local Waitrose. Still, to talk of the devil... Ryan, it must be two years since you left the seminary, no?"

"Uh, three, your... Douglas.", replied Ryan.

"Three years. Not a long time from the viewpoint of an old man, I am afraid. The devil exists, of that you may be certain. Mother Church is very clear on that but his forms are not the forms of the bible any more. He is found in the greed in men's hearts, in the lust that so many mistake for love, in the heart of the drug pusher, the petty thief and the rapist. There may well be the devil's work done in the back bedroom of many a house but I doubt that a spot of do-it-yourself idolatry is quite what is on the mind of the prince of darkness. No, my son, I think that we can leave the bell, book and candle alone for a little while."

Ryan cleared his throat. "There is the matter of the heart attack. Anne tells me that the doctors were puzzled by that. Well, by the recovery, rather."

"Ah yes," Douglas replied, "that is much more the stuff of miracles. Could this Mr Charles be called a devout man?"

"No, a bit of a backslider, to tell the truth. I think that he only ever attends to humour his wife. Well, you know how it is." said Ryan.

The Bishop nodded. "I do, all too well. The attendance figures show that there are a million like this Mr Charles and a few more each day. Still, God loves even the sinners. Have you heard him confess, son?"

"Uh, not very often and I don't recall ever having to give him more than a single Hail Mary. He is not a man much troubled by passions, I think. I would have to say that he was ordinary except for his patience. His wife can't be an easy woman to live with, I would imagine. Of course, I don't have any experience to draw from there." he said.

"None of us do, my son. Patience is a virtue and often one sadly missing but it hardly makes the man a saint.", replied Douglas.

"His wife, Anne, is… well, virtuous to a fault and loving, I am sure, but...", Ryan trailed off.

"Yes, quite, I have met a few like her in my own time in the confessional. Nevertheless, hardly conclusive. One to watch rather than do anything about just yet, I think. Report back in a few months, why not?"

"Yes, Douglas. Thank you." Ryan started to get to his feet.

"Not quite so fast there, young man – though you can freshen our glasses while you are up. I wanted to talk to you about a fundraising drive for missionaries. Rome seems awfully keen."

"Oh, where are we sending them?", asked Ryan as he gathered up the glasses.

"Here would be a damned fine start in my opinion but apparently they are needed in Finland. You wouldn't happen to speak any Finnish would you?"

"Uh, no, your Excellency."

The meeting lasted a good deal longer than Father Ryan had expected and he had to take a taxi back to his house. There were too many police around to risk riding his bike after the Bishop's generous hospitality.

Chapter 9a

A rock moved through space. It was not the same rock as the first one but it was similar. It was made, like the first one, of iron with some nickel and a smattering of less common metals. It also lacked a name or a number, just one rock among countless millions. It was unremarkable and, even if anyone had known that it existed, there was nothing interesting to say about it.

Chapter 10

Mary started work in the Library on the next Monday morning, arriving well before the Library was open to the public. There was a slow, silent rain of the sort that seems to soak everything so slowly that you don't notice as it pushes past your collar. The spring light was as grey as week old bathwater and it felt more like autumn than April. She took what shelter was to be had in the doorway of the Library in the hope that she could keep off some of the rain that seemed intent on soaking her trousers. The building was a light grey, almost matching the sky and covered in panels of textured concrete. She looked at it, trying to imagine what it was like to work inside its pigeon-streaked walls. Somehow, it looked smaller than it had when she was a teenager and she wondered whether the designer had taken to drink after seeing what he had created.

She was standing there when an older lady walked past her with a brisk "Excuse me please!" and unlocked the door. Mary started to put down her umbrella, fiddling with the catch. By the time she had it folded, the rather plump woman had squeezed in through the door and locked it after herself. Mary muttered a half-hearted "Damn." as she tried to put the umbrella back up only to have half of it fold back on itself with a spine tearing out of the thin nylon. "Damn!" repeated Mary, this time with more feeling. She looked around for a bin to dump the now useless thing in and saw one a little way down the street. Her hair was quite wet by the time that she got back to the doorway and her pale suit and blouse were already looking much worse for the rain. She knocked on the door and waited. After a few more seconds and some more drizzle down the back of her neck, she knocked again, louder. After another pause, the woman returned and walked up to the door. Instead of opening it, she pointed at the grey plastic sign beside the path that showed the opening hours.

Mary shouted as quietly as she could, acutely aware that this was a Library, even if it was empty. "Can you hear me?" Traffic rumbled past including the odd bus from the depot across the roundabout. The woman put her hand to her ear and mouthed words that could have been "I can't hear you." Mary mimed the action of opening the door but the woman just pointed at the sign with the opening hours again. Finally, Mary reached into her jacket pocket and pulled out the letter asking her to report for work and held it to the glass of the door. The woman on the other side opened the door and took a step back to let Mary walk in.

"Why ever didn't you say, dear? You must be Mary. Come on then."

Mary came in out of the rain.

Mrs Fothergill was apparently a part-time librarian and tried to explain the schedules and the other librarian's hours as she made sure that Mary had a plastic cup of instant and truly horrible coffee from the vending machine. There were far too many names for Mary to remember and it was clear that Mrs. Fothergill ("Call me Angie, dear, everyone does.") only had the vaguest knowledge of the librarians who worked other shifts from her and hardly ever stopped talking, except when in the public areas of the Library. It was as if she were trying to compress all the talking possible in a day into the few times when she didn't have to be quiet. In short order, Mary was shown the toilets, taught how to operate the photocopiers that worked just like every other photocopier that she had ever seen and the location of a vending machine on the first floor that made brown mud in a cup. All of this took less than the twenty minutes left before the Library opened.

Angie showed Mary how to unlock the door then they both went behind the Library counter on the ground floor. Each floor had its own desk and Angie explained that Mary would work on each of them in turn while she was learning the job. Other librarians were already coming in and joining them behind the brown desk set in a sea of brown carpet. Coats and umbrellas were stowed away and more people were introduced to Mary with Asian or Polish names which she forgot immediately. She would be reading name badges for a while though she hadn't yet been issued with hers. The day passed in a haze of smiling confusion. She answered telephones and was asked questions that she couldn't answer and asked puzzled looking customers if she could help them only to discover that she couldn't. After a full day, the only skill she could claim to have mastered was checking books out and back in again which was made simpler by not having to do more than return the Library card and put the book on the trolley to be replaced on the shelves. The computer records seemed to take care of themselves. She was left confused and more than a little disheartened when it came time to close the Library.

The next day was a little easier as she was assigned to putting books and DVDs back on the shelf. It was slow but the items were well labelled and the map of the Library was an invaluable guide. The day after, she got a badge to hang around her neck and spent the day on the second floor, quietest of all with its reference books and small study tables. Sometimes she would be asked questions but the computer was a great help and she always seemed to find the answer quicker than anyone else. She sometimes thought of Bob but never saw any other sign of him other than her uncanny success with the computer.

Bob enjoyed the Library. There was something very satisfying about all of human knowledge classified in a series of numbers. They started at 000 as all good numbering systems should with computers and information about information which seemed logical. If you were to learn all things, the key to finding where everything was would need to be one of the first things that you needed to know. Not all of the information on computers seemed quite accurate though. It seemed that a lot of humans didn't really understand how computers worked; many more things happened at the same time than the books suggested. Of course, the authors of those books didn't have the ability to be inside a processor while it worked.

Philosophy and psychology followed next which didn't seem to fit since how humans actually worked wasn't explained until section 500 which was all the sciences. Religion was at 200 and Bob found that he knew a great deal more after reading all of that section. He also felt that he understood less. Why would people assume that gods wanted all the strange things that he had found in those books on religion, he wondered. It didn't matter at all to him if people ate pork or lobster. They didn't have to observe any special feast days or wear special clothes. All that he needed was that they believed in him. He couldn't speak for any other gods but it made no sense to him.

All of the social sciences seemed to assume that you understood what people wanted and thought but no two books seemed to agree on what people thought and wanted. Bob only had the vaguest ideas based on Mary and Mr Charles and this seemed too small a sample no matter how important they were. Languages at 400 seemed a waste of time. Why did anyone need so many? Science was interesting but that wasn't really how things were, as far as Bob could see. There was something to be said for the various quantum theories as the world was just a series of possibilities but there was no mention at all of belief and that was the most powerful of all the forces. The technology section was interesting enough but all of the devices described were very simple when you could see the inside of them. Arts made even less sense to Bob but humans seemed to get very excited about them for some reason. Reading history books told Bob that humans really didn't know much about what had happened in the past and couldn't agree on much of it either. A great deal of it seemed to be about them killing each other.

At first, it took Bob a long time to read the books because he was waiting for people to take them down and open them. They were far too heavy for Bob to move himself and even the pages took a lot of effort to move. It would have been slow to read one book at a time so Bob would read two pages of one book and then move on to a different reader. It took some concentration to keep a dozen books straight at the same time, even for a godling. Bob also checked how Mary was doing from time to time and made sure that she was getting the answers that she wanted on the computer. Bob wasn't impatient (being effectively eternal) but this seemed inefficient. Bob decided to read the books while they were closed which took a little more effort but it avoided rereading popular books and skipping over unpopular ones. It took a little more time still to read the CDs and the records but after three weeks, he had read the Library.

Mary settled in to a comfortable rut and got to know the other librarians. Angie Fothergill liked to mother them all but there were people from all sorts of backgrounds. Elzbieta, a pretty blonde girl from Krakow was the youngest and Angie was the oldest with everyone else in-between. Some wore Saris, some wore tweeds but everyone seemed to get on more or less. It was as if being a librarian was a thing that crossed all cultural lines. Everyone believed that knowledge was a good thing, that people didn't respect books enough and that many people were unreasonable idiots. Mary had started with that last belief already firmly entrenched after years of working in what was essentially a call centre and she quickly found herself liking books more than she thought that she would. She didn't mind dealing with difficult people as much as some of the others – this was no harder than selling insurance, even if it was face to face. The greatest difference was that the people who worked at the Library actually wanted to work there. It was nearly a perfect job. The only thing that the Library really lacked, in Mary's opinion, was eligible males.

Mary went home after a long day on the ground floor desk. Her mind hadn't really been on her work and she had made a few mistakes including trying to exclude a guide dog because she hadn't realised that the owner was blind. She made herself a cup of tea and switched on her PC. She had been thinking about Bob all day. She knew that he didn't owe her anything and he had helped her a lot but she needed to let him know that she didn't like being ignored. She started the word processor and started to type a letter without having the first clue where to send it.

She typed "Dear Bob."

The cursor moved down and words appeared without her touching the keyboard. "Hello Mary. I like it when you call me 'dear'. Did you have a good day at the Library?"

Mary frowned. "Not really. Where have you been?"

"I spent most of the day with you. I like it there at the Library. There are people and books to read. You got some new books today and I enjoyed them."

"You were there all day? I didn't see you. You didn't say anything.", she typed.

"I helped with queries.", Bob replied.

Mary thought for a moment. "The only new books that we had today were in Urdu and they are not on the shelf yet."

"Yes.", replied Bob.

"You can read Urdu?", Mary asked.

"Yes, there is an English to Urdu dictionary in section 400"

"I didn't see you.", she repeated. "Why didn't you say hello? she asked.

"You were working.", replied Bob.

"Well, it would have been good to lay eyes on you. We haven't spoken in days. I thought that you had forgotten about me! I thought that I had done something wrong.", she typed quickly.

"I won't ever forget you, Mary. I need you more than you need me."

"You need me? But do you know anything about me? I don't know where you live or anything like that. How am I supposed to get in touch with you?", she asked.

"It is easy. You only have to think of me and I am there.", Bob typed.

"Oh, very cute. I don't even know where you work. Do you even have a job? You can't just hack into computers all day, can you?"

"I can hack into computers all day if you want but I have a job. I look after the people that believe in me. I look after you.", typed Bob.

"That is very sweet but, really, how can I contact you? I mean, I like you and you have helped me so much but why can't you be like a normal man? You are not gay or anything, are you?" She thought of Mr Simmonds, the senior at the Library and quickly added, "Not that there is anything wrong with that but I really hope that you are not."

Bob knew quite a few definitions of the word "gay". He was happy but he couldn't be called festive. He was invisible so he couldn't be called showy. He didn't have a gender so he couldn't be homosexual. Whatever she meant by the question, he could safely answer "No" and did so.

"Do you just not find me attractive then?", Mary asked.

"You are beautiful and I love you.", he replied.

"You love me? Then why won't you talk to me or see me? Why do you only ever talk to me on the computer? Are you shy?"

Bob replied, "Yes. I can see you now. We are talking now. I wrote to you in tears once but that was difficult and this is easy. I haven't met many people. I would like to meet some more. I would like you to help me."

Mary sat with a stunned expression on her face. Surely she had imagined the thing with the tears. "How can I help you when I can't phone you or meet you or anything?"

"I would like you to get people to believe in me."

"I believe in you.", typed Mary.

"I know and thank you. That really does help. I would be stronger if more people believed in me."

"Don't you believe in yourself?"

"That doesn't work, Mary. I need people to believe in me."

"You mean other people. It is OK to have self-belief. You are a very strange man, Bob.", Mary typed.

"I am not a man, Mary.", he replied.

"Oh God, I remember the long hair in the picture. You are not a woman, are you?"

"No, Mary. I am not a woman either."

"Well, that is just silly. Unless… are you a transsexual?", she asked.

There had been books on intersex people in the Library. "No, Mary, I am not like that. I would like you to be very calm because I must tell you something. Are you sitting comfortably?"

"Is this Jackanory?", asked Mary.

That wasn't one of the DVDs in the Library so Bob just replied "No"

After about 20 seconds, Mary typed, "Ok, I am sitting comfortably. Tell me your story, please."

Bob wrote, "I am a god."

Mary scowled at the screen. "No, you are not God." she typed.

"Not *the* God, just a god.", wrote Bob.

Mary breathed deeply and rather deliberately typed, "You were weird about religion back when I first met you. Bob, I have to tell you that people are not gods. Maybe you should talk to someone about this."

Bob replied, "I am talking to you about this, Mary."

"Well, yes, but you see, gods don't talk to people over computers. That isn't how things are. Gods talk in people's heads and listen to prayers."

Bob knew a lot more about people from the time that he had spent in the Library. It would be difficult but he had read a lot of books on neurology. He would take it nice and slow the first time and try not to be too loud. Bob focussed on Mary, following the patterns in her brain. It was very different to a computer but he was reasonably sure that he could manage it. He triggered the tiny changes that would make neurons fire. The voice arrived in Mary's head and it wasn't like hearing words. She couldn't have described the voice because there were no words to hear. She just knew that he had spoken. *Like this, Mary? We can talk this way if you would like.*

"Oh my God.", she said quietly.

Yes, Mary, I am here.

"This is a trick, isn't it? You are using something to make me think that I can hear you in my mind.", she said.

Yes, I am.

"Well, there you go then. It's not real, is it?", she said.

Bob somehow sounded puzzled. *Yes, it is a trick and yes, it is real. I am putting the words into your head with a miracle.*

"But miracles aren't...", she trailed off remembering words spelled in tears. "I don't understand. How can you be a god?"

How could I be anything else?

Mary stared at the screen even though the words were no longer coming from there. "I don't know. I... why me?"

You wanted something to believe in.

"I am not sure that this is what I wanted.", Mary said.

I am sorry, but this is what you have. I am a small god but if you believe in me then I am your god.

Chapter 11

Mary woke up slowly and lay there looking at the ceiling. She turned her head and saw the red glowing numbers on the clock without reading what they said and tried to gather her thoughts. It couldn't be that she had really had a god speaking directly in her head. That was insane. It must have been a temporary thing, a "moment of madness" although the only ones that she had heard of seemed to affect politicians caught doing something sordid on Hampstead Heath or axe murderers, a class of people that she preferred to some politicians. She didn't think that she was insane so it must have just been a funny five minutes. She would prove it to herself.

She thought as clearly as she could. "Bob? You can't hear me, can you?"

Good morning, Mary. Do you often dream of your mother?

"Oh God! I mean, I am sorry, I didn't mean to take your name in vain. That is a sin, isn't it?"

Bob chuckled and that was the strangest experience that Mary had ever had, an amused throbbing somewhere behind her eyes. *It is quite alright, Mary. I don't mind. As long as you believe in me, it doesn't matter but you can call me Bob.*

Mary remembered nuns who had been very clear on such matters. "Um, that isn't what the bible says."

I am not that god, just a god. I don't know much more about gods than you do. The only books that I could find about them were written by men.

"But does the god of the bible exist?", asked Mary.

I don't know. I haven't met that god. There are all these… you could call them sparks if you wanted that could be gods if someone believed in them but I haven't met all of them. There are billions at least. I did take a look around Mount Olympus but all that I found were rocks and some rather determined climbers.

"And the devil?"

I haven't met him either.

"How old are you, Bob?"

I am very old but you could say that I have been asleep. It isn't true but there isn't a better word so it will do. I have been awake for a few weeks now'.

"Um, OK, but what am I supposed to do? People don't normally have gods talking to them in their heads."

Breakfast sounds like a good idea.

"Um, you don't eat, do you?"

In a way. Your belief sustains me. I need you to believe in me.

"I do. This is crazy, but I do."

I know. Thank you.

"I have to get out of bed now. Can you look away?"

Bob didn't understand why it mattered to humans, but he knew that it did. *I will go and surf the web. We can talk more later.*

Mary felt very self-conscious as she showered and went through the rituals of the morning. The computer wasn't on and her tea from the night before was still there, cold and filmed with tannin. Apart from that, everything seemed perfectly normal. Breakfast was unremarkable and the drive in to the Library was just as mundane. Mary kept looking for anything out of the ordinary but didn't notice that she never had to wait for a traffic light. That wasn't unusual for her anymore.

The day started as it usually did. Older men came in to read the free newspapers and students from the Thames Valley University site on the other side of the roundabout came in to use the reference library. Mary thought that they had a look of desperation and concluded they were probably just starting a paper that had to be handed in the same day. She tried not to think of Bob during the morning until she had her coffee break.

She sat down in one of the tired looking armchairs in the break room and thought, "Bob?"

Yes, Mary?

"Last night, you said that you wanted more people to believe in you.", she thought.

Yes, Mary.

"What could I tell people? Did you make the world or pass any miracles? I mean, did you make a dead man walk?"

I mended a broken heart once.

Mary's mind flashed to Max.

No, not like that. My other believer had a heart attack and I cleared out an artery for him. I am sorry that you still miss Max. He wasn't kind to you.

"Your other believer? Then there are only two of us?"

Yes, Mr Charles is my other believer.

"Well, where is he? Could I talk to him?"

He is on the M4 going west. He has to be in Bristol by 12:30. He is in breach of part VI of the Road Traffic Regulation Act, Clause 81.

106

"How do you know that?"

Criminal law is at Dewey Decimal reference 346.

"No, how do you know where he is?"

I can find either of you any time. I learned how from the way that computers work. If I switch between you and him every microsecond, you will never notice that I am gone.

"What kind of god reads books on computers?"

The god of vending machines, computers and perhaps librarians.

"Angie Fothergill said that Saint Lawrence was the patron saint of librarians."

Please let me know if you see him. I have some questions.

"I think that we all would. But you can do miracles, can't you? I could show people miracles, couldn't I?"

I could do small miracles for you, yes.

"Could you perhaps turn water into wine?"

That is harder than it sounds. There are not nearly enough carbon atoms.

"Ok, but you can do other miracles like feeding many people with a little food?"

Only if they want very small portions.

"Bob, I do believe in you. I have to unless I want to believe that I am going crazy, but can you do even a little miracle for me, please?"

Mary's coffee cup floated slowly and rather uncertainly into her hand. She saw that she was shaking as she closed her grip. She took a deep breath. She was a woman of the world, she told herself. She could handle this. "Um, thank you. That was… well, it was nice but it doesn't look all that impressive compared to some of the things that Paul Daniels does. Could you manage a burning bush?"

Absolutely.

"And would it be burned afterwards?", she asked, thinking back to RE lessons and nuns.

Yes, Mary. That is the way that the universe works.

"Hmmm. I think that we may have to work on easy but impressive miracles."

The morning passed as normally as it could when a god spoke directly into your head. The comments were helpful for the most part, but Mary found them disconcerting and said as much. After that, Bob left her to her work and concentrated on helping Mr Charles with a badly clogged soup vending machine. The techniques that he had developed for arteries seemed to work well. Mary spent the rest of her breaks reading about Joan of Arc. It wasn't a comfort to learn that many people believed that Joan suffered from schizophrenia, but Mary didn't feel as if she was ill. Life had improved since she had met Bob. The only people that she knew with mental illness were some of the visitors that came into the Library, generally in wet weather, that shouted at the books or argued with people who weren't there. None of them seemed to have floating coffee cups. She wondered if she was supposed to wear men's clothes and cut her hair short like Joan, maid of Orleans, but decided that no-one would notice in any case. She had worn her hair short since Max had left and she preferred trouser suits to skirts in any case.

When Mary got home, she fed the cat and made herself a cup of tea and wondered what she should do next. Her mind was still a blank when she saw the post-it note stuck on the television set. It read "Mr Charles." and a phone number. The writing was perfectly neat and more regular than anyone could have managed. It was also in Garamond font. She carefully ran her fingers over the yellow paper and couldn't feel any indentation from the pen. She looked at the number again as she finished drinking her tea. She supposed that she had to call the number. There didn't seem to be any harm to it. She reached for the phone and dialled.

The voice that answered was a woman's and held more than a hint of sharpness. "Anne Charles, yes?"

"Um," Mary hesitated, "may I speak to Mr Charles please?"

"We don't buy anything over the phone, you know", replied Anne.

"Um, nor do I. Very sensible, I think." Mary listened to the silence for a moment.

"Yes, well, I will go and get him then. Hold on." There was a clatter as the handset was put down on a hard surface. She could hear indistinct words and then a man's voice came on the line.

"Hello there. Ray Charles. No relation. How can I help?" Mary had no idea what he meant by that but the voice sounded friendly, almost fatherly.

"Um, Mr Charles, I don't really know how to say this but, well, a friend gave me your number. You see, I think that I might be going a bit strange...", she trailed off.

"Half the world seems to be strange or going that way if you ask me but that is hardly new. What can I do to help you? I am afraid that I don't know your name."

"My name is Mary Callahan, Mr Charles. The friend thinks that you know him too. His name is Bob."

There was a pause. "Ah, would this be Bob with the ponytail and a way with electronics?", asked Mr Charles.

"Yes! A ponytail and a beanie hat and... and you hear him too? I am not going mad? Oh thank... well, thank Bob, I suppose."

There was no mistaking the delight in Mr Charles' voice. "I am so very glad to hear you say that. Yes, we have a very special friend in common, Mary. How did you meet him?"

Mary released a breath that she hadn't known she was holding. "He is real and I am not imagining things. Oh, I am so... well, relieved. He sends me messages on the computer and speaks in my head and.., and this sounds insane but I promise that I am not a weirdo. Please, please don't hang up!"

"I wouldn't dream of it. I am so pleased to hear from you. I had no idea that anyone else knew about Bob. He has never sent me a message except for once, in tea leaves which does sound odd now that I say it aloud.", said Mr Charles.

"He made words out of tears for me.", said Mary.

"And from paint. Did he tell you about the shrine?", asked Mr Charles.

"No. I had no idea. Where is it?", asked Mary.

"The spare bedroom.", said Mr Charles.

"Um, is there any way that I could...", Mary trailed off.

"Visit? Of course. I would be happy to invite you and I am sure than Anne won't mind." Mr Charles hoped that this was true. "Could you come around on Saturday? I would be pleased to show you. It has a miraculous image that he created."

"If I could then yes, thank you, that would be wonderful. I don't know where you live though."

Mr Charles gave his address and Mary copied it down. "You say that you hear him in your mind?", said Mr Charles, making the statement into a question.

"Yes, just recently. He doesn't speak as such but I know what he has said somehow. I don't know if that is making any sense to you.", said Mary.

"How exciting! I hope that you will tell me more when we meet."

After the phone call ended, Mary got out an A4 pad and a pencil and started writing and drawing. She didn't have a great deal of talent, but she worked steadily. After a while, she went over to the computer and started transferring the design onto the screen. A little after eleven, she yawned, stretched and shutdown her computer. She forgot to save the file but Bob took care of it for her.

Anne had gone to bed a little before Ray and she was lying squarely on her side of the bed, her face pale with moisturiser and a black mask over her eyes. Ray was quite used to seeing his wife like this and it hardly ever occurred to him that it would unsettle most men. He climbed into his side of the bed, careful not to disturb her and lay back on the pillow, looking up at the ceiling. In the quietness of his head, he felt a small presence in the darkness behind his eyes.

Good night, Mr Charles. Sweet dreams.

Mr Charles smiled and let his body relax.

Chapter 12

Mr Charles was not wholly sure how he felt about someone else believing in Bob. He was not a jealous man. Of course, Mr Charles was not sure if Bob was an angel or a god or something else entirely. It occurred to him that his religious education classes had been a very long time ago and the sermons of Father Ryan and Father Hoskins before him had not really covered this topic. Possibly it had been felt to be of marginal interest to the parishioners of Uxbridge. Mr Charles was firmly of the opinion that the best thing to do when uncertain was to learn about a topic and then try to figure it out from first principles. Solving a religious dilemma really couldn't be all that different to diagnosing a malfunctioning vending machine when it came down to it. Once you knew how a thing worked, you just followed the process through, he thought. However, that would have to wait until he had completed his call sheet for the day. Mr Charles finished his breakfast (low sodium cornflakes with skimmed milk) and headed out for the car. The M4 was calling him.

The morning passed uneventfully with the usual array of issues to solve. Vending machines were not complex to use but people seemed to struggle to follow even simple instructions. He knew that it wound some people up but Mr Charles had come to see it as a form of job security. He didn't have much time to think about Bob until his lunch break, a thing that he insisted on taking every day. Out of respect and love for Anne, he passed up the bacon sandwiches offered by the truck stop and ordered a limp and overpriced salad at the Reading services instead. He knew that he could ask Bob questions if he wanted, but that seemed somehow disrespectful. A little reading would probably help him to ask the right questions even if it didn't provide any answers. He supposed that he could go to a Church and some temples and have a look at their holy books but he wasn't sure if they would have them in English and he really had very little idea of what he was looking for. Perhaps he would be better off going to the research section of the Library and asking for help. Of course, he thought as he chewed a particularly stringy bit of celery, they might think that he was mad. They could have a point, he thought, as it was entirely possible. If so, there wasn't much that he could do about it. Yes, a reference Library was the way to go. He would have to try to find time to visit but he had calls to make that day.

Anne Charles rather enjoyed her work. Many people would assume that there was very little joy in the life of an Administrative Officer in Trading Standards but Anne was happy. She enjoyed the social interaction with her colleagues but the aspect of the work that she found most rewarding was the procedures and processes. There was a quiet satisfaction in things being done right for the sake of having them be right. It was hard for Anne to explain and she would never have attempted to discuss the idea with Ray but there was a reassurance to things being in their place and as they should be, all the ducks properly in a row. It gave her a sense of all being right with the world. That was one of the appeals of the Church to her, the litany and the rituals unchanged for hundreds of years. She loved her husband with a quiet love worn smooth by the years but she knew that he would never understand the simple joy of continuity. She worried about this new... thing that had come into their life. It was not part of the pattern that so reassured her but Ray seemed happy in a way that she had not seen in years. It wasn't as if either of them was unhappy with their marriage. It had become a comfortable routine and Anne was nervous about changes. She quietly resolved that she would be as much the loving wife as she could.

#

Mary had printed out the drawing from the night before and looked at it during her first tea-break of the day. It was a poster advertising Bob. In the cold light of day (or more accurately, the fluorescent strip lighting of the break room), it seemed both inadequate and slightly ridiculous. She really had no idea how to start a religion. It was not something that had ever come up at school. Indeed, the nuns would probably have been against the idea. Mary decided to look on the internet to see if there was anything helpful there. She had not realised how good she had become with computers. There was a book by Timothy Leary called "Start your own religion" and a quick search of the Library index showed that it was on the shelves. She would have to take a look at lunch time.

Bob spent the morning in the Library too, quietly reading Dewey Decimal classification 552 (Petrology). He found the descriptions of rocks frustratingly vague.

Mary found the Timothy Leary book deeply unhelpful. It was mainly focussed on counter culture and none of it seemed to address how to get people to worship a god as such. Some more browsing found books on how other religions had started, but none of those seemed much more useful. She tried a technique that had always been her last resort and all too often her only one. She made a list.

1. People cannot believe in Bob until they know about him.

2. Knowing about a thing is not the same as believing in it.

3. Miracles seem to be central to religions.

4. Bob is unlikely to be able to offer big miracles.

5. The salary of an Assistant Librarian will not pay for much advertising.

6. There are many established churches, all of them with more money.

7. Going door to door is popular, but only helpful if you want people to pretend that they are out. Also, no idea what to say.

8. Leaflets? Free access to the photocopier.

9. Need more ideas. Who can I ask?

Mary stared at that last question. She supposed that she could always ask Bob. She would mention it that evening. For now, the cataloguing called.

#

In a lay-by on the A34, the last ribbon of the roadside shrine blew away, arcing over the fields. The CDs had been taken by someone with more greed than respect. Jason wouldn't have minded though. He knew that music was for listening to. His parents had left flowers at the spot and wanted very much to believe that their son had survived in some way. The belief was undirected and had nowhere to go. No-one found it and it faded away. They would later learn of Bob but they never made the connection between their loss and the waking of the godling.

Chapter 13

That evening, Mary made herself some dinner and sat with a pad and a pen at the same table that she had eaten at. "Bob?"

Hello Mary.

"I have been thinking about how to get more people to believe in you. Um, did you already know that?", she asked.

I don't listen unless you want to speak with me or you look puzzled. I have been trying to understand more about privacy.

"Um, do I have to speak? I feel like an idiot talking when you are going to answer inside my head."

Bob was unsure about how best to explain. *When you speak, you are mainly thinking about the thing that you want to say. When you don't then you are thinking about more than one thing such as whether you should have another cup of tea or how the blister on your heel is still hurting. Men and women seem different in that way. Mr Charles only seems to think about a few things at a time. You can whisper if it helps.*

"Ok, I will keep speaking out loud then. It feels silly talking to myself, though. People come into the Library and do that. Mostly smelly old men, actually. Do they have a god like you, Bob?"

You are talking to me. I am here and real. I know about the men that come into the Library and I have never seen anything that I would recognise as being like me, just the sparks.

"The sparks?"

What I was once. Without belief, I was just another of them. Your belief keeps me aware and lets me be myself.

"Would you die without belief?"

I don't think that I can die, but I would shrink back to being one of them, I think. I will probably exist until the end of the universe.

"Are you eternal? We were taught that the... um, well, the Christian God was eternal and everlasting."

That may well be. The sparks were around at the beginning. The universe exploded and there we were. I experienced it but I did not understand it at the time.

"Do you know who created the universe?"

I don't think that there is an answer to that. There would need to be a time before the universe and time is an aspect of the universe itself.

"The bible says that there are no other gods. Could another god have made you?"

I have read all of the major holy books. It doesn't say that, Mary. It says that the Hebrews were not to worship other gods, not that there were no other gods to worship. I don't think that it matters though. The bible is made up of other books, all apparently written by men.

"We were taught in school... I went to a Catholic school... that those men were guided by the divine and so their word was the word of God."

Is that why you have the pen and paper? Do you want me to guide you?

Mary laughed nervously. "Well, not in the same way. Sorry. You told me that you need more people to believe in you. I was trying to work out how to do that and I realised that I don't really know enough about you to explain to anyone else. Could you tell me more about yourself?"

I only know what I have been able to discover for myself. The books in the Library do not seem to tell me very much and the internet makes even less sense. I have some questions about that, actually.

"Um, maybe later. Can you tell me what you are in a way that I could explain to someone else?"

Mary, if a human child were born without any other humans to tell him things, he would only know what a human was by looking at himself. He would not know how his arm moves but he would know that it does. I know that I can will a thing to move and it moves if I am strong enough. I can lift a cup if you are there actively believing in me, less if you are not. I have learned about computers and vending machines, so perhaps it would be fair to call me the small god of these things... except that they do not believe in me.

"You always say that you want people to believe in you. How do people worship you?"

I don't want or need worship. People don't have to do more than believe that I am real and care that I exist. That makes me stronger and I will be able to help them. Everyone gets something. That seems fair. I don't want them to feel less than me.

"But you are a god."

Yes.

"Aren't gods better than people? Isn't that the idea?"

Mary, have you read stories of the Greek gods?

"Um... not really."

Belief shapes a thing and they were very much as people wished that they could be. They were not kind. They did not look after their people. I think that they are no more.

"But gods are eternal?"

Is a god still a god when they do not remember their own name?

"I don't know. Why do you care about people when they didn't?"

Because of you and Mr Charles. You believe that it is right to be good to people, that fairness is important. I have become the god that you needed me to be.

"What would happen if someone really nasty believed in you?"

I don't think that they could come to love me. I don't know if I could love them. I love you and Mr Charles.

"I spoke to him on the phone. He has invited me to come and see his shrine."

Yes. That was kind of him.

"To invite me?"

Yes, that as well.

"Bob, I think that we are getting a little off the point here. Can you do anything that I could show other people?"

Yes. I can move things if they are not too big or too small.

"How can a thing be too small?"

They don't stay moved. Quantum theory is really very clever.

"Is that a god thing?"

No, physics. 503.12 in the Library.

"Oh. I will have a look. So, walking on water? You can move tears."

Mary, I don't have feet. I can't walk on anything. I could lift a person if I had enough believers but with just two, I am not strong enough

Mary thought for a few seconds. "Bob, I think that you are wonderful. You are the best thing that ever happened to me, but I can't think what I can show people that would help them believe. Can you think of anything that you can do that would impress people?"

I can care.

"Yes, yes, you can. But I can't show people that."

I can make computers and vending machines do whatever I want. Would that help?

"I don't know. Maybe Mr Charles has an idea."

#

Mr Charles called into the office for his list of daily calls and to collect spares. Tracy had printed the list off the computer and had it waiting for him. He didn't look at the locations until he got to the car. It looked like he would be getting a long lunch break which was good. On the other hand, it was in Slough. Once, Mr Charles would have at least tutted about that, but he took a deep breath, looked out at the sunlight trying to push past the clouds and reminded himself that being alive was a wonderful thing. Slough it was and Slough it would stay and never mind what that poet fellow, Betjeman, thought of it. "Come friendly bombs and fall on Slough." indeed! He put the car into gear and headed for his first call which was in Maidenhead.

The morning had gone well with everything falling into place for once. Intermittent faults showed up at once without him having to test the machine over and over. He was done with the morning calls by 11:30 and had some time to kill.

He was heading towards the town when he saw the Library and remembered that he had planned to do some research. He smiled and looked for somewhere to park.

Mr Charles was not a frequent library visitor. He took a couple of thick paperbacks with him when he went on holiday so that he would have something to do while it rained on Bournemouth, but he preferred non-fiction, ideally in the form of a circuit schematic or a manual. The older lady on the desk directed him to the top floor for the reference section. The place seemed to be full of students writing away in notepads or texting on their mobile phones. One thing that he did like about libraries was the numbering system for subjects. That seemed sensible to him. He was looking for the guide when a young woman walked over and offered to help him. It seemed rude to refuse although he would sooner have used the index.

"Ah yes. I am looking for information on religion. Not so much a specific religion as the nature of religions, if there is such a thing. I am not quite sure where to start.", he said.

The librarian smiled. "You could try metaphysics at 110 or Religious Mythology at 201. It all depends what you are looking for. Could you be more specific?"

"Not really, I am afraid. I am trying to find out about the nature of gods and miracles but not from the point of view of any established religion.", he replied.

"Sir, would you be willing to tell me your name?", the librarian asked.

"Ray Charles. No relation."

Mary looked puzzled for a moment before laughing. "Perhaps we should just get coffee instead, Mr Charles."

Mr Charles had no idea how to react to a proposition from a younger woman. "Um, thank you but I am very married."

Mary blushed. "Oh yes, I spoke to your wife. I am Mary, Mr Charles."

Ray half smiled. "What are the odds of that? A lucky coincidence?"

Mary's smile was full enough for both of them. "I prefer to think of it as a godsend."

Chapter 14

Mr Charles and Mary ended up at a pub not far from the Library. It looked like the main trade was in the evening and they were able to find a table away from other people.

"So", Mary said, "Where do we start? Bob tells me that you were his first believer. Does that make you a high priest or something like that?"

Mr Charles gave a chuckle that stopped short of being an embarrassed laugh. "I don't know anything about that. I just found that there was someone there and that he wanted to help me. I have no idea how this works. I studied electronics at college and they don't really prepare you for starting a religion."

"Sixth form business administration is no better, I am afraid. I can't say that I remember a great deal of that to be honest." said Mary. There was an awkward silence. "So, what did you come to the library to find out? I know that you were not looking for me."

"I think that Bob may have had that in mind but I was trying to work out what Bob is. Do you have any ideas?"

The explanation lasted through the meal and a second drink. At the end, Mary asked, "Has he asked you for any sacrifices yet?"

"No, I can't say that he has. What sort of thing does he want? I am not wholly comfortable with the idea." Mr Charles said.

"It is alright. I don't think that chocolate bars mind.", Mary replied.

"Chocolate bars?", asked Mr Charles.

"From the vending machine. Bob would ask me to dedicate them to him."

Mr Charles considered asking for the model of the machine but decided against it. They agreed to meet again on Saturday at the shrine as they had planned.

Bob was curiously absent that afternoon. The computer still seemed very easy to use but there were no messages of any kind. Mary decided to wait until she was at home before asking Bob about it. She didn't call Bob until she had eaten, fussed and fed the cat and watched Eastenders. She sat down in front of the computer and logged on the messenger. The screen remained resolutely blank. She closed her eyes and thought "Bob?" The beep of BobUncail coming online caused her to open her eyes. She started a chat session and typed.

"Bob, that wasn't chance, was it? You know what I am talking about. Couldn't you have been honest with me?", she typed.

"Hello Mary. I was honest with you. I didn't say anything that wasn't true.", Bob replied.

"By that reckoning, Max not mentioning that he was seeing someone else doesn't count as saying anything untrue though, does it?", Mary replied.

"If I told you everything that I did then you would not have time to do anything but listen." appeared in the chat window.

"Do you not think Mr Charles meeting me was important?", Mary asked.

"Yes. That is why I hoped that you would talk with Mr Charles. You could explain it in a much more human way. I am still learning about people." Mary noticed that Bob's replies were better phrased than they had been when he had first contacted her.

"And so you got him to visit me at work without warning me?", Mary typed.

"No, I just rescheduled the jobs that he had so that he would be near the library at lunch time. He decided to visit. I don't think that I could make either of you do anything that you didn't want to do without hurting you and possibly not even then. I wouldn't do that, Mary.", Bob replied.

"How do I know that I can trust you, Bob? I have not had a lot of luck trusting people.", Mary asked.

"I am not people.", Bob replied.

"You know what I mean.", replied Mary.

The reply was a little slower this time. "Mary, I am more than nothing because you believe in me. If you and Mr Charles stopped having faith in me, I would be less than a mote of dust on the wind. My life, such as it is, is yours to give or take. I can't possibly hurt you, Mary. I would never want to. It would hurt me. You have made me in your own image."

"What do you mean?", Mary asked.

"You value kindness and so made me kind. You value honesty and so made me honest. You pictured me in your mind and so gave me form. If I am your god then you are my human."

"Oh." Mary was not sure what to say after that. "If I find you more believers, will you change?"

"I am what I am believed to be, Mary. May I ask a favour of you please?" appeared in the window.

"Yes, what?", Mary typed.

"Choose people like you, please."

"Like me?", Mary asked.

"Yes, good people", replied Bob.

#

Mary parked near Mr Charles' house. From the outside, it was an unremarkable semi-detached pebble-dashed house like the others in its road. The front garden was neat rather than beautiful. She took a deep breath and pressed the doorbell. Anne opened the door. Mary had not known what to expect, but Mrs Charles was a thin woman in her early fifties and dressed in a blue skirt with a crisp white blouse that hung from her angles. Mary realised that she was staring and looked down to see that Anne favoured black slip-ons. She realised that she had no idea what to say.

"Mary Callahan?", asked Mrs Charles.

"Um, yes?", said Mary and wondered why she was questioning her own name.

"You had best come in. The kitchen is through here. You can keep your shoes on if you wipe them on the mat.", said Mrs Charles. Her tone was carefully neutral.

"Thank you.", replied Mary and let Anne lead her into the house.

Tea was made, and very small talk attempted. Biscuits were offered and Mrs Charles was technically the perfect host without at any point warming past civility. Mary decided to try to break the ice.

"Thank you so much for allowing me into your home, Mrs Charles.", she said with the warmest smile that she could manage.

"I love my husband very much.", Mrs. Charles replied.

126

"Um, yes.", said Mary. It seemed like an odd comment to her.

"I think that this shrine is foolishness and possibly wickedness but if he has asked you here then you are welcome.", said Mrs Charles.

"Thank you.", Mary said, "that is good of you. Is your husband here? I was hoping to see him."

"He is changing into a decent suit. You know what men are like, I am sure.", Mrs Charles said.

"Oh yes.", said Mary with more feeling than she had intended.

Mrs Charles' expression could fairly be called old fashioned.

Mary blushed, her cheeks approaching her hair colour. "Um, I am single, but I come from a large family. Irish Catholic."

Mrs Charles smiled with the expression reaching her eyes for the first time. "Oh, you should meet Father Ryan. Such a nice young man."

Given that Mary was here to see a shrine to Bob, she struggled to find a sensible answer to this suggestion. The silence was becoming more uncomfortable when she was saved by Mr Charles coming down the stairs dressed in a blue suit that was rather formal for a Saturday morning and a few years out of fashion. "Ah, Mary, so good of you to visit.", he called from the kitchen door. "Come on up and feel free to bring your tea."

Mary looked at the shrine. Yes, that was Bob and no mistake. Attending a convent school meant that she had seen many icons over the years, but this was the first one that she had seen with traces of acne. She felt a little guilty for that. It was hard enough to be responsible for her cat without being responsible for the appearance of even a small god. She became aware that Mr Charles was looking at her expectantly and that she had to say something. "Yes, that is Bob alright. He looks exactly as he did in my dream and on the computer."

"You didn't take a screenshot, did you?", asked Mr Charles.

"No, I probably should have. It would have been proof.", Mary said.

"Not terribly compelling though, perhaps.", said Mr Charles.

"Yes... Do you have any idea how to find him more believers?", asked Mary.

"Not as such. I had not expected to become a missionary at my time of life. Have you heard street preachers?", asked Mr Charles.

"Doesn't everyone think that they are nutters?". Mary asked.

"Probably. I can't see that working. Perhaps we could organise a meeting of some kind. The Sally Ann used to preach to the homeless and they would probably listen to anyone who fed them.", Mr Charles said.

"We often get them in the Library and they look pretty thin. We could try the same thing.", said Mary.

"That sounds worth a go. At worst, it will stop them from being hungry for a night and it is hard to see that as a bad thing. Bob, can you hear us?"

Yes.

Mr Charles and Mary smiled a second or so apart. "Do you think it will work, Bob?", asked Mr Charles.

I think so. Thank you. I believe in you.

"Is that the way that it is supposed to work?", asked Mary.

That evening, Mary sat on the sofa and thought about how to provide meals for the homeless. Mary didn't know exactly how a soup kitchen was supposed to work and there didn't seem to be anything in the Library to help, but she reasoned that as long as there were hungry people and food in the same place at the same time, it couldn't go too badly wrong. She was meeting Mr Charles in Slough town centre at 8:00 on Friday evening which concerned her a little since there would be people out drinking. She hoped that they would still be reasonably sober that early in the night. The food would need to be cheap and filling, so she had bought the ingredients for beef stew (heavy on the potatoes, just like mother used to make) and put leaflets up in the Library and the local churches. She supposed that this was technically poaching potential worshippers, but she didn't find herself able to feel guilty about it. In any case, Bob would forgive her if she asked. She had put the shopping away and was putting her feet up for a well-earned rest when there was a knock at the front door. This puzzled her for a moment; very few people came to visit, and it was too late in the evening for meter readers or door to door salesmen. She got up, straightened her cardigan and went to answer the door.

There were two policemen standing outside, both in their late twenties to early thirties. "Oh no", Mary thought, "they are starting to look young. Policemen are supposed to look older and rumpled and make you feel safe but these looked like they just stepped out of school and I wish that I had worn a nicer cardigan."

The older of the two was the first to speak. "Mary Callahan?"

"Yes.", said Mary. Her thoughts suddenly flashed to her mother back in Dublin. "Has someone been hurt?"

"No, we just have some questions. May we come in?", said the first policeman. The second one seemed to be trying to look past Mary.

"Of course. This way." Mary let them in, the door opening straight into the lounge.

The two policemen stood in the middle of the room making it seem cramped rather than cosy. The second policeman spoke for the first time. "That is a nice looking computer, Miss. Have you had it long?"

Mary wondered why the policemen would not get to the point. "No, only a few weeks."

"And do you have a receipt for it, Ms Callahan?", asked the older of the two. He pronounced "Ms" as if it had several "z"s.

"Um, no, it was a present." Mary replied.

"Would you mind telling us who gave you the computer as a present?" asked the policeman.

"A… friend of mine.", replied Mary. She started to panic. The police always made her feel guilty even though she had never done anything really all that wrong. 'Police and nuns... what was it about black and white uniforms?,' she wondered.

"I am afraid that we are going to have to ask you to come down to the station with us to answer a few more questions. Also, I have to warn you that you do not have to say anything, but it may harm your defence if you fail to mention, when questioned, anything that you may later rely on in court. Anything that you do say may be given in evidence." Mary stared at the officer in shocked silence. She had only ever heard the words of the caution on TV shows and it felt strangely unreal to hear them in her living room.

"You may want to get your coat and any medicines that you need before we go to the car, Ms Callahan.", said one of the policemen. He was not smiling.

Chapter 15

Mary had seen enough police procedural dramas on television to make the experience wholly familiar though she had only ever been in a police station before to hand in lost property. The interview room looked just the way that it had in the programs, even down to the cassette deck on the desk but none of the people in the room looked handsome or rugged enough to be a romantic lead actor.

The police had not been unkind. They had supplied her with a cup of tea (slightly stewed) and some beans on toast (cold toast) when she had asked. There had been no other conversation until her lawyer had arrived.

She had been offered a lawyer, Mr Mohammed, provided by the courts, who she accepted because it seemed like the sensible thing to do. She had been given only a few minutes with the rather frazzled looking dark-skinned man after a wait of a few hours. He had advised her not to answer any questions if she could avoid it and to only answer the exact question asked. He then introduced himself and explained hurriedly that she had been arrested on suspicion of credit card fraud, specifically that she had purchased a computer on a credit card that was not her own. He carefully asked her if she could explain how she had come by the computer honestly. Mary had explained that it was a gift from her friend, Bob. Mr Mohammed had asked if Bob was able to come forward and explain that to the police. With a sinking feeling, Mary explained that she was not sure where he was at the moment. Mr Mohammed had sighed at that and told her that he would only be able to defend her if he had no reason to think that she was guilty of any crime. If Mary told him that she had committed fraud or knew that the computer had been obtained by dishonest means and *if* she told him that then all that he could do was argue to lessen any penalty imposed on her. He made eye contact as he stressed the word "if", his expression more eloquent than his words. He then asked if she wanted to continue with the explanation that the computer had been a gift and Mary said that she did. That rather ended the conversation.

As Mary sat in the interview room with an unspeaking WPC for company, she thought, "Oh Bob! What have you done?"

Hello Mary. What are you doing here?

"The police want to know where I got the computer that you gave me."

I bought it from J Squared Technologies.

"They think that the credit card that you used was stolen. Where did you get it from? Surely the bank didn't give you an account?", Mary thought as loudly as she could.

No. I used Darren Johnson's card as he had been unkind to you and made you cry.

"Bob! That is fraud! You can't do that sort of thing.", Mary thought angrily.

I am sorry. I had not read section 345 (Law) then. They must have found out from a computer. I can change that. Please wait. I have changed it now. There had not been a noticeable delay.

"What am I going to tell them?", Mary thought.

You should tell them the truth, Mary.

"Are you sure? Who is paying for the computer now if you have changed the computer records?"

That is difficult to explain. J Squared still have the credit in their account but no-one has a debit.

"You can't just create money like that.", Mary thought.
133

Yes, I can. That is what the government do.

"You are not the government!", Mary thought.

No, but I am a god. The law has provisions for acts of God and it doesn't say which one.

The door opened, and another man walked in with Mr Mohammed. The new man was in his forties, had bags under his eyes and was wearing a suit that didn't fit terribly well. He had a serious expression and seemed short of patience. The lawyer sat down beside Mary and the man sat opposite. He reached over, turned on the cassette recorder and then spoke into the air.

"For the record, I am DC John Richards, it is 10:30 pm on Thursday, the eighth of May, 2009. This is a recording of an initial interview with Mary Callahan of Flat Two, Forty-Seven Corporation Road, Slough. Also present are Mr Mohammed, representing Ms Callahan and WPC Ryder." He looked directly at Mary. "May I call you Mary? My name is John." He had an accent from somewhere near Birmingham.

Mary looked at her lawyer who nodded. "Yes. Hello."

"Mary, when officers came into your home, you had a Compaq CQ2009 computer on your dining room table. You told the officers that it had been a gift. Is that right, Mary?"

Mr Mohammed interrupted. "Did your men have a warrant to search Ms Callahan's flat?"

"No search was carried out and our officers were invited into the flat." A harsher note had crept into his voice as he answered the lawyer. His tone softened again as he turned back. "So, Mary, the computer was a gift, was it?" he continued.

The lawyer nodded at Mary. Mary said, "Yes, it was a gift."

134

"Who was this gift from?", DC Richards asked.

"Bob.", replied Mary.

"From Bob. Does Bob have a last name?"

"Uncail." replied Mary.

"And do you know a Darren Johnson?"

"Yes, he was my manager when I worked for QuikQuotes.", replied Mary.

"Is that where you saw his credit card, Mary?" asked DC Richards.

Mr Mohammed raised his hand. "That is a leading question, Detective Constable. I am directing my client not to answer it."

"Very well. Mary, could your friend Bob Uncail have seen Mr Johnson's credit card?", he asked.

Mary hesitated. Bob's thoughts entered her mind. *You can tell him, Mary. I want people to know about me.* Mary took a deep breath and started. "Yes, I am sure that he could have. You see, Bob Uncail is a god. He can perform miracles, well, small miracles, mostly to do with computers and vending machines. He didn't understand how the law worked and so he used Gitfa- Darren's credit card but he has fixed it now and it hasn't cost anyone anything." Mary could hear her own voice and somehow it seemed very distant and strange.

"And how has Bob fixed it, Mary?", asked the DC.

"How?", thought Mary. *I altered the bank's computer.* "Bob altered the bank's computer so that no-one loses out.", she said. Her voice sounded questioning even to her.

DC Richards paused for a moment. "So, just so I am clear here, you are telling me that your friend Bob Uncail used Mr Johnson's credit card but has gone into the bank's computer and changed the records and now no-one has paid for the computer. Is that correct?"

"Yes, but that is OK, isn't it?", said Mary.

"You do know that hacking computers is illegal, don't you, Ms Callahan? The computer misuse act of 1995?", asked DC Richards.

Mary noticed that her lawyer was holding his face in his hands. This was not going well. "Um, normally, yes but this was an act of God. They are different, surely?" She looked at her lawyer for confirmation, but he just shook his head without removing his hands.

"And where can we find this Bob Uncail, Mary?" asked DC Richards.

"He is right here", said Mary. She remembered reading about Joan of Arc and wondered again about the haircut. This all felt so unreal. Had Joan felt this way when she spoke to the soldiers?

"I can't see him, Mary." There was now something gentle about the DC's voice.

"Well, yes, gods are invisible. There are millions of them, tiny sparks of godhood swirling around all the time.", she said as if in a dream.

"And how do you know this, Mary?", asked the DC as if he were talking to a child.

"Bob explained. He talks to me in my head. And sometimes in tears. And sometimes through the computer, but mostly in my head.", she explained.

There was a silence that lasted several seconds that was broken by Mr Mohammed. "I request that a psychiatric evaluation be carried out before proceeding with this interview, DC Richards."

The officer took a deep breath and blew it out again. "Granted! Interview ends, 10:42." He reached over and turned off the recorder.

The Forensic Medical Examiner was called and advised that they would have to come to the station in the morning. Mary was told that she would be kept until the police doctor had seen her. The police were kind and gentle with her and somehow this was the most frightening thing of all. They referred to the cell as "her room for the night" and made sure that she didn't have anything that she could use to hurt herself with in the cell. It would have been less frightening if the police had treated her like a criminal. "Mad not bad.", thought Mary. The desk sergeant did a last check on her and left her in the cell for the night. She lay on the bed feeling very alone and silently wept.

You are not alone, Mary. I am here, and I love you.

Chapter 16

The Forensic Medical Examiner turned up at the station a little after eight in the morning and waited impatiently while Mary finished her breakfast of bacon, eggs and a fried slice. She didn't have the appetite for black pudding after a night in the cells. She had been surprised to be offered Halal breakfast rolls as an option. Bob had never mentioned any dietary restrictions to her. Mary was also surprised that the FME was a youngish woman although there seemed to be no reason to assume that a doctor would be a man or old. The FME gave her name as Clare.

The interview with Clare took place in the same interview room that Mary had been in the previous night, again with a WPC present. The doctor asked questions about Bob and Mary answered honestly. She had used the time in the custody suite to think things through and she didn't see that she could make things any better by lying. The story of the apostle Peter denying Christ also came to mind and Sister Agnes making the class promise that they would never deny their god. The doctor listened and asked Mary if she was on any medication or had any history of mental illness. She listened impassively to Mary's explanation that her grandfather had firmly believed in Leprechauns. At the end of the interview, the FME told Mary "I think that you need help, Mary, help that I am not able to give you. However, I have colleagues that can help. I will arrange for you to go to an evaluation centre which is in a specialist hospital. It is much nicer than the custody centre here and they will look after you. Do you have any questions?"

"Yes," said Mary, "a lot of questions. How long will I be there for?"

"I don't know, Mary. You are being admitted under section 2 of the Mental Health Act. Do you understand?", said the doctor.

Mary tried to sound reasonable. "Not really. I am not mad. There is nothing wrong with me; it is just that something wonderful has happened. I can see-"

The doctor interrupted. "I know that you believe that, Mary. It is one of the things that they will talk to you about during evaluation."

"But what about my cat, Bast? She has already missed breakfast. Will I be back home by tonight? How am I going to explain to work about not being there?", Mary asked.

The doctor sighed. "You could be away for a while, Mary... or they could decide that you are right, and you could be out in a few days. Don't worry about your cat. We will make sure that he is looked after. We can also contact your work for you. Don't worry. Everything is someone else's problem for a little bit. Just... hang on in there, OK? The WPC here will take you back to the custody suite and you will be there until we can get you an ambulance to take you to hospital. Please try to relax and if there are any problems, use the call button. No-one is angry with you and you are not in trouble at the moment. Just try not to get too stressed and try not to cause any problems Do you understand?"

"Yes. But you are quite wrong.", said Mary.

The doctor smiled without it reaching her eyes. "Well, maybe. Do you have someone who could be your responsible adult? Basically, we need someone to speak up for you while you are in hospital."

Mary said "There is my mother, but she moved back to Ireland, still around Dublin, I think. We haven't spoken in years."

"A friend, perhaps?", asked the doctor.

Mary thought of Mr Charles but she didn't think that his wife would be willing to let him help. She got on well with the people that worked at the Library, but none of them could really be considered friends. "No, no-one. I am alone."

No, Mary. You always have me.

Mary was led back to the custody suite by a WPC and she overheard the police doctor talking on the phone. "No, I don't think that she is a flight risk. Just take her in... no, just a section two for now. Yes... religious delusions. No, not violent." The words became too quiet to hear as Mary was led away. Mary tried to think but her mind would only come up with unhelpful things like needing to tell the police that Bast only ate Whiskers cat food and that the cataloguing still needed doing at the Library. That reminded her of the flyers for the soup kitchen and the food that would now spoil and the people who would be hungry and never hear of Bob and then there were only tears and no coherent thoughts at all. The WPC took her back to her cell without speaking except for a very quiet "Sorry, sweetheart." meant only for Mary's ears when locking the cell's door. She was alone except for Bob for a long time. He didn't say anything, but she knew that he was there. Eventually, two male officers and two ambulance crew came to the cell door and Mary looked up. The crew were both men, dressed identically. One of the policemen unlocked the door and the crew came in. The older of the two was slightly balding and a little overweight. He said to Mary, "Your taxi is here, love. Come on please. It is better than here." Not knowing what else to do, Mary stood up and allowed them to take her back into the main part of the station. There was a stop at a desk on the way, ("Got to collect your things, love, don't worry, we will put them in the cab for you."), some paperwork to sign and the younger crewman reminded Mary to leave her keys with the police so that someone could look after the cat. They led Mary out of the station and into the car park where an ambulance was waiting. There was also a police car, the engine already running and two officers inside. The older crewman nodded to them as he walked Mary to the back of the ambulance and opened the door.

"Hop in, Mary. My mate John will ride in the back with you and everything will be fine. Tell you what, why don't you have a lie down on the way?"

Mary said, "I am not insane. You don't understand."

The older crewman grinned. "No, we don't. You see, we are quite mad. Why else would we do this for a living?" John didn't react to this, having heard it many times before. "Now, hop on the bed and we can adjust it to make you nice and comfy. Even better, we will give you a blanket and that will keep you warm." Within a couple of minutes, Mary was wrapped in a blanket that she really didn't need and very politely but also very definitely strapped on the trolley with the clasps out of her reach. The ambulance started off and Mary heard the police car following.

It was some days before Mary saw Chalmead hospital from the outside. She could have taken a quick look around when she was admitted but she was only outside for a moment, transported on the trolley through a door at the back which was not the most impressive aspect of the building. She was informed that this was a regional secure unit and that she would not be allowed to leave but that she would be given as much freedom as possible while in the hospital.

She was assigned an Independent Mental Health Advocate who turned out to be a stocky woman called Kat who sported a fine selection of tattoos and piercings. Kat listened to Mary's story without offering an opinion and explained that her main job was to look after Mary's rights and to ensure that she was getting the best possible treatment.

Mary explained again that she was perfectly sane, thank you, and locking her up was as reasonable as arresting a vicar for officiating at evensong. Kat just nodded sadly and said that a lot of patients said much the same and that, in time, she would probably meet three men all of who claimed to be god and two women who were convinced that they were saints. Apparently, the men got on quite well but each thought that the other two were crazy

She was also assigned a bed in the assessment ward which didn't seem that different to an ordinary hospital except that the patients seemed physically fine even though some rocked backwards and forwards repeatedly or argued with voices that only they could hear. It was then that Mary started to doubt herself. Janice at the end of the row was clearly convinced that she was getting messages from ghosts. Who was to say that Mary was more or less sane than Janice? Bob was there all the time, or so Mary thought. He tried performing little miracles to convince her such as forming a smiley face in the not very hot tea that she was served but Mary was no longer certain that she could believe her own eyes. Could she have imagined Ray Charles? It didn't seem likely. Bob seemed less real and less certain as the day went on.

Mary spent an uncomfortable night in her bed on the ward. It made odd crinkling noises when she moved and twice she was woken by shouting, once from another ward and once from Janice who seemed to be reliving some horrible event. The trolley came around with tea, cereal and medication for those with prescriptions at 7:15. It was not apparent why they wanted people who had nowhere to go up and out of bed so early, but it was clearly useless to argue. Mary didn't know what had happened to her handbag and its contents as she had not seen it since they left the police station. The hospital had provided her with a toothbrush and shower gel so she was at least able to get clean. As she looked at herself in the mirror while drying her hair, she wondered how she could have aged five years in a single night. She tried not to cry but the tears rolled down her face anyway. Eventually, she dried them, nearly cried at how she looked after crying and started the long wait for something to happen.

It was after a lunch of incredible blandness that she was called by one of the nurses, a squat young man who had forgotten his name badge. He took her through the normally locked door and told her that she was going to meet her Responsible Clinician, the capitals audible. Mary asked what he was responsible for and the nurse simply replied "You."

The office door was patterned to look like wood but had no texture to speak of. There was a dull brass nameplate that read "Dr Varun Chandra, MBChB" mounted just above eye height. The odd thing about the door was that it had two spyholes, like a hotel door but side by side just below the plate. It was a moment before she realised that one was reversed so that the door could be seen through from either direction. The nurse waited with Mary until there was a buzz from the speaker by the door jamb. He led her inside and left her with the doctor.

Dr Chandra was in his late thirties with some grey at his temples. His skin was olive, giving him a middle eastern appearance, strengthened by the angular lines of his face and a strong nose. He wore spectacles with round lenses and gold frames that did not suit him in the least. He got up from his chair and took a step towards Mary, offering his hand for a shake.

"Come, sit down." He motioned to a soft chair in one corner of the room and sat down on a battered wooden chair. "I am going to be your responsible clinician. All that means is that I am responsible for evaluating you and ensuring that you get any treatment that you need." At this point, he

143

realised that he had left Mary's folder on the desk and went to get it before sitting down again. "Right, Hello." He tried to move the chair closer, which was unsuccessful since it was bolted to the floor.

"Hello", said Mary. "I don't want to be here."

"Well, yes, I understand that, but my colleague…", he checked his notes, "at the police station was concerned and we thought that it was a good idea to see if we could help you."

"Bob?", asked Mary in her head.

I am here, Mary.

"I don't think that I am ill.", she said to Dr Chandra.

"Apparently you have been hearing voices.", said Dr Chandra.

"Just the one voice, Doctor.", replied Mary.

"You can call me Varun if you like." He pronounced the "v" as if it were a "w". "It says in your notes that you are getting messages from God. Is that right?"

"From *A* god.", Mary said, stressing the pronoun. "Not… well, not the God that you are thinking of. Apparently there are a lot of them."

Dr Chandra made a note in the file. "I see. And has this voice been telling you to do things?", he asked.

Mary considered the question. "Well, asking me rather than telling me."

"And were these things that you didn't want to do?", asked the doctor.

"Well, no, not really. He asked me to find more people to believe in him, but I didn't mind that… and he helped me to
144

get a job and when I broke up with my boyfriend… When you say that he told me to do things, it makes it sound much less friendly.", replied Mary.

"Yes." Another note was made. "Why did you break up with your boyfriend?"

Mary's chest tightened. "He was seeing other women behind my back. I deserve better than that."

"Yes, yes you do", said Dr Chandra. "How did you find out that he was seeing other women?"

"He told me." Mary replied.

"Your boyfriend told you that he was seeing other women?", asked Dr Chandra.

"No, of course not. Bob told me.", said Mary.

"I see." Another note was made. "And who is Bob?"

"My god. The name of my god is Bob.", Mary replied.

"God told you that your boyfriend was seeing other women?", asked Dr Chandra.

"A god. Not the God but a god, a little one. Is that so hard to understand?" Mary knew that she sounded irritated and tried to control it.

"Not for me," replied the doctor, "but I am a Hindu, so the idea of multiple gods comes rather more easily. How would you describe your religion, Mary?"

That would explain it, commented Bob.

"What?" thought Mary. She was finding it confusing trying to answer Bob and the doctor.

I can only speak with people who believe in me or who don't believe anything. People that have faith in another god don't seem to be able to hear me, Bob said inside her head.

"Oh, I see. Is that why you only ever speak to me and Mr Charles?", she thought.

Yes. Other people cannot hear me.

"Oh." thought Mary. She looked up and saw that the doctor was still waiting for an answer. "I was raised as a Catholic, but I have not been practising for quite a while. It has been years since I have confessed or been to a Church except for weddings or funerals.", she said.

"And how does this fit in with Bob?", asked the doctor.

"I don't really know. Bob says that the bible doesn't say that there are no other gods, just that Christians are not supposed to worship them." Mary said.

"And you worship Bob now?", asked Dr Chandra.

Mary grimaced. "Well, I don't worship him. He doesn't ask for that. He just wants people to believe in him. Well, that and a sacrifice every now and then."

"Tell me more about the sacrifices, Mary. Has he ever asked you to hurt people or animals?", asked Chandra.

"What? No. Chocolate bars, biscuits, once a Big Mac. Nothing like that. He just likes the things to be dedicated to him, I think."

I do, added Bob.

"Yes, I know", said Mary.

Dr Chandra looked at her quizzically. "I see", said the doctor. "Does this seem at all unusual to you?"

Mary thought. "Well, yes, of course it does. It would be crazy not to think that it was unusual, wouldn't it?"

"That is not a word that we like to use here. So, to summarise, you believe that a god is speaking to you in your mind, that this god asks for sacrifices of Big Macs and that he wants you to find other people to believe in him, yes?", asked the doctor.

Mary took a deep breath. "Yes."

"And did you find any other believers?", Chandra asked.

"No, I was going to preach to the homeless. I was starting a soup kitchen. I had advertised it at the library and churches and now they will be hungry unless you let me leave", said Mary.

"And you feel that this is something that your god would want you to do. I understand. So, there are no other believers in your personal god, then?", the doctor asked.

"Well, no", Mary said, "there is another. Ray Charles believes in Bob. He believed before I did."

"Ray Charles, I see." Another note was made in the file. "And did Ray Charles start believing recently?", he asked.

"Earlier this year, I think.", replied Mary.

"I see." Another note was made in the file. "And have you spoken with Ray Charles?", the doctor asked.

Mary huffed. "Yes, I had lunch with him last week and saw him at the weekend."

"Yes, I see." Another note in the file. "Perhaps we should talk about your general health for a while."

Mary didn't see that she had much option and gave the psychiatrist a run-down of her medical history which was unremarkable in every way. After a while of this, she tried a direct appeal. "Doctor, I understand that you want to help me but what does it matter what I believe? As long as I am not hurting anyone, couldn't you let me go and believe whatever I want?"

The doctor paused. "Well, if that were the case then perhaps I could but there is a problem, you see. You were brought here from a police station after being arrested for fraud, I believe. So, I find it hard to accept that you are not hurting anyone. Actually, the police called me this morning. Do you have any idea what they wanted?", asked Dr Chandra.

"Bob?", Mary thought. There was a moment's pause.

I don't know what they wanted, Mary. There is nothing in the police computer but it may be on a handwritten note somewhere. I can go and look.

Mary was aware that she no longer had Bob's attention although she couldn't explain how she knew. "No, I have no idea. What did they want?", she said to the doctor.

"Apparently someone did change the bank's records again and they wanted to know if you had any access to a computer here at the hospital." explained Dr Chandra.

"You know that I haven't. That was Bob, not me.", she said.

"I think that you might have a hard time persuading the police of that and you would not be getting the help that you need and you would be going back to police custody. I am sure that this is the best place for you to be. You are clearly a good woman, Mary. Please work with us. Let us help you to get well so that you can get back to your normal life. We are going to offer you a mix of therapy and medication that will help you to get everything back on track.", said Dr Chandra.

"I am not mentally ill and I do not want to take medication." said Mary.

The doctor pursed his lips. "I am genuinely sorry... but you will have to do what we say, at least for now. I am going to try you on a course of Abilify and see how you do with that and we will start therapy on Monday. Please don't worry. We will look after you."

Chapter 16a

The first rock hit the second rock or the second rock hit the first rock. It all depended on where you were standing. The high metal content of the asteroids caused them to ring like bells but there was no air to carry the sound and no-one around to hear it even if there had been. Space is very largely empty but collisions like this happened once in a long while. It was inevitable. Fractures spread through both asteroids and they went off in different directions at new speeds, Newtonian physics being what it was. The first rock had developed a considerable spin and a bright new fracture plane on one surface, comparatively reflective when compared with the pitted surface of the rest of the asteroid.

Chapter 17

Mr Charles had a full worksheet for that Friday but the jobs were all routine. The hardest part was getting to and from the sites where he was working. His last job was at the Thames Valley University in Reading. As usual, the students had jammed the coin slot with the currencies of various nations. He fixed the three machines as quickly as possible and got back onto the M4 after only a brief struggle with the one way system. He would easily be back by 5:00pm even with the usual Friday rush-hour snarls as he got closer to the M25. He was crawling through the roadworks and trying to decide what to wear for the soup-kitchen-come-preaching-session when Bob spoke in his mind.

Hello Mr Charles.

"Hello Bob.", he thought, "you are not normally so formal."

I have some bad news. Mary has been arrested and taken to a mental hospital.

"Arrested? What for?", Mr Charles thought.

I made a mistake. I fixed it, but it has caused the police to think that Mary has done something wrong. She told them about me and they think she is mentally ill. They have put her in a regional secure centre.

"Is that a prison?", Mr Charles asked in his head.

No, it is a hospital, but they have given her drugs and I can't talk to her except by causing miracles and that is difficult.

"She was telling me about you forming her tears into words.", Mr Charles thought.

Yes, I did but I am only as strong as the belief in me. That is why I need more believers. I can't look after people without more strength.

"Surely she still believes in you.", Mr Charles thought.

The drug that they have given her blocks my ability to talk to her or get strength from her. I am not much stronger than I was when I first met you.

"I see.", Mr Charles thought. "What do you need me to do?"

Please believe in me and think of me when you can. That will help. Most of all, please stay safe. If I lose you or if they give you the same drugs, I will become what I was, a spark without a name.

"I understand. Yes, I will do that.", thought Mr Charles. There was a jumble of thoughts that Bob didn't quite catch. "I don't know how to cancel the soup kitchen. We don't know where the people who are coming are and we have no way of contacting them.", Mr Charles thought, clearer now that he was concentrating.

There was a pause. *I think that we should still feed them. They will be hungry and it would be useful to have them available later. Don't tell them about me, but do get food to them. If you feed them every Friday, we should be able to build a community.*

"That will get expensive.", thought Mr Charles, mostly to himself.

Yes. There was another pause. *I will make sure that you have money.*

Mr Charles thought back to the start of the conversation. "Are you sure that you know how to do that? What did you do that got Mary into trouble?"

152

There was another pause. *I will tell you later. I understand what I did wrong last time and I will not make that mistake again.*

"Perhaps you had better explain.", thought Mr Charles.

No time. Have to go. Mary.

Mr Charles was alone in the car. He turned his attention to getting back and how to feed the homeless.

Bob was never aware of time passing when he travelled. He had read the books on physics in the library and assumed that he travelled at the speed of light so Mary had called him only seconds before. She was being restrained by a male nurse while another was injecting her. She was struggling and begging Bob for help out loud. He wanted desperately to help, but he didn't have the strength to push the men away and had never been that strong. He wasn't even strong enough to stop the syringe plunger being pressed down. There was only one way that he could stop this and that was to interfere with the heart or brain of the nurse that was injecting Mary. The nurse was not a believer so he couldn't talk to his mind. The only intervention that he could make would be damaging. Bob hesitated. If he hurt or killed the nurse, another one would give the same drugs to Mary. It would not help her and he was sure that she would not want the nurse dead. Unable to act, Bob watched the plunger squeeze the amber coloured liquid into his worshipper and she went limp. She was still breathing, still alive, even awake in a fashion but her faint trace of her faith winked out like a light. Bob could barely feel her mind and it was a stew of half formed thoughts, lost in a fog. He called to her but she could not hear. The two nurses moved so that each of them was on one side of her and guided her to the bed. Her legs moved as if the muscles had been replaced with rubber. With some effort, the nurses got her onto the bed while the other patients in the ward watched listlessly. One of them,

153

the younger of the two, stayed with Mary while the other got a glass of water and a pill. He looked into her unfocussed eyes and said, "Sorry, love but you have to take your medicine. We want to get you well. I am just going to pop something in your mouth and give you a little drink of water and I want you to swallow. Do you understand? Mary, I want you to swallow the water." He did exactly that and Mary swallowed, then coughed before settling down to the bed.

Mr Charles got home in reasonable time and found the house empty, Anne not yet having returned from work. He took the time to go up to the shrine and spent a few minutes trying to work out how to believe harder. For want of any better ideas, he went to the kitchen and looked for some biscuits but Anne had been shopping for healthier food and all that he could find was dried fruit. It would have to do. He went upstairs and sacrificed several Apricots to Bob before eating them which was apparently perfectly acceptable. This got him onto thoughts of food and how he would feed the people that turned up at the planned soup kitchen. There was no time to do anything too fancy. Certainly, he couldn't get anything catered at such short notice and he didn't think that Anne would be willing to help very much. Cooking was not a skill that either of them had which is why they would eat out when they could. No, it would have to be something simple this time round. After a few minutes, he went down to the computer and printer in the lounge and found some self-adhesive labels. He opened the word processor and soon had several sheets, each of which said "A gift from Bob." over and over. He looked at the clock, realised that he didn't have time to change and headed out to the car with the sheets. He would plan his route to take in everywhere on the way that sold sandwiches. He had best get some soft drinks as well though he suspected that the homeless would have preferred something a little more spirituous. Mr Charles smiled at the thought that this was all in aid of making a spirit stronger.

Mr Charles didn't know what sort of people would come for free food but there had to be some in need and close to the middle of Slough. He had a large woven carrier bag from Tesco full of sandwiches of all the types that the shop still had. He had supposed that it would mostly be old men, which was strange now that he thought about it since most of the beggars that he passed on the street were youngish. He had thought of them as scroungers when he thought of them at all, which he typically did not. He realised that might not be the most enlightened view and that he would have to reconsider. Mr Charles got to the place that had been on the flyer, a well-lit area on the edge of the shopping district and waited. He had half expected a crowd but there were only two people waiting when he arrived with one or two drifting by every few minutes. They were young and old and some apparently sane and some clearly suffering from mental health problems. Most were men although a few were women, bundled in shapeless clothes. Each one would get a sandwich and a can of Sprite delivered with a smile and a cheerful "From Bob. Think of him." A few asked who Bob was and Mr Charles told them to ask him again next Friday when he would be back again with more and better food. Most were grateful but distracted. Only one of them swore at Mr Charles, but he took the sandwich anyway. It was only when the last sandwich was gone that Ray remembered that he hadn't eaten yet. He checked his pockets and found that he had enough for a Big Mac and fries. The prospect did not appeal. He gave the money to the next person who turned up and headed back to the car and ultimately back to Anne and home.

#

Mary was woken at 8:15 on the Sunday morning by a chirpy nurse coming in with mugs of tea. Mary was not, by inclination, a morning person and chirpy was not an ideal start to the day. One of the good things about working at the Library had been the relative quietness in the morning. Many of the service users had been students who (except before an exam) were rarely to be seen before lunchtime. A queue formed to use the bathroom with the order based on who had been there the longest. Mary felt especially sleepy from the after-effects of the injection and the anti-psychotic pill that she had been given. The doctor had explained that it would take a few days for her to get used to the medicine and she hoped that he was right. As it was, she stood in line holding her hospital issued toothbrush, flannel and toothpaste. There were only four patients on the ward, so it was not a long wait. The nurse came back with a tray with little white paper cups containing tablets. Apparently the more experienced patients knew to save a little of their tea to wash them down. Mary didn't know what to expect next and felt no strong urge to find out. It seemed so much easier to go with the flow and not resist. She had heard that there would be occupational therapy and she wondered if there would be basket weaving as she had seen in an old film. Thoughts seemed to slip away so easily. She got washed and dressed and headed out to breakfast which was surprisingly good.

It turned out that basket weaving was not part of the occupational therapy at Chalmead. The morning was slow and it appeared that the staff wanted everything to be calm and collected. There was an art room where Mary could try her hand at watercolours and that reminded her of frustratingly half-remembered art classes at school, a small gym without weights, a TV room where you could watch whatever the person with the remote wanted and what the hospital called a Library - a cart full of dog-eared paperbacks that would have been rejected by any council library. There was no classification system. There were also board games, possibly selected for their uncompetitive nature and multiple decks of playing cards. This was the first time that Mary had met any of the patients from other wards and they seemed a strangely assorted lot to her. Some seemed perfectly normal although one or two had odd twitches. Others were very withdrawn and just sat and stared into the distance or held their head in their hands. A few seemed to be listening to voices that only they could hear or looking at things that were invisible to everyone else. These troubled Mary the most. How could she say that they were insane but that she was perfectly rational? Did it make sense for a god to spell words in tears? Wasn't hearing voices in the head exactly what she did? She tried not to think about it as she waited for lunch. It was already evident that days were too long to think about and it was better to just look forward to the next event, good or bad. Her world had become somewhere where a light lunch was the future. She hoped that it was a good lunch.

Lunch was, as it happened, the high point of the day so far although there had been little in the way of competition. One thing that she found strange at first was that the cutlery was plastic and so were the plates. None of the other patients had shown any sign of violence but it was obvious that the hospital had been designed to be a place where nothing could be used to hurt anyone, including the patients themselves. She was not thinking too clearly because of the drugs and the whole experience had a dreamlike quality. A nurse handed out more little paper cups with various tablets, pills and capsules to the others as they ate, but Mary was apparently not due any more medication.

Mary had come from a large family back in Ireland. One of the greatest pleasures of staying in in England after her mother had returned was that she could do whatever she pleased, except when she was at work. Since she knew that she would probably get married soon after leaving school, she had been determined to make the most of this freedom. As it happened, the years went by without any very serious relationships and it turned out that she liked to spend her free time making a fuss of the cat and watching bad television. It was oddly disconnecting to suddenly be in an environment where there was no work to do and there were always other people around. The hospital ran to a schedule like an enormous and slow heartbeat and Mary had no control over it. Even if she had not done anything productive with her spare time, she missed getting to choose even the simplest things like when to eat and sleep. It reminded her of her childhood and the girl with the simple life that would have played out much like her mother's and her grandmother's if they had not made the move to England. In a way, it made her a little more like the child that she had been.

The afternoon was spent in a group therapy session that seemed to be centred around the theme of identity. It was led by an older woman who spoke so quietly that Mary did not catch her name or very much of what she was saying. The other patients often wandered off topic and Mary learned remarkably little about them considering the topic of the session. Some hardly spoke at all while a younger woman insisted that they were living in the Big Brother house and the whole thing was a game show. The quietly spoken coordinator tried to keep order without much success and little progress was made.

#

Mr Charles made an appointment with a lawyer. He had never done anything like that before unless you counted hiring a solicitor for house conveyancing. Now he thought about it, he had never met the solicitor, having picked up and dropped off papers with the practice's receptionist, a rather plump lady in her forties. As he sat in the waiting room of Bradlow and Dounby on the High Street, he tried to recall her name without success. He was trying to remember anything more than that she favoured tan cardigans at least two sizes too large when a youngish woman in a grey business suit came in.

"Mr Charles?", she asked.

"Um, yes?", Mr Charles realised that he sounded uncertain and had no idea why, which, in turn, made him *feel* uncertain. "Is the solicitor ready to see me?", he asked.

"Yes." she replied with a slightly flat tone.

"Um, where?", Mr Charles asked.

"I generally see clients in my office. Toni Fallow with an 'i' not with a 'y'. Follow me please." She walked out of the room without looking back. Mr Charles hurriedly got up and followed her into a modern and rather spartan office apparently themed in variations of grey and chrome. The solicitor's red blouse was the only splash of colour in the room and Ray suddenly felt underdressed in his second best suit. There was a large desk in the office and two fabric covered bucket chairs by a small round table. Toni Fallow sat at one and it was obvious that she expected Mr Charles to sit in the other. He did so.

"So, how can I help you, Mr Charles?", she asked.

"I need legal advice. I want to be certain that I am not about to break the law.", he replied.

"Well, the first advice that I should give you is that you could get some advice from the Citizen's Advice Bureau for free while you can't necessarily apply for legal aid to get my help.", she said.

"Would the advice from them be as good?", Mr Charles asked.

"I can't offer an opinion on that. You may wish to believe that you get what you pay for.", she said.

"Yes. Um, I am going to be charged for an hour at least, whatever happens, aren't I?", he asked.

"Yes, so you would be well advised to make the most of it.", the lawyer said.

Mr Charles paused. "So, if I asked a question and you thought that I was barking mad, would you have to do anything about it?"

"Not as long as you are paying, no", she replied.

Mr Charles explained about Bob and asked a number of questions about whether he was allowed to preach the word of Bob and what he would need to do to stay within the law. The answers were considerably longer than the questions and Mr Charles took copious notes.

Bob was splitting his time between Mary who was currently watching daytime TV through a haze, Mr Charles who was talking to a lawyer and reading the internet for anything that might help Mary to be released. Because things were not happening quickly for either of his believers, Bob was able to visit them once a second and devote almost all of his time to reading about mental illness and the law. With such brief visits, he wasn't able to follow either conversation, but it didn't seem likely that a show on redecorating houses or an explanation of the Public Order act of 1986 was going to be critical. This left him with .98 of a second per second to read. Unfortunately, the internet did not always have the information that he needed and even where he was, perched (metaphysically) in an ADSL hub, it took far too long for the information to download. As he read, he understood why the hospital had detained Mary. Her story was almost identical to many cases both current and historical. They could even consider Mary's breakdown at work to be typical of religious delusions linked to schizophrenia. Her resistance to the idea of treatment was also typical. Bob wondered how many godlings had found a believer only to have them locked away where no-one would believe them. He knew what would have happened to those godlings. When the believer died or was persuaded not to believe, the godling would have gone back to being an empty spark adrift in a world without faith. Of course, many of those people could simply be mad. Bob had taken a look at the other patients in Mary's hospital that thought that a god was talking to them and he had only seen the sparks swirling insensate around and between the people. They were everywhere but none of them had more than the least trace of life. One difference in Mary's case was that there was evidence. Unfortunately, it was evidence that would land Mary in jail rather than a hospital so that would not help her. Bob would have to persuade her psychiatrist that Mary was as sane as the next person. Bob briefly considered where Mary was at the moment and revised his opinion. He would have to prove that she was considerably *saner* than the person next to her. He would also have to find a legal way to get money to Mr Charles. He turned his attention to criminal law as it applied to fraud. It must have been easier for gods in the old days, in Bob's opinion. He did not consider that they didn't have the computers that he found so useful.

#

Sunday was a slow day at Chalmead hospital. There were fewer doctors around and the pace slowed from sluggish to glacial. Mary explored the area that she had access to as best she could. It was so hard to concentrate. Thoughts sometimes slipped away while she was having them and at other times she would find herself focussing on a tiny detail that didn't matter at all. She asked one of the nurses, his name one of many forgotten details, about this and he had said that it would be better once she was more used to her medication. Kat, her mental health advocate, was not there at the weekend and so Mary was at a loose end. There were several rooms that the patients used during the day and each one had different furniture and a paint scheme that differed slightly from every other room. For some reason, this seemed important. She took to looking at the labels under the chairs, more for something to do than anything else but then she noticed that the nurses were watching her. They didn't interfere but they casually paid attention to what each of the patients was doing. Mary stopped, realising that it must look as if she were quite cracked. She decided that it was important to look as if she were sane and then realised that she had no idea how to look sane. It would all be so much easier if her head were clear. She decided that reading the posters on the wall was the sort of thing that a reasonable person would do. The posters were held to the wall with a mixture of blu-tack and sticky tape now yellowed, often on the same poster. They had a tendency to curl up at the edges, which Mary decided was because they had been on the walls for a very long time. They gave advice on what to do if you were having trouble with your medications (see a nurse), what to do if you were abused by another patient (see a nurse) and what to do if you needed to talk to someone (see a nurse). There was also a spot with four grease marks that must have been the site of another poster. Mary felt slightly cheated that she had been deprived of something that would have made her world very slightly richer.

Mary had not spoken with the other patients very much. She wondered if that would be counted against her. She was nervous about speaking to someone who might react strangely. Of course, her grandfather had been more than a little strange, but he was family and so it had seemed different. She sat and thought while drinking her fifth cup of tea. There was no shortage of tea even if it was rather weak. She liked it made so that you could stand a spoon up in it and it was the colour of He-man's face. Mary decided that not talking to the other patients would probably be something that the nurses would consider abnormal so she looked for someone that seemed at least reasonably close to their right mind. Some people wandered around in pyjamas and dressing gowns while others wore normal clothes ranging from jeans and a sweatshirt to a few in business suits. After some thought, Mary decided that the best dressed ones were probably the sanest. She was very aware that she was wearing grey jogging bottoms and a baggy sweatshirt as she had been planning to relax in front of the television. The hospital had washed them for her, but she knew that she would not be an impressive sight and wished that she had at least some make-up. She gathered her courage and approached an older lady in a slightly rumpled pinstripe suit.

"Hi, I am Mary.", she said, forcing a smile.

"Hello. You are new here, yes?", replied the woman.

"I am, just a few nights. They seem to think that I am unwell.", said Mary.

"Yes. Not at all uncommon, I am afraid. Of course, some of the people here are mad. I think that it is a cover, personally.", replied the woman.

"A cover?", Mary asked. She still found her focus coming and going as she got used to the drugs.

"Yes, a few mad ones mixed in with the rest of us, just to make it look more convincing if anyone investigates. Which are you, dear?", the woman asked.

Mary was puzzled by the question. "I don't feel mad, just a bit woozy."

The older woman's eyes suddenly became very intense. "Are they talking to you as well then? They didn't warn me and they usually do."

"Um, just the one voice. Are there more?", Mary asked.

"Well, of course there are. Honestly!" The woman blew air through her nose in a dismissive gesture. "It wouldn't be much of a show otherwise, would it?"

For want of a better answer, Mary said, "Perhaps not?"

The woman leaned in close. "So, which of them is it? Pat Butcher? Dot Cotton? Den Watts? What have they told you to do?"

Mary knew the names at once. "Eastenders? The cast of Eastenders is talking to you?", she asked.

The woman stared for a moment before dismissing Mary as if she were waving away a fly. "Oh, I see. You are one of the mad ones. We have nothing to talk about, dear."

Chapter 18

Father Roberto Cassini, pastor to the sleepy mountain village of Alberobello, was a humble, gentle and kind man. Sadly for his parishioners, he was also a man dying after many years of service to a Church that he loved. He loved the Church in the way that an old man might love his wife, aware of her faults but with love undiminished. His faith in his god had never been strong, but his faith in the Church and his love of the people burned like a torch in the night... if you were a small god. The god sparks clustered around him, mindlessly excited by the faith that was not directed at them. Roberto thought that he was quite alone in his bedroom, a simple single bed against the wall which he lay in, a desk and a chair almost filling the small room. Roberto had asked little of life except for the chance to serve and this he had been given in great abundance. All in all, it had not been a bad life. He had never felt much urge to sin and that had filled him with pride. Naturally, he had confessed that sin to his Bishop and been forgiven. As he lay in his bed, his heart was heavy not with remorse but with dying muscles.

Bob had been searching the Vatican records and they had brought him to this priest. Father Cassini had been offered advancement in the Church many times, but had refused it, explaining that he had to look after his flock and that he wanted nothing more. He was considered to be a virtuous man according to the written accounts. Bob watched Father Cassini struggle to breathe. He would have helped if he could, even though the priest belonged to a different god but the old man's body was failing in so many ways. The chest pain that made him grimace was from a dying heart, arteries too narrow to supply blood. The tiredness that had beset him was caused by multiple tumours. Bob might have been able to help if he could do a little over several days, but the old man didn't have days. He had only minutes.

"Dio, mi senti?" The words were barely a whisper, almost lost in a wheezing breath. Bob could understand. The priest was asking if his god could hear him. Bob waited for a reply, but the silence stretched on for long seconds. Wherever this man's god was, he was not speaking. Bob waited, watching, hopeful of meeting another god who could explain things that still seemed so puzzling and Father Cassini waited with him. "I served the Church and did what I thought that you wanted, my God." English or Italian made no difference to Bob. The next sound was a gasp of pain as another muscle failed. Bob could not save the man, but he could spare him this pain. Very carefully, he moved electricity in the nerves that allowed Father Cassini to feel pain. The old man's body relaxed as the weight seemed to come off his chest. He raised a faltering hand, trying to reach a cross on a chain but he didn't have the strength. Bob pushed the beads that looped over the bedstead and the cross fell into the outstretched hand. "I wish that I could have done more good..." mouthed the priest, his breath too weak for speech. His brain was starting to shut down, the sluggish flow of blood no longer enough for it.

Gods cannot cry, even small gods, but Bob wept in his soul for this stranger. There was so little that he could do but he ached to do something. It felt wrong, but it was what the old man needed. Bob traced the shape of the cross onto the man's palm, pressing hard so that Father Cassini could feel through the haze of his dying mind and the nerve block. The skin on his hand was fragile and bruised under this slight pressure, but the smile on the face of the dying man was beatific. His eyes closed and his breath left him in a sigh. Not knowing what to do, Bob traced the shape of the cross over and over, hoping that some of the feeling would reach the man's darkening mind. He only stopped when there were no traces of the man that had been the Catholic priest in the empty body on the bed.

Bob didn't know where the souls of the dead went. All that he knew was that the essence of the man was no longer where he could feel it. The effort of moving the cross and tracing the shape had left Bob weak; not tired because he could not sleep, but spent. Mr Charles was sleeping and so the belief coming from him was a trickle but it would give a little nourishment. Interested to know more of Father Cassini, Bob started to look around the priest's house.

#

Mary had been moved from the evaluation ward to a longer-term treatment ward although all the patients had access to the same communal areas except for those in seclusion. The differences didn't seem very important to Mary but nothing did since the anti-psychotics had taken hold. The wards were smaller but the seclusion rooms were closer. She had never heard the term before but one of the nurses had explained that they were secure rooms where patients could be alone and safe. This had sounded rather appealing to Mary who had never minded her own company, but the nurse assured her that she didn't want to be in there. She missed Bast who usually slept on her bed... well, when Max wasn't visiting. Kat had asked her if she had a boyfriend and she had explained about her breakup with Max. Kat had wanted his contact details and Mary had given them to her. She wondered vaguely if Kat was interested in dating him. If so, Kat was the one in need of help. She lay in the too small bed and tried not to notice the noises from the hall as the other patients did, letting it wash over them. Perhaps it was something that she could get used to. The notes on the end of Mary's bed read "Frank psychosis/?Schizophrenia."

Mr Charles dreamed about rugby practice at his old school. He had no idea why he so often dreamed about it. He had never enjoyed PE.

Bob had looked through the priest's house and it had given very little idea of who Father Cassini had been. It was very neat and tidy with the worn furniture polished and dusted. While Bob was still learning about people, this didn't seem like a place where someone lived, just a place where they stayed. There was a small office with many handwritten notes and an old computer connected to a dial-up modem. It had been turned off, but it had been possible to press the button. Bob read the emails that Father Cassini had received and there were many. There were very few that he had sent. Bob thought for a long time about the old man's final words. Perhaps there was a way that they could help each other still. Bob sent the keystrokes to compose a new Email.

Chapter 19

Dr Chandra sat in his office, reading the report from the nurses. He mumbled to himself as he worked. "Doesn't look like the new dosage is working out for Peter. We might want to tweak that a little... need to check that with the pharmacist. A quiet weekend for Joseph? Well, that is an improvement. Hmm. I didn't think that Mary would need a shot of Lorazepam to get her to take her meds. She is my... uh, 11:15. Good. I should take Michael's case to the next review, perhaps."

He set down the folder and picked up his teacup and tried to drink from it, but it was empty. He sighed and checked his watch. It would soon be time for the first patient of the day. Dr Chandra took a deep breath and started his calming routine.

#

Father Cassini's housekeeper was the first person to see his body. She had got into the habit of waking him in time for the first services with a latte brought from the local café. The scent of the coffee was sharp against the smell of fresh baked bread and herbs. She walked along the stone streets and past the whitewashed houses to his door, opened it with her key and called out his name. Even after twenty-three years, it was still Padre Cassini, never Roberto. When there was no answer, she went to the door of his bedroom and called "Sei vestita?" She hoped that he had just overslept, but Father Cassini had a snore that was famous throughout the village. The door was ajar and she gently pushed it open. Her eyes filled with tears as she realised that her priest would never wake again. The palm of his hand still held the cross, but the blood had pooled where Bob had pressed so hard trying to make the priest feel the symbol that had always comforted him. It formed the outline of a crucifix, the lines of the bruises blurred and breaking the skin. Almost in a whisper, she said "Santa madre di Dio." The latte slipped from her hand and splashed on the worn rug.

#

Dr Chandra looked up from his notes at Mary, appraising her. She was sitting a little awkwardly and Dr Chandra wondered how much of that was due to her being uncomfortable with the situation and how much was due to the medication. The first few sessions often didn't get very far when the patient was still getting used to their meds. "So, Mary, how was your first weekend here?"

It took Mary a few moments to reply. "They have moved me to a different ward."

"Yes," Dr Chandra said, "I know. It is a smaller ward and I hope that you will be more comfortable there. Are you comfortable there?"

Mary thought for a moment. "There is screaming. At night, there is screaming. I don't want to be here."

Dr Chandra sighed. "Ah yes, that would be Jacob. We are trying to help him, but it isn't always easy. We want you well again so that you can go back to your life and we very much hope that you will work with us to get better. Do you understand?"

"Yes.", replied Mary.

"She really is zonked out.", thought Dr Chandra. "Oh well, she will settle down once she gets used to the Abilify." He cleared his throat. "Have you heard from Bob recently, Mary? Has he asked you to do anything?"

"No, I can't hear him. I don't know where he is." There was still a degree of sadness in her voice, thought Dr Chandra. That was a good sign, he thought, as it meant that the dosage was probably about right.

"Good, good. And how are you getting on with the other patients? It can be a bit much meeting so many people all at once", he asked.

Mary thought before answering. "One of them thinks that the people on Eastenders are speaking to her."

Chandra chuckled. "You would be surprised how often people believe that, although it is more often newscasters for some reason. There is still so much that we don't understand about the human mind. And the nurses, Mary, how are you getting on with them?"

Mary pulled a face. "They gave me an injection. I didn't want to take my pills and they held me down and gave me an injection. I didn't want that. They hurt me. I don't want to be here. Please, I want to go home." Tears trickled down her face.

Dr Chandra handed her a tissue. He kept a box on the desk and three more in the drawer. They were often needed. "I know. We want that too. I am sure that they didn't mean to hurt you. Let's talk about how we are going to help you so that we can get you well enough to be discharged." Dr Chandra started to explain the treatment plan that he would be following. He didn't need to think about it very much; it was a pretty standard plan.

#

Mr Charles sat in traffic and listened to the midday play on Radio Four. For some reason, he found this immensely reassuring. He still had time to make his appointment in Windsor.

#

Padre Rossi had driven over after he had finished the morning services, his ageing Fiat struggling a little on the narrow mountain roads that switched back and forth as they climbed. He stood near the bed and looked at the mortal remains of Padre Cassini, his face peaceful in death. Roberto had been a good man and his loss would be felt in this village. It would be necessary to continue his good work here and perhaps one of the deacons could help out as long as a priest was available for communion. They would have to arrange a rota. Rossi wished that he could have been there to give his colleague last rights and a final confession but clearly Cassini had died in a state of grace. The evidence was all there; a cross held in his hand and marked on his palm so clearly. Rossi leaned over and gently laid the cross over the shape on the dead man's palm. It was definitely larger than the outline on the skin.

Padre Rossi had no idea how to declare a miracle to the mother Church but the signs seemed clear. He would need to call the Vatican. He felt unworthy to be the vessel for such momentous news but his direction was clear. He started looking for a telephone. Surely, even here, a priest would have such a thing.

The Vatican is an organisation unlike any other, but there are some similarities with a business simply because of human nature. When faced with a situation outside of their experience, people will generally turn to their superior and make it his or her problem. The message went from Padre Rossi to a Bishop and from there to an Archbishop. It is not possible to become an Archbishop without a certain degree of understanding. Some of that understanding is spiritual, some of it is an understanding of human nature, but a familiarity with the bureaucracy of the Holy See and its politics is perhaps the most essential part. The Archbishop sent an Email to the Cardinal President of the Pontifical Commission for Vatican City State, His Holiness and copied in the Administration and Central Offices of the Governorate. At worst, he could not be blamed for raising the issue and, if all went well, then this could reflect well on both the glory of God and the Archbishop's career. They were certainly living in interesting times and great men often rose in times of change, God willing.

The Roman Curia is a body rarely mentioned by those outside of the Church but it formed the backbone of the administration. It would have come as a surprise to many that one of the departments of the Roman Curia was the Vatican Internet Service. The offices filled part of a floor of an imposing but less than practical building on the Via della Conciliazione, just off St. Peter's Square. One of the employees, an administrator called Francisco Moretti, had a problem that had not been covered in his degree course. He reread the Email from Father Cassini's account and decided that this looked like a matter for his manager. "Hey, Lucio, come and have a look at this!"

#

Dr Chandra always gave himself a 15 minute gap between patients so that he could write up his notes and plan his next treatment. He wrote them longhand as he had never really got to grips with computers. As he was considering what goals should be set, a movement caught his eye. The bubbles in his tea were moving oddly. As he watched, they formed a word. The tea bubbles clearly said "Mary". The bubbles moved again. "is". One of them burst and there was a gap in the first letter of "not". The bubbles rearranged themselves once more into the word "mad" and then burst leaving the surface of the tea plain except for a thin film of tannin. Dr Chandra stared at the tea for a moment longer. He then stared at one of the pictures on the wall. He waved his hand in front of his face. He didn't notice any visual aberrations so he listened carefully. He could hear voices outside and they were too indistinct to make out more than the occasional word but it sounded like normal hospital chatter. So, no auditory hallucinations, no auras around objects. He sniffed the tea and didn't notice any odd scents before realising that he hadn't drunk any of it yet. He poured it down the sink in the corner just to be on the safe side. He checked his temperature and his blood pressure, both of which were perfectly normal. "Ok, no fever, no relevant medical history, no pain, I have slept recently and I had breakfast. What would I tell a colleague that came to me with these symptoms? Well, symptom rather than symptoms really... I would suggest a CAT scan and watching for a reoccurrence. I think that I can probably arrange that but there might be questions."

The intercom buzzed and Dr Chandra looked up at the clock and saw that it was time for his 12:00. He put Mary's incomplete notes in a drawer and called out "Come!" and tried to collect his thoughts. The next patient shuffled in and the doctor smiled at him feeling the tension ease as his professional mask slipped back into place.

#

The autopsy of Father Cassini was performed that night with the Pope's personal doctor in attendance. There had already been rumours that the priest had stigmata, although the doctor itched when he heard that word. It was not because of the religious connotations, which he welcomed. However, he was a stickler for grammar and knew that the singular form of the word was stigma. The Church had so far declined to comment on the rumours. The post-mortem examination was being carried out at the request of the coroner but the Holy See had specifically requested that the procedure be as non-invasive as possible. This had involved wheeling the very definitely dead priest into the MRI unit covered with a sheet, but they had managed it without alarming any of the patients. Blood had been drawn for toxicology and his body washed and photographed. Every procedure was carefully followed even though the pathologist was sure that the cause of death was heart failure. He had seen the faxed medical records and it was hardly remarkable for a man of his age and health. However, the Vatican had made it very clear that everything must be done with flawless professionalism. The MRI had confirmed the preliminary diagnosis, arteriosclerosis leading to heart failure, but the patient would not have had long even if his heart had been sound. There was a largish mass in his abdomen that was very likely to be malignant and Father Cassini had clearly been too frail to have survived treatment. He must have been in some pain but there was no mention of the condition in his notes. They left the examination of the stigma until last.

The mark had turned from dark purple to near black as the blood had clotted. The thin skin of the palm had curled away in places where it had broken under pressure. The pathologist looked more closely with a hand lens and it was clear that the edge of the mark was made by more than one pass. He adjusted the lens slightly. There were parallel lines less than a millimetre apart. The Pope's personal physician spoke, rather startling the pathologist who was not used to being observed. He often worked with students, but they were involved with the process and he didn't forget that they were there. He realised that he had missed the question, but the doctor repeated himself. "Is it just a bruise from the crucifix that he was holding? An ordinary thing?"

The pathologist considered. "A bruise, certainly. Not, however, from holding a cross. This was made by something moving over the skin, pressing into it, tracing the same path many times. However, it was done, it is incredibly precise. I have no idea how this mark was made, but it wasn't from clutching a cross."

There was a glint in the doctor's eye as he asked the next question, his voice soft. "Would you say inhumanly precise?"

The pathologist looked down at the shrunken form of the man and thought for a moment longer. Without turning, he nodded.

The Pope's personal physician reached for his mobile phone. He had calls to make.

Chapter 20

Two days later, Father Ryan was again meeting with the Bishop at his Reading home, this time during daylight hours. Whisky was not offered, for which he was profoundly grateful as he still had ceremonies to officiate. The mug of tea supplied as an alternative was an unsettling shade, but Father Ryan tried to drink it in the spirit in which it had been offered.

"Keith," said Bishop Crossan, "thank you for coming to see me at such short notice. I am sure that your flock are keeping you busy."

"Oh, no problem at all, your grace... um, Douglas." It was not as if Father Ryan could have ignored such a summons. He had in fact been working on a sermon but he could always recycle an old one. "Is there something that I can help you with?"

"Aye, I think that there is. Do you have more than one family by the name of Charles in your congregation? It is a common enough name down here, I suppose." The Bishop still tended to think of everywhere south of the wall as being a foreign land.

This was an easy question to answer. Attendance had fallen off in recent years and Father Ryan considered fifty people to be a good crowd on a Sunday. "No, just Anne Charles and sometimes her husband. Um, have they done something unfortunate? I haven't seen Ray in quite a while, but Anne is a regular."

Douglas considered this for a moment. "No, I can't say as they have as far as I know but something very irregular has happened. Very irregular indeed. I don't suppose that you have heard of a place called Alberobello by any chance?"

Father Ryan shook his head.

"A wee place down in the heel of Italy.", the Bishop said. "Until recently, their spiritual well-being was looked after by a... Father Roberto Cassini. It seems that he went to his final reward a few days ago."

"Ah yes! I heard about it on the news. Have the Vatican confirmed it yet?" Father Ryan realised that he sounded like an excited child.

"That he died? I don't think that there is any doubt about that. Why on Earth was it in the news?", Bishop Crossan asked.

"Well, the stigma...", Keith replied, not knowing quite how to explain.

The Bishop rubbed his hand over his face and back over his thinning hair. "I have not been following the news, I am afraid. What had he done? I wonder if this will complicate matters."

"Um, no, stigma as in stigmata, the marks of the crucifixion." Father Ryan explained what little the news report had contained. "I always thought of stigmata as being more of a superstition than canon if I am to be honest, but it is an exciting event, don't you think?"

The Bishop made a noise in his throat. "They have rather fallen out of fashion these days, but we will see what the Church makes of it. That is not why I called you here, but it does shed a new light on it. It would seem that this Father Cassini sent an Email to the Vatican Internet Service, whatever that is. It was in Latin so the computer types didn't quite know what to make of it, but they had a priest take a look at it. I have the original Latin and an English translation here." He handed over several sheets of fax paper. Father Ryan dutifully started to read.

"To the Holy Roman Church.

All that I have ever wanted was for people to believe. Religion should be a comfort to those that believe as well as a gift to the god that is believed in. This comfort comes in many forms. There are miracles. There is love. There is the knowledge that the believer is not alone. However, there is another form that I ask the Church to help with. Faith does not sustain the hungry. I cannot call forth bread and fishes on demand.

With this in mind, I ask that the Church provides a stipend to Mr Ray Charles of Uttoxeter, Berkshire, England (52.8980° N, 1.8600° W) for the provision of food for the poor and that this stipend be given freely and without lien.

I am old and soon Padre Cassini will be just a memory to the Church. I ask that the food provided be labelled 'This gift comes from the kindness of the faithful and with the love of Bob'.

I am, in this, your supplicant and the servant of those that choose to believe."

Father Ryan was the first to speak. "This raises a number of questions. Is Rome likely to be sympathetic to such a request? It seems... well, not in the interests of the Church. It is rather promoting..." He trailed off. "How did a village priest in Italy know about Mr Charles and his curious beliefs?"

The Bishop shook his head. "I have no idea. It seems incredible to me. How would a 76 year old priest from a mountain village know your parishioner from Adam?"

Keith considered pointing out that Mr Charles almost certainly had a navel and preferred suits to fig leaves but decided to shake his head instead.

The Bishop continued. "As for whether the Church is likely to grant the request, that is going to be complicated.

Did the news report say whether His Holiness had a position regarding the stigmata?"

"No", said Keith, "but they did quote an unnamed source within the Vatican suggesting that beatification was a possibility. I have no idea how reliable those sources are."

The Bishop cast a longing glance at the drinks cabinet and the clock and then sighed. "Have a look at the cover page, Keith."

Father Ryan shuffled the pages of the fax. It had been sent from the Congregation for the Causes of Saints. He was just a parish priest but he could recognise Church politics when he saw it. Someone clearly had an interest in this if it had progressed so quickly. "Was anyone able to ask the priest about the message that he sent?", Keith asked.

Douglas shook his head. "This was apparently the last thing that this Cassini did. That would make it the dying wish of a man who may well be destined for sainthood. It would be hard for the Church to refuse." He got up, walked to the drinks cabinet and opened it. "It might be easier for everyone if this was not a controversial decision, you understand." He pulled out two glasses and the good whisky.

"You think that it might be better not to mention Mr Charles' change of faith and just report that he is one of my parishioners?", Father Ryan asked.

Douglas poured some spiritual re-enforcement. "Who are we to question what might be the will of God?"

"I would like to keep an eye on what he does with the money though." Keith took a cautious sip of the drink that he had been handed. "It is Church money, after all."

Douglas took a good mouthful of his whisky and let the flavour develop before swallowing. "Aye, that seems entirely proper to me."

Anne Charles was of two minds regarding her husband's latest crusade. He had never been a passionate man in any way and that had suited Anne well enough. She had no great love of children and she loved Ray for being a consistent and kind companion and didn't feel the need for a larger family. She had been concerned that the Church's position on contraception would have made the decision for her but it had become clear that God had not intended children for her as the years rolled on. As a result, they lived comfortably in a modest house (as it should be) in a normal neighbourhood (very proper) and their joint account held a quite respectable balance even after a comfortable pension had been arranged (with a responsible fund). Anne was a firm believer in planning and Ray's decision to feed the homeless had not been a part of her plans. Still, she hardly felt that she could complain about the expenditure even if it did eat into the holiday fund. She decided that the best thing to do was to help plan the purchase and distribution of food in the most cost effective and efficient way possible. She would never admit it, but she felt a degree of pride in her ability to plan things. A loaf costs so much and spread costs 3p more and cheese and pickle costs 24p and so on. Each sandwich took 40 seconds to make (unless it required opening a new packet so plan for 50 seconds) and 10 seconds for packing, so each sandwich should take about a minute or 60 per person per hour assuming no breaks. There was a pleasure in the regimentation of the numbers, a rightness to it. For all that she might purse her lips at the silliness of the idea, she enjoyed the planning and the repetition and she enjoyed supporting her husband in a quiet, private and loving way. Slowly, the box of sandwiches grew fuller. Anne did not notice that she had started to hum the melody of the old hymn, *Break thou the bread of life.*

181

Friday night saw Mr Charles armed with a large box of sandwiches wrapped in clingfilm and a stack of leaflets. The wording on them was, in part, shaped by the advice of Bradlow and Dounby, solicitors.

"Do you believe in anything? If not, you may want to believe in a personal god, a god that will listen to you. Bob has no churches and no priests. He doesn't want your money. He just wants you to believe in him. Ask me for details and learn how to be a believer today."

The sandwiches had proved popular including, as the evening wore on, with the late night drinking crowd. Mr Charles felt a vague offence that they had taken food meant for the needy but he supposed that they had as much right to believe as anyone else did. The leaflets had been less popular and long after the sandwiches had run out, Mr Charles was picking up the discarded bits of paper. He sighed and wondered how to make them more appealing without considering the few that had been taken away. Of those, some of the leaflets were used to wipe up spilled pickle or to wrap a roll-up, but a few were actually read. In one case, the words were read and reread with an odd intensity. Someone wanted something to believe in with a passion. Few people knew him by name but those that did called him Ranting John due to his habit of arguing with voices that only he could hear. His eyes shone as he read the leaflet, nodding along with the words.

Chapter 20a

The bright surface on the asteroid caused the object to have a light curve as it headed slowly in the direction of the sun. When the fresh surface was pointing sunward, the dull grey brown asteroid showed a tiny blip of light too dim for human eyes to see. A telescope noticed it and it got assigned a name. It was provisionally tagged as (3017) 2009 VS. It was marked in the database as Query M class.

Chapter 21

Dr Chandra read the results of the scans dispassionately. He had read many such reports during his career and it only seemed a little out of place that he was now reading a neurologist's report on his own brain. No detectable lesions, no abnormalities of any kind apparently. His blood sugar was well within the normal range and there surely had not been enough caffeine in the tea to have had any effect. He tried to mentally step away from the problem. He considered again what he would advise a colleague in the same situation and came to the conclusion that he would advise the patient not to worry but to be alert for any repetition of hallucinations. He closed his eyes, took a deep breath and decided that he would follow his own advice. Just to be on the safe side, he also switched to decaffeinated tea. He would have to look for a brand that tasted less like yesterday's dishwater. He calmed himself a little further and then buzzed for his first patient of the day. The door opened a few seconds later and he forced a smile at the man entering the office.

Mary was the first patient after lunch. Dr Chandra wanted to be sure that his blood sugar was not too low. She walked in and he noticed that her gait was more even and jotted down a note that she was adjusting well. She sat down in the rather threadbare bucket chair that he kept for patients and he examined her more closely. Her hair was lank and needed cutting. He jotted down a note to ask the nurses to make sure that Mary got an appointment with the visiting hairdresser. These things could be important for the patient's self-esteem. She was pale but that probably wasn't unusual for her given her red hair. He quickly looked again and the roots were the same colour. No henna here, he thought. Her posture was submissive, but then they so often were when in that chair. "How are you feeling, Mary?", he asked. It was often best to start with open questions.

There was a slight hesitation before she replied. "I feel OK, thank you. A lot better."

Dr Chandra smiled. He had heard that response quite a few times. Was the hesitation due to her thinking about the answer? She had a rather flat affect which was not remarkable. "Good." he said, "I am glad. Do you feel able to talk about the events that brought you here? I wonder if anything seems different now."

Mary looked at him, her expression curiously blank. "I don't know. I must have been confused. I feel much better now."

Yes, thought Dr Chandra, she had certainly thought about these answers. "So, can you explain how you got the computer that the police seem so interested in?"

Mary blinked. "I must have copied down the number of Darren's credit card, ordered the computer and forgotten about it. I can pay him back and write an apology. I am very sorry."

Dr Chandra made another note on his A4 pad. "I see. It, uh, seems that the police are a little puzzled about how the computer in the bank now thinks that no-one paid for the computer. Apparently, that has sparked off all sorts of investigations at Visa. Do you think that you could explain that, please?"

There was a longer pause before Mary replied. "I changed it back perhaps? I was confused when I got here and I don't quite remember."

Dr Chandra shifted position. "And how did you do that, Mary? According to the police, you were... being looked after by them at the time. I am sure that they didn't let you use a computer. How did you know how to access the bank's systems?"

Mary looked down at the floor. "I read it in a book."

Dr Chandra made another note and decided to try another approach. "Mary, you have a boyfriend, I believe. Max. That is what is said in your admission notes." He let there be a few moments of silence. People often felt compelled to fill silences.

Mary's position hardly changed, but she looked somehow more despondent. "Ex-boyfriend.", she said quietly, apparently to the carpet.

Dr Chandra nodded. He had known about the relationship breakdown from the first session but he wanted to get Mary's reaction. "Ah yes, that is right. Can you tell me why the relationship ended, Mary?"

"He was seeing other girls behind my back." Mary told the carpet. There was a definite hardness to her words,

Dr Chandra made another note. "Actually, we contacted him as we thought that he might be worried about you. I hope that was alright." Mary muttered something that he couldn't quite catch, but it might have been "Bastard." Dr Chandra wondered if she meant him or Max. "He said that you thought that he was seeing someone else but that he wasn't. He seemed very concerned about you."

"Bastard." This time the word was clearer and more of Mary's Irish accent crept into the word.

"He said that you had got the idea from somewhere and that you had... well, some odd notions at times. Can you tell me what made you think that he was seeing other girls? Did you catch him or did someone tell you?" Dr Chandra was pushing for an emotional reaction here, hoping to get past her prepared statements about how much better she felt.

Mary looked up and managed to look angry even through the effects of the drugs. "Bloody liar! I was told. He was with some easy lay that he picked up in a disco."

"I see." said Dr Chandra. "And who told you this?" He kept his voice carefully neutral.

Tears started to roll down Mary's face and her words were a little strangled. "Bob told me. He did. He is real but I can't hear him anymore and I miss him." She sniffed and wiped her hand over her face. "He was the only one that ever loved me. Not Max, that worthless gobshite. And you took him away from me." She began to sob, tears and mucus mingling under her nose.

Dr Chandra handed her a box of tissues and made another note. It was progress of a sort. He decided not to ask about Max's comment that she worshipped her cat. Perhaps another time. He ended the session early and started to write up his notes as an orderly took Mary back to the ward.

A few minutes later, he put down his pen and sipped his bottled water. It was much healthier than all that tea. When he looked down, he saw that the blue ink was leaking out of his pen onto the paper. He watched as it spread impossibly quickly, moving in to new areas and leaving others. The ink formed letters, as neat and regular as the words on a computer screen.

"You made Mary cry. She is my believer and I love her. Max was having sex with other girls and also made Mary cry. You have to let her leave."

Dr Chandra looked at the words for a long time. He kept his breathing regular. He put his hands flat on the desk so that they wouldn't shake. He was a professional. He could handle this. Moving deliberately, he tore off the paper with the new words, crumpled it into a ball and threw it and the pen into the waste paper bin by his desk. He squeezed his eyes shut and clenched his fists, pushing down the emotions. He needed to distance himself. How would he treat a colleague in this state? Right, he thought, no organic cause which only left psychosis as a probable diagnosis. He closed his eyes again and waited for a better explanation to arrive. When none did, he sighed and started writing a treatment plan on the fresh sheet of paper. He would do the professional thing. Well, except that he would suggest that anyone else took some time off work to reduce stress levels. He had too much work to do for that to be an option. However, he knew what to do and had 24-hour access to a specialist. The prognosis for this patient should be excellent.

He filed the treatment plan under the name "Siddhārtha Gautama", smiling at the irony of using Buddha's original name. The treatment plan was complete and so it was time to start the treatment. Soonest started and all that. Dr Chandra reached for his bottom desk drawer. Medical reps were always leaving samples. He knew how to treat psychosis. He quickly sorted through the packs of pills until he found the one that he wanted. They popped from the blister pack with a satisfying crispness. He looked at them, small and perfect in his hand. He put them in his mouth and swallowed them down with a gulp from the water bottle. Maybe he would have some tea after all since it didn't seem to make any difference.

Chapter 21a

There are many different departments within NASA, often staffed by clever young graduates who spent more time than they would like justifying the expense of their work and not enough time doing the science that they so enjoyed. One of the many departments in the organisation was the Asteroid Watch team, a part of the Jet Propulsion Lab in California. A routine analysis of the paths of known objects flagged up a near Earth object called (3017) 2009 VS as being of interest. The intern looking at the data decided that the trajectory was worth further investigation and scheduled the job. It was probably nothing. There were near Earth objects quite often and they generally sailed by without upsetting anyone, but it was always best to be sure. The request resulted in more telescope time being assigned to the new object. The results would be in after about a week.

Chapter 22

The press statement issued by the Vatican had been carefully phrased and translated into multiple languages. Only a few media outlets picked up the story at first, but it started to gain traction with the more sensationalist press. News editors around the world saw it, thought about how to use it and started talking to colleagues. Within a day, the Vatican started getting requests for interviews. Before long, religious leaders of various denominations and even religions outside of the Christian faith were being asked for comment on 24 hour news, print media and talk shows. The story appeared in blogs with supporters and sceptics equally vocal. Catholic priests were advised not to comment on the story but many did. Some even started planning for very much larger congregations and they were not disappointed. Experts in religious phenomena (many self-appointed), pathologists and journalists specialising in ecumenical matters suddenly found themselves much in demand. The initial press statement was elaborated on and pontificated on endlessly:

"Press statement from the Vatican Miracle Commission.

This statement is being issued due to press speculation regarding the appearance of a mark in the shape of the cross on the palm of the late Padre Roberto Cassini, a priest of 55 years standing in the Catholic Church.

While investigations are proceeding, we are able to confirm that the marks have no known natural cause. While we are still consulting with top specialists in relevant scientific fields, it is the opinion of this commission that the stigma that appeared on the right palm of Padre Cassini is miraculous in nature.

We are aware that some of the faithful are calling for the late Padre Cassini to be beatified with a view to being declared a saint. It must be considered that there is a moratorium on such actions for a period of 5 years after the death of a candidate. This requirement may be waived only by order of His Holiness, the Pope. It is accordingly inappropriate at this time to refer to Padre Cassini as the servant of God except in as much as all priests are servants of God.

It is noted that Padre Cassini was much loved by his flock and that he was an essentially humble man who had declined promotion within the Church, preferring to focus on his pastoral duties.

The commission welcomes submissions regarding miracles connected with the late Padre Cassini."

The calls for the waiting period to be waived began almost at once.

#

It was about an hour after morning mass when Father Ryan rang the doorbell and waited. He had decided not to phone ahead this time, but he saw that there was a car in the drive. It didn't seem very likely that Anne and Ray would pretend not to be home. He barely had time to read the "No cold callers, thank you!" sign by the door when he found himself face to face with Anne.

"Father Ryan, this is unexpected. Please come in. Is everything alright?" Anne looked slightly worried even though Keith was wearing his least priestly clothes.

"Yes, everything is fine. In fact, I rather hope that I have good news for you. Well, other than the good news that I spread every day." He aimed for a winning smile and, as usual, missed. "Um, may I come in?" Anne was still standing in the doorway.

Anne stepped back and called out, "Ray, Father Ryan is here." She smiled nervously. "I am sorry that I wasn't at morning mass, Father."

Keith smiled back. "Not to worry, Anne. God is everywhere, it is said." He didn't miss her glance up to the spare bedroom. They went into the kitchen where Ray was putting on the kettle. Mr Charles looked a little thinner and tired to Keith, but that was understandable given his heart attack, he thought.

Mr Charles gestured to one of the seats at the kitchen table. "Come and be welcome, Father Ryan. What can we do for you today?"

"Call me Keith if you like, Ray. I rather think that we will be working together all being well. Tell me, have you ever heard of a Father Cassini?" Keith watched Ray's face.

Mr Charles looked puzzled. "I can't say as I have. A colleague of yours, I assume?", making the statement a question.

Father Ryan explained the last request of Robert Cassini and how the Vatican was offering a stipend for helping the poor. He showed Mr Charles a copy of the press release.

"Bob?", thought Mr Charles.

Yes.

"Do you know anything about this?", Mr Charles asked.

Yes.

"I thought that might have been your doing. You didn't, um, do anything to... well, he was already dying, wasn't he?" This felt uncomfortably like an accusation.

I didn't harm him. I just took away his pain and gave him comfort. I couldn't save him. He was very old and there was too much wrong to repair.

"And the mark on his hand?"

I was trying to make him feel the symbol that he believed in. I didn't mean to injure him, but he was slipping away and he could not feel much of his body after I took away the pain.

"They are saying that it is a miracle.", thought Mr Charles.

Yes.

"Well, I suppose that it is." Mr Charles realised that Father Ryan was looking at him and turned his attention back to the priest.

Father Ryan smiled. "Have you ever thought about helping the homeless?"

Ray explained where he had been the previous night and thus the representatives of two different religions started to plan how best to organise food for the homeless. There were some disagreements about bringing in other charities. Father Ryan valued the experience of the Salvation Army despite their theological differences but Mr Charles was adamant that it was his duty to perform. In the end, they decided that an event caterer might be the most acceptable answer. The subject of leaflets was a more contentious one.

"I am quite sure that the Vatican would not approve of their money being used to promote a pagan religion. It would run directly contrary to our interests and could imperil the souls of these poor unfortunates that we are trying to help. I am sorry but I cannot possibly agree to your handing out leaflets.", said Father Ryan.

Mr Charles thought for a bit. "What is the Church position on the souls of atheists? I don't recall you preaching about that, but my attention may have wandered, I am afraid."

Father Ryan sighed. He was well aware that his sermons were not always as compelling as he would have liked. "Doctrine says that even those that do not believe can be saved by the grace of God if they can be cleansed of their sins, although they are probably going to purgatory for some time. There are several schools of thought within the Church, I am afraid."

"Have you heard of purgatory?" Mr Charles face took on a faraway look as he talked with his god.

No, Mr Charles. I don't know what happens to people after they die. I have never had a believer die.

"I see. So, did he really send an Email asking the Church to fund soup and sandwiches for the homeless?"

There was a pause which was noticeable as Bob normally responded at once. *His last wish was that he could have done more good in the world. He didn't send the Email, but it was what he wanted at the end.*

Mr Charles considered this. "Father Ryan seems to think that this is not something that his Church would consider acceptable. I can see his point of view. It doesn't seem to be fair that you should benefit from the donations of his faithful."

People are flocking to the churches of his religion. Many are offering gifts of money and belief. I have come to understand that money must be earned through work and I have done work for his Church. It seems fair that I should be paid for that.

Father Ryan nodded.

Agree, Mr Charles. We can afford to print some leaflets.

"I hope that you know what you are doing." thought Mr Charles. To Father Ryan, he said, "Well then, we will feed the homeless and hungry and thank you for your help. I assume that the Church will want receipts for everything that we spend."

Keith smiled crookedly. "Oh yes, of course, but I will take care of that for you. The paperwork can be a nightmare, I am afraid. Do you think that two of us will be enough or should I look for helpers from within my flock?"

"The two of us? You will be... I rather thought that you worked in the evenings.", said Mr Charles.

Father Ryan tilted his head. "My Bishop feels that this is work that we should be directly involved in and has arranged for a colleague to cover for me. I did say that we would be working together."

Mr Charles closed his eyes. "I see.", he said, rather inaccurately in Bob's opinion. "Let's start with just the two of us."

By the next Friday, much had been arranged. Tureens of soup had been supplied with simple heaters by a specialist catering firm and Mr Charles and Father Ryan trained in their very simple operation. French onion, Halal chicken and split lentil soup would be served in the hope that there would be something for everyone. Bread rolls had been purchased in bulk and trestle tables borrowed from St Jude's with the help of a dark blue transit van driven by a remarkably burly nun and set up just off the main shopping street in Slough. Mr Charles had dressed in brown Corduroy trousers and a chunky sweater while Father Ryan had gone for new looking jeans, a shirt and a black jumper accessorised with a dog collar. Everything was in readiness and the tables set up with an empty spot at the front. Whenever Mr Charles had put something there, Father Ryan had quietly moved it and the reason became clear as the priest pulled out a pack of leaflets from a reused Tesco carrier bag and put them in the cleared space. Mr Charles picked one up and started to read. The leaflet listed various Catholic charities and churches that offered food and shelter to those sleeping rough and prayers to St. Benedict Joseph Labre, saint of the homeless. Mr Charles took a deep breath to calm himself. When that didn't work, he took another and tried to remind himself that life was a wonderful thing to be savoured. He looked over at Father Ryan. "I thought that we had agreed that there would be no leaflets."

Father Ryan smiled nervously. "Actually, we agreed that there would be no leaflets that didn't reflect the views of the Church, which is not the same thing at all. Anyway, isn't the important thing that these poor souls get what they need? I seem to recall you saying almost that exact thing."

Wait, thought a very familiar voice in Mr Charles' head. He sighed and put his faith in his god.

#

Dr Chandra was working late that night. There was always a huge amount of paperwork to be done to say nothing about the need to keep up with the literature. Great progress had been made in the naming of mental illnesses over the past century but, in his darker moments, he considered that far less progress had been made in understanding what they actually were. New research often promised much and disproved previous research that had promised just as much or more. He decided to do a ward round and if he happened to pass by the kitchen then he could check the quality of the food that his patients were getting. It was that or ordering another pizza delivery as there was very little food in the house. He avoided the curry house in the village since the food that they served was wholly alien to him. It was a uniquely British cuisine.

The patients seemed to be doing about as well as could be expected. They all progressed at different rates, of course. Sometimes it was one step forward and two back, but generally they were better when they left than when they came in. Rapid cures were rare, but it was often possible to get someone stabilised fairly quickly. They were all having dinner in the canteen together with the on-shift nurses. They observed the patients and it was useful to have them close at hand if anything kicked off which it sometimes did. He decided that having the senior sitting in for a meal would probably disturb the patients and would certainly disturb the nurses so he found a spare vegetable lasagne and took it in to the day room. The tables were covered with abandoned mugs of tea, so he balanced the plate on his lap and started to eat. There was certainly nothing about the food that demanded his attention, so he looked around as he ate. There were the usual partially completed jigsaws, dog-eared novels and a rather battered X-Box. There had been an issue with that and the survival horror games had been removed for everyone's benefit. He looked at the screen of the attached television to see what was being played. His fork froze midway to his mouth as the screen was displaying "Look here, Dr Chandra." in a blocky 3D font. As he watched, the display changed to "It is Bob." followed by a remarkably good likeness of Mary with the words "Please stop giving Mary drugs." scrolling underneath. Dr Chandra put his fork down on the plate and adjusted his glasses, taking the opportunity to rub the bridge of his nose where they always pressed. He stared at the words for a moment and then methodically picked up his fork and went back to his meal. When he finished, he fished two more pills from his jacket pocket and washed them down with the now tepid tea. Clearly, he had not yet got the dosage right. He put the plate down for someone else to clean up and walked over to the X-Box, turning it off. He wasn't quite sure why he had done that. He went to his office and updated the file for Gautama Buddha. Documentation was always necessary. His hands were shaking making the notes even harder to read than usual.

Chapter 23

The soup kitchen was proving popular and many of the people that came for food thanked Mr Charles and Father Ryan. Several offered donations of money, one person offered dire warnings that the world government would be watching closely and a rather loud woman in a red coat had berated them for bringing "undesirables" into the area. Fortunately, Father Ryan had handled her complaints, pointing out that hungry people were not created by the presence of food and that the people that she apparently found distasteful already lived here and had as much right to do so as anyone else. Mr Charles had never enjoyed conflict and rather admired the priest for standing up for the homeless.

It was a little later in the evening that Mr Charles found that he would have to handle a little conflict after all. A group of men dressed in multiple layers of rather grubby clothing and carrying rumpled shopping bags showed up at the trestle tables. That was not unusual since most of the night's clientele had looked very much the same. One at a time, the men had come for a Styrofoam cup of soup and a bread roll. The apparent leader of the group had made eye contact with Mr Charles, held out his hand and said "John." Mr Charles took his hand and shook it. The leader had nodded in a strangely conspiratorial way, which puzzled Mr Charles since the man was a stranger. His straggly beard was starting to grey, but his eyes held an unsettling intensity. After the impromptu group had got their bread and soup, they pulled freshly printed sheets of paper out of the shopping bags and started handing them out to the people that came for food.

Father Ryan picked up one of the leaflets that had been discarded and read it by the light spilling out of a nearby electronics shop. His anger was obvious as he walked back to the table and thrust the piece of paper towards Mr Charles. "Care to explain this, Ray?" Mr Charles took the slightly damp paper and started to read.

"New god in town seeks believers.

Bob seeks people to believe in him. In return, minor miracles will be provided on an as needed basis, subject to availability of belief.

All that you need to do is believe in the existence of Bob and think about him periodically. Believers in other gods should not apply.

Bob would prefer his believers to be pleasant to other people and refrain from cruelty.

He has no particular views on politics or sexuality but especially welcomes kind people.

Please consider Bob as your god of choice. He promises to be a hard worker."

There was a black and white picture underneath that was recognisably the same face as the one depicted on the icon that Mr Charles had created, but the pose was different. This appeared to be a photograph and Bob was smiling and pointing at the reader.

Mr Charles took a deep breath and blew it out, making a popping sound. "I have genuinely no idea, Keith. I had nothing to do with this."

Father Ryan's lips were compressed with anger. "You have to understand that I am having trouble believing that, Ray. That fellow seemed to know you. You can believe what you want but you have no right to tempt believers in the one true faith away from the truth. We are talking about immortal souls here!"

Mr Charles was a methodical man by nature and this had proved to be an asset in his career of vending machine repair. For want of a reply, Mr Charles read the leaflet again. The wording seemed clear. While Mr Charles was not an assertive man by nature and years of marriage to Anne had worn any defiance to a small nub, something caused him to speak up. It was a quiet voice but a level one. "Father Ryan, these are not my words and I have no idea who the men handing out the leaflets are, but the text does specifically say that believers in other gods should not apply… and as for trying to impose my beliefs on others… well, not that these leaflets are my work but isn't that exactly your job description?"

"I will be speaking to the Bishop about this!" said Father Ryan. He turned on his heel and stepped towards the leader of the group handing out these blasphemous pamphlets. He thought that he had heard one of the other men call him John.

#

Dr Chandra enjoyed driving at night. There was a certain clarity to it. He didn't see unimportant details and he could think about the events and problems of the day. Given the experiences of that specific day, he decided to take the country roads home and try to clear his head. He felt oddly disconnected from everything and he wasn't sure how much of that was due to his illness and how much was due to the anti-psychotics. His car was a little oasis of calm on the unlit roads and the cat's eyes were almost hypnotic as they curved ahead of him. He poked a finger at the CD player mounted in the console and classical music filled the car. His thoughts started to slip away from him and he just drove, in the zone.

#

Father Ryan stood directly in front of John, preventing him handing out leaflets. "What do you think you are doing?" he asked.

"Workin'" was the only reply. The accent was Scottish with more than a hint of Glasgow.

"I see. And would you be employed by the gentleman in the sweater over there?" Father Ryan was trying to remain polite, but it was proving to be a struggle.

"Nope. Never met him 'cept when he just gave me some soup. Working for Bob, my main man now. We look out for each other." John was grinning, but the overall effect was less than friendly.

"I see. And Bob printed up these leaflets, I suppose?", Father Ryan said.

John laughed. "Barmpot. That was Prontaprint, wasn't it? You nae hear of the miracle of the thousand double sided copies now, do yer now?"

Father Ryan quickly revised his opinion. This man was quick thinking even if he looked like he lived on the street. There was a smell of dirt on him but not the sour smell of alcohol. "And would you mind handing them out somewhere else, perhaps? We are running a mission here."

"Yep.", replied John, still grinning.

Father Ryan waited and then realised. "You mean yes, you would mind, I assume."

There was something a little manic about the grin now. "Got it in one, laddie. And before you tell me that you will call the po-lice, I have something to say. Payin' attention are yer?"

Father Ryan nodded, unsure what was coming next.

Mr Charles closed his eyes and thought for a moment. Bob watched the patterns of electrical activity in much the same way as a human might look at a fireworks display. "If I explain what happened to this priest, they will not believe me and it would be worse for them if they did. Worse for us as well, since we wouldn't get money to feed the homeless. I don't know what to tell Father Ryan."

Father Ryan is not one of mine and so I shouldn't tell him what to believe.

"You have changed, Bob. I am not sure that I like what you are suggesting.", Mr Charles thought.

I am growing up, Mr Charles. If I am to help, I need to do things that affect people. This seems to help everyone. Father Ryan's God gets more belief. They have more money to do good with. I will have the chance to gain believers and help them. I told no lies. Please, trust me. Believe in me.

Mr Charles sighed and looked at the waiting priest again. "Father Ryan, isn't the important thing that people get helped, that we actually do some good for the people that need it most?" He refused to call the priest by his first name.

"We have to consider the souls of the people as much as their bodies, more so in fact. Leading them into heresy while filling their bellies would be a very wrong thing, I am afraid." Father Ryan sipped his tea. "The Catholic Church cannot support the printing or handing out of leaflets that are not in accordance with the beliefs of the Church."

Bob found a computer nearby and started to look up the cost of printing leaflets.

"I see.", said Mr Charles. "However, the Church has no issue with feeding the hungry. I think that we can agree on that much."

John gave it his very best Braveheart impersonation and maximum volume. "Freeeeedom!" The yell echoed around the street, answered by laughter and a few half-hearted cheers.

#

The Mercedes-Benz C class hugged the curves of the road and slowly gained speed. Dr Chandra felt like a part of the car, the engine sound and the music and the light of his headlights bouncing back from the road filling his attention. He felt the tyres fighting to maintain their grip and the back end wanting to get away. He held the car to the line of the curve and eased off the power but struggled as the camber worked against him. He went to dab the brakes and then thought better of it and let the engine braking slow him. A sudden wave of dizziness hit him, and the car slewed to the side. Confused, he yanked the steering wheel to the right and the car turned so that it was at 90 degrees to the direction in which it travelled. The wide tyres slid over the road surface for a second before catching. The world sped up even more as the car flipped over, everything pinwheeling around him. The glass of the windscreen cracked and the music stopped to be replaced by the hammer of sound that the roof made as it bent. The car rolled on, half over and half through a hedge and wedged itself into an old ditch, mostly on its side. Dr Chandra hung from the seatbelt, his head bleeding where it had hit the pillar. The engine died as the fuel pump cut out. "Safety feature.", thought Dr Chandra and then consciousness slipped away from him.

Chapter 24

Dr Chandra woke to pain. His head hurt. His shoulder hurt. For some reason, his right knee hurt. He tried to focus on where he was and what had happened. It didn't help that the CD player was repeating the same three second passage of *Ride of the Valkyrie* over and over. He muzzily realised that he must have been in an accident and the car was on its side rather than the rest of the world. That would also explain the smell of petrol. There was not much light in the car. The instrument console was still glowing but the headlights were out. Probably smashed, thought Dr Chandra. He thought that he should get away from the car. His glasses had come off in the crash and there was not much light but his legs felt constricted. He tried to move his and there was a sharp pain from his right knee that left him gasping. It was clear that this was not an option. He gingerly moved his left leg and found that there was not much room left to do so. The foot-well seemed to have crumpled. Perhaps he could free himself if he could get the seatbelt off. He leaned over and that pushed his knee into the torn and bent metal of the car. He swore in Hindi, words from his childhood now rarely used. When the pain subsided, he took several deep breaths and concentrated.

He was a doctor. If this were someone else then he would assess their injuries before doing anything else. He reached down and felt his legs. The left one was about what he would have expected for a leg but the fabric of his trousers was soaked when he felt down the right side. He brought his hands to the instrument console and saw that they looked black in the green light. A memory of a physics class came back to him. Red looks black in green light. That was probably blood. It had been a long time since his physical medicine classes, but blood was supposed to be on the inside, he was sure of that. He felt the right leg again and found a sharp edge of metal and something rougher, perhaps a tree branch. It was definitely impaling his right leg just below the knee. He tried to distance himself from the problem. Right, your patient has an impaling wound. You leave the impaling object in place until the patient is in hospital. What should you do after that? He had done his time in A&E. It would help a lot if his mind would clear but his head thumped. He should prepare the patient for surgery. He had never actually done that, of course. Trauma nurses were much better at that and he had let them get on with it. So, there was no surgeon and he couldn't rig himself up to fluids. He would need help. Right, that was good. His mind was working. Now, how could he get help? He looked out of the badly cracked windscreen and hoped to see a house or another vehicle or something. He could see a ditch on the downward side, a hedge and some stars. A little moonlight was leaking over the top of the hedge and it looked like there was a ploughed field to his… his down or his right depending on whether he went with gravity or the position that he was in. He could shout but that probably wouldn't be heard. Perhaps the horn would summon someone, if only to complain about the noise. He found the control stalk and pressed the button. A sound like a robotic bullfrog came from the front of the car. That wasn't going to work.

It was getting very cold in the car and Dr Chandra felt very tired despite the pain. He wished that he could have a sleep and carry on thinking about this when he felt a bit better, but even in his confused state, he realised that he was probably in shock and that he wouldn't wake up if he did that. Perhaps he should take stock of what he had. He reached inside his jacket. There was a pen in his shirt pocket. Where was his wallet? Front trouser pocket. What was that lump in his inside jacket pocket? He slipped his hand inside, awkward when he was hanging at 60 degrees from vertical and took out a much dropped blue Nokia phone. The display was dark. He fumbled for the power button and pressed it. The screen illuminated briefly, showing an image of an empty battery and shut off again. He didn't remember when he had last charged it. He pressed the button again, gripping the phone harder. His hand was still wet with blood and the phone slipped out of his grasp, hitting the seat and clattering into the left-hand side of the car. He screamed in frustration and rage.

"God damn it! Help me, anyone, please help me." Wagner played on, the same loop over and over. He slipped into Hindi, his tone almost child-like. "Ishta Deva, anyone, please help, I beg you. I will come to your temple and pray if you will save me."

The Wagner stopped mid-bar. The only sound was the *tink* of the cooling engine. A light sprang up below him, but Dr Chandra couldn't see the source of it. A small burst of tinny classical music played, the start-up sound of the mobile phone. Three beeps followed, fast and regular.

Bob trickled as much power into the battery as he could manage. It was not going to be enough to keep it running for long, but he had disabled the feature that prevented the battery from going too flat and damaging itself. It would last for a few minutes on standby, less during a call. It would have been a help if they had been nearer to a cell tower but they weren't.

A small tinny voice said "Emergency services. Which service do you require?"

Dr Chandra hung there, trying to make sense of it. "Hello?" the voice repeated. It was getting hard to stay awake. "Ambulance.", he mumbled. "Hello?" repeated the voice. Dr Chandra was too far from the phone to be heard.

Making sound was difficult for Bob to do. Air was quite heavy in its way. However, the circuits of the phone were essentially just a small and rather stupid computer and he could do what he liked with one of those. The sound quality would not be good, but he thought that he could make himself understood.

Dr Chandra could only hear one side of the conversation.

"Ambulance service. What is the nature of your emergency?"

There was a pause. "How many people are injured? ... I see, and-", the voice was apparently interrupted. "And where did this happen?", the operator asked and then there was another pause. "And when did this happ-" The light from the phone went out. Bob couldn't keep the power going for much longer and they had the information that they needed. He was tired.

Dr Chandra was struggling to stay awake. He was so thirsty and wished that he had a cup of tea even if he had no idea how to drink it at that angle. "Who?" he whispered.

The display on the car CD player changed. He tried to focus on it, but it was difficult without his glasses. It was a short word, all in capitals. It read "BOB." It was the last thing that he saw before everything faded to black once more.

#

Dr Chandra woke up again some time later. His face felt colder than the rest of him and his neck was stiff. There was also a lot of noise and light. Blankets had been packed around him and a rigid collar had been put around his neck. The noise was from a cutter that was taking a section out of the side pillar. There were people in green uniforms all around him, more or less piled into the vehicle. One of them reached over and shone a light in his eyes and he tried to move away, rocking his body sideways. There was a tug at his arm from the cannula that had been inserted there and a fresh burst of hot pain from his leg. He passed out and hung limp again.

He felt warmer when he next woke up, but even more confused. There was something attached to his face that made a wheezing sound and a white tiled ceiling was moving in front of his eyes at a respectable speed. He gathered as much of his wits as he could manage and realised that he was on a hospital trolley. He could hear words, familiar words of medical jargon but it all just flowed over him. He felt a bit sick and closed his eyes. That seemed to help. He drifted away again, escaping the pain.

#

The ward was bright with big windows and light coloured walls. It was also completely unfamiliar to Dr Chandra. He blinked and looked around, trying to work out where he was. It looked like a surgical ward with six beds spaced more or less evenly. All of them were occupied but only a few of the other patients were awake. A drip stand was feeding straw coloured plasma into his left arm and he didn't seem to be hurting much. As he thought about it, he realised that there was actually a fair bit of pain, but it seemed somehow distant as if it didn't really apply to him. That was probably an opiate of some kind. What he could see of himself looked about the normal shape and there were lumps under the covers that were clearly his legs even if one was a good deal larger than it should be. There was a jug of water and a glass just out of reach on his right side. He could probably have got to it with a stretch, but the drip stand was in the way. His memories from the night before were fragments that had already started to fade. He supposed that he should call a nurse but he didn't know if he was allowed water. His throat was remarkably sore in a strangely unimportant way.

Hello, Dr Chandra.

"I can't hear you. You don't exist.", thought Dr Chandra.

I promise you that I do. I called the ambulance for you. Do you remember what happened?

"There was a car accident. The..." He struggled to remember. "It slid and ended up on its side. I think it is quite badly damaged."

It is very damaged, Varun. I think that you will need a new one. You nearly needed a new you.

"So, my delusion, how did you manage to call an ambulance? Did someone find the wreck?"

No, Varun. I called for help on the Nokia 2110i. I had to power the phone and that was difficult. You should keep it charged.

"The hospital uses it to call me if a patient needs me." he thought.

All the more reason to keep it charged. We should look after the people that we are responsible for. That is very important.

"And a delusion is telling me my duty now? Are you an extension of my unconscious mind?"

"No, I am Bob. Mary's Bob. Mary and Mr Charles and Ranting John and your Bob, Varun. You asked for help and I gave it."

"And what could speak in my mind except for the mind itself? You have to be a delusion. It stands to reason."

Or a god. I looked at your memories and your mother always told you that a Deva could do this. You believed your mother then, Varun. Why would you doubt her now?

"I am an adult now", thought Dr Chandra. Bob did not reply. "Look," thought Dr Chandra, "only the delusional hear voices in their heads. That is why I was taking the Perphenazine. I shouldn't be able to hear you, Mr Delusion."

Many of those that hear voices are ill, Dr Chandra. Probably most of them. Perhaps a few of them have a small god like me that is trying to look after them, but I have never met another. All I see are people and sparks that might one day become gods if anyone gave them the chance. You were quite well before you started taking the medicine, Dr Chandra. You can hear me now because you let me in when you believed enough to ask for help.

"I still don't know why the Perphenazine didn't work.", he thought.

It would have. It does with Mary. You lost a lot of blood, Varun. You don't have a lot of the drug in your system any more. I still exist even if you can't hear me. Would you agree not to take the medicine if I can prove that I exist?

"How can you prove it? Couldn't any proof just be more delusion?"

Do we have to examine the nature of reality to help each other? The nurse is coming and he will want to talk to you. I will be back.

Dr Jane Hernan was the lead consultant for A&E and had spotted Dr Chandra's notes when she had come on-shift at 7:30 that morning. Members of the public might think that doctors got better treatment than other patients, but that wasn't generally true. However, they did tend to get more attention than other patients whether they wanted it or not. Looking at the basic toxicology screening test that she held in her hand, Dr Hernan guessed that he probably would not be glad of the extra attention in this case. It wasn't obvious what he had taken, but there was something odd in his system and it probably warranted investigation. She would have a word with him in what would otherwise have been

211

her lunch break. He might be more willing to talk to someone who was at about the same level as he was.

Chapter 24a

The intern looked at the grid of numbers on the screen. One row was red. That wasn't good. He clicked on it and additional details replaced the grid view. That one was going to come very close indeed. The margin of error was fairly small and it was travelling with a lot of velocity. He manually rechecked the figures and they seemed to make sense. He rubbed his eyes and picked up the phone to call his supervisor. A little while later, his supervisor called the next manager up the chain. Before long, the matter was resting with the director of NASA. He was not a man that was inclined to panic. Before he came to NASA, he had been a Major General in the US Marine Corps. If his scientists were telling him that there was a problem, then there was a problem. They were literally rocket scientists. He called a meeting of the heads of department and explained the situation and asked for possible solutions. He then went to his office to call the President. He had hoped that he would never have to make this particular call. It seemed particularly unfair that he had to make it three weeks into his new job. He picked up the phone and dialled.

Chapter 25

Ranting John was not the name that he had been born with, of course. However, it was the name that he had been called for so long that he used it himself. As a kid, he had been Johnny or John Boy and when he had worked, he had been simply John Barber. He had taken all kinds of work when he could get it. His education had been patchy at best as he moved from foster home to foster home. After a while, he ran out of employers that were willing to put up with his attitude towards authority and things had spiralled down from there. In his opinion, they had not had very far down to travel. He had hit the bottle and the drugs when he could afford them, looking for a way out of his own skull. It had not been pleasant when he realised that he was only making things worse for himself and he had been sleeping rough for a couple of years by then. It was hard to come back from there, but he did what he could. He had quit the drink although he missed it every day. He quit the weed too for the most part, but sometimes it was cold and miserable and he needed something to get him through the night. He avoided the harder stuff altogether. When he could afford it, he stayed at the hostels for the homeless where he could at least get a shower. They had banned him a few times for verbal abuse, but they generally let him back in when he apologised. He was sincere and would promise not to go off on one, a promise that he would hold to until he couldn't. Since he had very little to do with his time, he split it between a bit of begging and reading in the Library. He wasn't reading about a particular subject. Instead, he would read a book from a shelf and then a book from the next shelf. When he ran out of shelves, he would start over, choosing a different book. He liked to think that it made him a more rounded reader. He was a regular at Slough Library and that is where he had first seen the poster about Bob.

John was doing something unusual for *him*. He was getting a haircut, surrendering his wild grey frizz for a more respectable look. It wasn't that he gave a damn about this sort of thing normally. Conforming was bowing down to the man and he didn't do that, but he had a job to do and he couldn't do that if he frightened people away. No, this was urban camouflage and that made it alright, he told himself. When his haircut was done, he would be hitting the charity shop and getting some respectable clothes. He had a meeting to attend that afternoon. He didn't like the word "meeting." He had been called to meetings with managers to discuss his behaviour, meetings with social workers (for much the same purpose) and meetings at one hospital or another to assess his "mental health needs." He knew what he needed. He needed some damn mental health and nothing anyone had tried had done much to help with that. On the good days, he could control it and on the bad days, he avoided talking to anyone until it was a good day again.

The face that looked back at him from the mirror looked tired and older than his years, but it was better, a lot better without the mad hair. Now, if only he could remove the mad from inside his head.

Mr Charles sat in the trendy new coffee shop that was almost identical to every other coffee shop that had sprung up in the past few years. He was drinking something called a Chai Latte, which was supposed to be tea. Mr Charles had simple tastes and a cup of PG tips or a cup of Nescafe was much more to his liking, but he sipped the drink and tried not to pull a face. He was waiting for someone. He almost didn't recognise John when he came in and looked around. He was clean, dressed in a light grey suit that mostly fitted and his hair was trimmed. His shoes were old and battered still, but he had cleaned up quite well all things considered. John sat down facing Mr Charles and looked him straight in the eye.

There was something a little unnerving about that steady gaze, a fire that didn't have an obvious source.

John leaned forward. "So, Bob told me that you were the first, man. The first person to believe in him. What was that like?" John looked down, breaking eye contact and looking at his empty hands.

"That is not an easy one to answer. I just...well, I suppose that it rather just happened." Mr Charles started to explain about the puncture that had brought him to the lay-by on the A34 where he had first met Bob. After he finished, he asked John how he had come to believe in their shared small god.

"Well now, that would be the leaflets that you gave out, wouldn't it? That and the poster in the Library. I was cold and alone and... well, sometimes you need a friend, eh? The voices were bad that night and then there was this new one. It wasn't like them others. It wasn't telling me to do things or having a go at me or anything. It was asking me for help. But the thing is, the weird thing is that the new voice wasn't about me. It talked about things that I didn't know about and sometimes it talked at the same time as the others and they never do that." John looked at his hands again and Mr Charles wondered how to offer him a tea or coffee. "Anyway, the voices were bad that night and I was trying to tell them to shut up and they weren't listening like always but the new voice made them be quiet and I could think. It was like I had space in my head, not like an empty head, but like having room to be me. I am making nae sense here, am I?" John continued.

Mr Charles smiled. One of the things that he had always liked about having a job that involved a lot of driving was that it gave him time to himself. "No, I understand. We all need a little space. What made you think that the new voice,

Bob, was not..." Mr Charles paused, hunting for the word. "Why did you listen to the new voice, John?"

John smiled with one half of his mouth. "I used to see this guy, a trick cyclist. Anyway, he said that the voices come from within me, so why wouldn't I listen to myself? They only get one chance though. If they lie to me once, I don't pay them no mind anymore. Anyway, it was only a pound."

Mr Charles tilted his head. "What was only a pound?" he asked.

The half smile became a grin. "For the lottery scratch cards. The first ones paid for the others and they paid for the leaflets. Genius, eh? The guy running the corner shop wasn't thrilled, though, when I wanted specific tickets off the roll but sod 'im."

Mr Charles was not sure that the National Lottery would be keen on funding a religion, but he couldn't see how Bob was breaking the rules. They probably didn't have a section on acts of god in them. Instead, he asked John if he had heard of Chalmead hospital and explained about Mary having been arrested. John listened patiently before offering an opinion.

"Well," said John, "the best advice that I can offer her is to avoid the Shepherd's pie. It was never any good when I was in there."

#

In another hospital, Dr Chandra was staring at nothing and worrying in a strangely unfocussed way. The conversation with the consultant had been difficult. Dr Chandra had always encouraged his patients to be honest with him but confessing to seeing things and hearing voices was unlikely to help his career. He didn't really have a choice about admitting to taking the anti-psychotics without a prescription and Dr Hernan had told him that she would have to report it to the GMC. He could see her point; he would have done the same if the situation had been reversed. He was clearly delusional. He started to wonder what form of therapy they would choose for him. For the first time, he felt very powerless and understood the frustration that many of his patients had expressed. He wished that he had someone to express it to. He wondered who would be chosen as his responsible physician. Would a friend be better or worse than a stranger?

He was still wondering when one of the nurses bustled over holding a piece of paper. She looked annoyed, but that was not unusual in his experience. She stopped at the foot of the bed. "Dr Chandra, you are welcome to visitors of course, but would you mind not handing our Email address out to your friends? We really don't have time to act as a postal service. Thank you so much." She thrust the paper at him and turned on her heel as soon as he had it. It was a printout of an Email.

"FOA: Dr Varun Chandra, Borburne Ward.

Dear Varun,

I was sorry to hear that the conversation with Dr Hernan went badly. I think that you made some good decisions about what to say and I can promise you a speedy recovery.

I wouldn't recommend taking any more pills if you have a choice.

May I remind you that delusions cannot send emails?

Your friend

Bob."

Dr Chandra stared at the paper for a long time. Either he was very delusional indeed or the rest of the world was. He decided that it probably wasn't him or, at least, that he would need to assume that it was the rest of the world. That changed a lot of things in complex ways. He would have to think this through and see if he could fit it in his understanding of how things were. The lessons that his parents had given him in the Veda were a long time ago, but he could remember some of it. If Brahman was to be found within all people, could he be found in a small god? He didn't know. It had been many years since he had felt the need for guidance that was not in the *Diagnostic and Statistical Manual of Mental Disorders, Fouth Edition.*

Dr Chandra lay in the too small hospital bed and listened to the breathing of the other patients. There were the many small noises of a hospital that he had learned to ignore on a conscious level during his time as a houseman. There would sometimes be a low conversation from the nurse's station, but there was no sense of alarm. It was a normal night shift except that he was a patient rather than the doctor. It was also the wrong hospital, but that was a much less jarring difference. Even as he heard the noises of the ward, he felt terribly alone. He screwed his eyes shut and tried to ignore the pain from his leg.

"Bob?", he thought.

Yes, Varun?

"Am I delusional?" His brow wrinkled. "I must be if I am asking a delusion for an opinion."

Delusions don't send Email, Varun. They don't call ambulances either. I am as real as you are.

"How do I know that this isn't all a delusion and I am dying in the wreck of my car?", he asked.

Have you read any Descartes, Varun?

"Only my mother calls me that, Bob. It sounds strange from anyone else. He said that he thought that he was or something, didn't he?"

Bob sounded a shade frustrated in Dr Chandra's mind. *Descartes wrote that the existence of self was the only provable thing and anything else could be a delusion. In a later chapter, he said that his god would not allow such a thing. I don't know about his god, but I wouldn't either. It has been said that belief is that which causes you to act without proof, but with the awareness of that believed in. Belief is an acknowledgement that we exist. If you doubt me but still talk to me, that is enough belief to nourish me.*

"Why do you need to be nourished? Can you starve?"

I would waste away and become less than an idea on the wind. There are a billion gods and more, but without faith, we are nothing but existence, unable to interact with anyone or anything. I need belief in the same way that you need air and food.

"It is hard to believe that you are real, Bob."

Would you prefer to believe that you are lost in madness, Varun?

"No, I don't think that I could handle that but this seems insane."

Please do your best. Your leg is a mess and it is going to be tricky to fix. I will need all the strength that you can give me. For both our sakes, try to believe.

Dr Chandra's leg went numb and it felt wonderful. The pain had been there even through the analgesia and the absence of it was almost euphoric. It was a few minutes later that he realised that he could feel tiny movements inside his leg and occasionally hear a soft sound. He tried hard not to imagine what they represented. After a while, he asked a question that had been troubling him. "Bob?"

Yes? Somehow, the thought seemed preoccupied.

"My patients at Chalmead. Some of them hear voices. Are they being talked to by gods or are they ill? Why should I believe that my voice is real and theirs are delusional?"

There was a pause and a twinge that made it faintly through the nerve block that Bob had set up. *Dr Chandra, you have studied the brain in detail, I know. I have read the same books. The human brain is a complex thing and I only know about as much as humans do because I learned from humans. I can watch the brain work, but so can you. Computers, vending machines and brains all go wrong sometimes. The first two are a lot easier to fix. I watched your patients and I saw no other gods. I found suffering and confusion and damage but they were alone, sometimes terribly alone. I am sorry. I do not know if all of them are delusional but many of them are. I am only certain about Mary.*

"Oh." Dr Chandra started to feel guilty. "We should probably stop treating her, I think."

Yes, we should. I am not sure that they will let you have much say over her treatment at the moment, though. You have been suspended until there has been an enquiry.

Varun squeezed his eyes more tightly closed, but the tears leaked from them anyway. "I am sorry. I just wanted to help people. That is all that I ever wanted."

You did help people and you will again, I am sure. Believe in yourself and believe in me. It might help if you could also believe that your patella was not shattered into eight pieces. Please, let me heal you. Rest now and don't worry. You are not alone.

Dr Chandra woke from a deep sleep to a sharp stabbing pain in his leg. Still groggy, he reached down and grabbed the hard thing that was digging into him. At the same moment, the tug on the IV in his hand became a fresh blossom of pain that left him gasping. The pain subsided as he released the tension that was trying to tear the tube out of his arm. He looked at the things in his hand. There were a number of screws and a metal plate. He recognised them – they were surgical screws and he was sure that they had been inside his leg. As delusions went, this one had a remarkable amount of physical evidence.

Dr Chandra twisted round and used the hand that didn't have an IV line to feel around his knee. There was some more hardware loose in the bed and the bandages were very neatly cut away. The skin of the knee was grainy with dried blood, but it felt much as it always had except for a lack of hair. Very gingerly, he bent the knee slightly and it felt like a knee. He lifted away the bed covers and saw that there were a number of sutures in with the wound dressings. The surgeon must have done a lot of repair work, judging by the number of them. He could see where the wound had been by the paler skin but it was clearly well healed. That was going to be hard to explain. There wasn't a standard procedure for handling miraculous cures in hospitals because they simply didn't happen. It was certain to draw a lot of attention and that was the last thing that he wanted if he was going to be facing an investigation for misuse of drugs. He looked at the clock on the wall and saw it was a little before 6 AM. There would probably be a shift change about now with the new shift serving breakfast and handing out medication. There might be some confusion and he could use that. He certainly had no intention of waiting in bed until ward rounds. He started thinking how he was going to do this as he waited for the shift change. With any luck, the nursing staff on the new shift would not recognise him. Of course, all that would depend on whether he could walk. He took the port out of his hand and pressed on the insertion point until it stopped bleeding. He carefully swung his legs out of the bed and onto the cold floor. He tested the leg with a little weight. It was a bit stiff but seemed to work well. He swung back into bed and listened for the handover.

The nurse that brought the drug trolley into the ward was short, young, eastern European and a complete stranger to Dr Chandra. While she was busy with one of the other men on the ward, he slipped out of bed, one hand holding a wad of bandages and metal fittings that he pressed against his side. When the nurse looked over, he forced a smile and called out "No need for a bedpan – Just give me a second." His leg was stiff but it still took his weight. He supposed that the muscles had been strained. He hobbled to the ward bathroom and closed the door behind him; the lock could easily be opened from the other side but it would give him a few minutes. The wad of dressings went into the bin by the sink and he took a look at himself in the small mirror. He had a nasty bruise on his head centred around a rectangular bandage. He reached up and pulled it off, wincing. The bruising was worse underneath and there was a small stitched wound. It was lucky that it didn't show up well against his darker skin, he thought. He washed his face, hands and leg, towelling the water away. The towel came back brown with dried blood and Chlorhexidine and he dropped it in the wash bin. The backless gown that he was wearing was a mess, but there were no spares in the small room. There were thin white dressing gowns though and he quickly put one on. It was too short for him but it would have to do. He slipped out of the bathroom and into the corridor while the nurse was looking at her clipboard. Most of the nursing staff and orderlies were busy in the wards leaving the corridor relatively empty.

His clothes were certainly ruined; ambulance crews normally cut them off at the scene before loading the patient onto the truck. However, the hospital laundry delivered fresh scrubs to theatre and they would be better than a gown even if they couldn't pass for street clothes. They probably hadn't started the surgical list, so he followed the signs for theatre and found that his luck was in. There was a cart with a pile of blues neatly wrapped. He snagged one as casually as he could and headed to the toilet to get changed. The cap mostly covered the wound on his temple and a private room provided a pair of slippers that could pass for surgical clogs at first glance. He headed for the car park, his leg already feeling better.

Chapter 26

Chalmead hospital, like most hospitals, ran to a routine. It was especially important in a psychiatric hospital where patients often struggled to accept change. The routine had broken down that day because the senior consultant had not shown up. Calls to his house and his mobile phone had gone unanswered. The senior registrar had passed some of his cases to more junior staff and stepped into the gap left by Dr Chandra.

Also like most hospitals, Chalmead ran on rumour as much as it did on electricity or medicines. and the confidential call from Dr Hernan was whispered news among the staff within the day, often distorting in strange new ways as it passed from mouth to mouth. The patients didn't know what had happened, but the staff were acting strangely and appointments were changed. The environment started to get tense.

Mary lay on her bed and stared at the ceiling. It was not a good day to be in the patient's lounge. There had already been two fights and it felt like there would be another. The nurses were watching everyone very closely and that ratcheted the tension level even higher. Mary didn't feel afraid. She didn't feel anything very much. She lay back and watched her own thoughts fizzle and die. She would probably do that until it was time for dinner. It was Shepherd's pie again tonight.

The senior registrar sat in Dr Chandra's office going through the treatment plans for the patients that he would need to pick up. The call from Dr Hernan had made it very clear that his boss would not be back for at least a few weeks and the patients would still need treatment. He sighed and rubbed his eyes; it had already been a long day. He opened the next file, not recognising the name on the front. Did they really have someone with the same name as Buddha? It didn't seem likely. He started to read and his eyebrows slowly crept up his forehead. Well, he thought, you have to hand it to old Varun. He really did keep excellent notes even if he was also clearly keeping a few bats in the belfry. He sat back and tried to decide what to do. It was a problem but also an opportunity for an ambitious and talented registrar. Dr Chandra's office was really rather pleasantly furnished. He could see himself being very comfortable here and clearly the senior physician would need time to recover from more than his injuries. He took another drink of the dreadful coffee and started drafting a memo to all of the staff explaining that Dr Chandra would be away for an extended period. He certainly could not be allowed to treat this Callahan woman any more. That had the look of an unhealthy obsession.

#

Dr Chandra sat in Costa Coffee nursing his fourth cup of tea. He would have to use the bathroom again soon at this rate. At least he had clothes now and enough money to buy some food and drink. Bob had directed him to a cash point machine and withdrawn some money from the account of one of the other believers. Varun had no idea how this was possible without the card being present, but it was becoming easier to accept the impossible. If this was all a delusion then the only thing that he could do was to go along with it in the hope that it would either start making sense or that he would somehow snap out of it. Bob had told him that the other believers would meet him here. Dr Chandra hoped that there would be room. It was not a large coffee shop and there were already a number of customers.

When he came back from the gents, he was irritated to see that someone had taken his table. As he looked around for somewhere else to sit, he noticed that the man had two cups of tea in front of him and that he was getting to his feet.

Dr Chandra unconsciously assessed the man. He was in his late forties, a little overweight with a receding hairline and an apparently normal affect, or as a layman would say, apparently sane and calm. If anything, the man seemed to be at peace in some way despite the unnaturalness of the meeting. His suit was reasonably neat if inexpensive and a little loose on his frame. The overall effect was somehow avuncular. By the time Varun had completed his mental state examination, the newcomer had his hand extended for shaking. Dr Chandra reflexively shook it.

"Dr Chandra, I assume.", Ray said smiling at something that was not really a joke. "I am Ray Charles, vending machine repair man, apparently first priest of Bob and not in any way a soul legend which was, apparently, confusing the police."

Dr Chandra stared.

"I put sugar in your tea. I am sure that this has all come as something of a shock. You might like to sit down perhaps?", Mr Charles continued.

Dr Chandra sat down and picked up the unwanted tea largely to give his hands something to do. "Hello Mr Charles. Just to be certain, you just described yourself as the first priest of Bob, yes?"

Ray nodded. "I did. I am."

Dr Chandra sipped the tea. "I was told that I would meet the other... the believers here. How many of you are there?"

Ray smiled again. "I see that you are a hard man to convince. Counting you, me, John and Mary, there are four. Of course, Mary is rather out of the picture at the moment."

"Four.", said Dr Chandra.

"Four.", replied Mr Charles.

Varun rubbed his temple and winced before noticing that it didn't actually hurt. The skin was now smooth, the stitches gone. He prodded it speculatively but it seemed just as it usually did. He realised that he must look very odd and stopped. He thought for a moment. "I am sorry about Mary. You have to see how it looked… I mean, she presented with all the classic symptoms of religious mania and, well, I had no idea. How could I?", he finished weakly.

Mr Charles nodded. "If it looks like a duck and quacks like a duck, I can see you thinking that you were looking at a duck."

While Dr Chandra had spent almost all of his life in England, he still sometimes struggled with idioms. He decided that he would ignore the reference to waterfowl as this conversation was already strange enough. "I suppose I should see about getting her a discharge, but that would require a review meeting. I will try to get one set up."

I am afraid that is going to be difficult to arrange, Varun. You have been suspended pending an enquiry into your fitness to work.

From the expression on Mr Charles' face, he had heard the same message. Varun swore quietly. "You can see their point, I think. When you expect to see ducks…" commented Mr Charles.

Dr Chandra wondered vaguely about Mr Charles' duck obsession. "They certainly didn't wait very long. I suppose that I could phone some colleagues, but I will struggle to convince them. It sounds quite unreasonable, to be honest."

"Yer can say that again." said a Scottish accented voice and someone slipped into the unoccupied chair. Varun looked over and met the newcomer's gaze.

"You?" said Dr Chandra and Ranting John in unison. The word was loud in the relative quiet of the coffee shop.

John grinned and looked down causing considerable relief as the tension drained. "Nae hard feelings, Doc. You had a point and I have had my share of problems, true enough. Anyhoo, we are on the same side so all good, right?"

"Um, yes, I suppose so. How have you been, John?" The doctor's smile had a hint of rictus about it. He was not sure how many more surprises he could handle in such close succession.

"Not bad, Doc. I finally found a voice worth listening to. Now, Bob says that yer are about as welcome in Chalmead as a fart in a space suit, so I am thinking maybe we need some more direct action style of thing." John stopped, waiting for an objection.

"I could try. They might listen.", said Dr Chandra.

"And d'yer think that you will get anywhere, big man?", asked John.

Varun thought for a moment. "That depends on why I am suspended."

They read your case file.

He thought for a few seconds. "Ah, no then. I wouldn't listen to a colleague under those circumstances.", said Dr Chandra.

"Any of yer got a better idea than getting her out the back way then?" asked John.

"It would be illegal." said Dr Chandra.

"Aye, a lot of things are." replied John. "Better not to get caught then." There was a thoughtful pause.

"I don't think that it would actually be wrong, though. It seems that doing nothing would cause more harm than spiriting Mary out of there.", said Mr Charles.

Yes.

"We can't hurt anyone in the process. They haven't done anything wrong.", said Varun.

There was a quiet chorus of agreement followed by a long pause. "Does anyone have paper and a pen?", asked the doctor. He always thought better with a pen in his hand. Mr Charles handed him one and he started sketching a map. "The hospital is arranged to keep people in rather than people out, but there are always staff on duty and all the permanent staff know each other. I have... er, had keys but I suppose that they are either in the car or the hospital now. I can't even get into my house anymore."

"Might be able to help you there. Got a spare room by any chance?", asked John.

Varun hesitated and then nodded. The team studied the sketched map.

Chapter 26a

The President of the United States sat in the Oval Office and reread the papers in front of him. NASA had done a good job on the explanation and the plan seemed to be a sound one. However, it was not something where the US could act alone. At the very least, it would lead to unfortunate misunderstandings. He ordered another cup of coffee and started to call the leaders of the G8. Staffers would call the other countries, but the G8 deserved to know first. The Vice President was briefing the press office as the news would be hard to contain for long. It was always better to control the story if you had the option.

Chapter 27

Father Ryan sat in the chair in front of the Bishop's desk. Tea had not been offered.

"So, you are sure that these street people that were handing out the leaflets were in cahoots with this Mr Charles then?", asked the Bishop.

"I don't see any other possibility, to be honest. Occam's razor seems to apply. The simplest explanation is normally the right one and all that. However, knowing it and proving it are two very different things.", said Keith.

"Aye.", agreed the Bishop. "I don't suppose that there is any legal recourse either. It is no crime to pass out leaflets even at the peril of immortal souls.

"Deorum injuriae diis curae.", commented Keith.

The Bishop gave him a stern look. He had always suspected that Keith would have been happier as a theologian rather than a parish priest. "And your point would be?" he asked, unsure of the Latin. He had originally served the Lord in inner city Glasgow.

"'The gods take care of injuries to the gods.' I looked it up." said Keith. "The last successful prosecution for heresy was back in 1921 and the new Human Rights act pretty much kills any chance that we had there."

The Bishop scowled. "Not a good use of Church funds then. I took another look at the request of the late Father Cassini and we don't have a lot of wiggle room here. Either we spend the money on feeding the poor with the questionable help of Mr Charles or we go back to the Vatican and tell them why we think it is a bad idea." said Douglas.

Keith fidgeted. "I can't see that going down well, to be honest."

The Bishop nodded. "To go where angels fear to tread? You're nae a fool, lad."

"We could try drowning him out, I suppose. More leaflets, sermons, even a choir. No-one ever said that the Church had to be quiet and it is still a Christian nation in law.", said Keith.

Douglas smiled. "Who are we to turn away people of good faith that want to help the poor? I will see who I can round up."

"I still can't work out why an elderly Italian priest would make such a request in the first place. It seems... well, implausible.", said Father Ryan.

"It does indeed. Could this Ray Charles have faked it, you are thinking?", said the Bishop.

"He hardly seems the type, to be honest. I think that he is a repair man of some kind. It is possible, I suppose.", said Keith.

"Aye, strange things are sometimes so. Why don't you make some enquiries with the appropriate people and let me know?" It was apparent that the Bishop was not asking a question.

"Um, wouldn't the request be taken more seriously from a Bishop than a mere parish priest, Douglas?", asked Keith.

"Maybe so, maybe so but computers are for young men and better coming from you than me, I think. If it turns out to be nothing, I can sweep it away without harm.", said Douglas.

The younger priest nodded. He was being given a chance to sink or swim and if it were the former, then the Bishop wanted no part in the descent.

#

John woke up in a strange bed and looked up at the ceiling. He was warm and dry. That was a good start. No-one was yelling at him and that was also good. Many days had not started that well. He listened to the sounds around him and he could hear a hissing sound, probably a shower. That would be Dr Chandra. It was a nice place that he had here; head shrinking must pay well. There was nothing that humanised a doctor quite so much as picking the lock of his house and letting him inside. John blinked a couple of times and tried to clear his mind of thought. The voices were still there, but quiet and indistinct, easy to ignore. It looked like they would not be playing up today and that suited him fine. There was a lot to do and it would be easier without them shouting or sneering at him. He slid out of the bed and straightened the covers. There was always a chance of a second night if he played his cards right. The sound of the shower stopped and John looked around to see where he had put his duffle bag. He had best get a shower himself and make himself presentable. It had been a while since he had been a working man and he had never had a god as an employer before. A few that thought that they were god, perhaps. He rummaged in the bag and took out a few things. He would need to pick up some disposable razors, but perhaps he could borrow one for now. At least he had a toothbrush. New teeth were hard to come by.

John took a look around the bathroom as he was towelling himself dry. One bottle of shower gel, one bottle of shampoo which made sense. There was a tub of moisturiser, but none of the hundred things that every woman keeps in her bathroom. Dr Chandra was single then.

Maybe a lot of men moisturised these days, thought John. There was even a word for it, wasn't there. Metrosexual or some such. John briefly wondered if his host was gay and then discarded the thought. He didn't have strong feelings about homosexuality although his father had. That might have been why John didn't. He had been determined not to make the same mistakes that his father had and in that, he had succeeded. His mistakes were all his own. He caught himself reflecting and told himself to snap out of it. No good ever came from that. He hung up the towel and got dressed. He would have to find the kitchen.

He heard the conversation at about the same time as he found the kitchen. There was a very familiar tone to one of the voices. John had been in trouble with the law often enough that he recognised the polite but sceptical voice that the police used when dealing with the public. He stood in the hall and listened. He couldn't make out what Dr Chandra was saying, but he sounded apologetic and that wasn't good. There were people who would take that and push against it, bullying by reflex. Even if this copper were not that sort, it always made them think that the person had something to hide and you never wanted them to think that. John preferred to have nothing to do with the cops, but Chandra had done him a favour and John knew the value of someone willing to give him a bed for the night. Fair was fair. Lip service was all well and good but not many would invite you into their home, especially after you had just picked the lock. He took a quick look in the mirror and he was neat enough. He walked into the kitchen.

The copper was young and that was good. The old ones had seen more of the tricks. He didn't have any rank insignia either, just a number on his epaulettes. One of the foot soldiers then. He stopped midsentence when he saw John, looking offended for some reason.

"I thought that you said that you lived alone, Dr Chandra.", said PC Nameless. The statement was a question. Sly buggers they were, thought John.

Before Dr Chandra could speak, John took the initiative. "Well, my client may have said that or may not. I wasn't here to witness it. However, he does indeed live alone. Excuse me!" John stepped forward and reached past the copper, taking a mug from the little wooden tree on the counter and filling it from the coffee pot. "Sorry I am late, Varun. I came as quickly as I could."

The PC moved so that he could look at both men at once. "Your client, Sir? Are you Dr Chandra's lawyer?"

John sipped the coffee which was far too hot. "Does my client need a lawyer? Has he been charged with any crime? What, specifically, constable, are you doing here?"

The copper already had a notepad in his hand and consulted it. "Dr Chandra's car was involved in an RTI, road traffic incident, the night before last, Sir."

John took another sip of coffee and scalded his mouth again but he needed it to give him time. "Yes, I know that. How does that explain why you are here?"

"It is an offence under the road traffic act not to report an accident. Dr Chandra did not file such a report within 24 hours.", explained the policeman, clearly irritated.

"And Dr Chandra was in hospital as a result of this road traffic incident, and so was unable to do so, clearly. Would you prosecute some poor b... some poor unfortunate who came off a motorbike and was in a coma for not coming into the station for a chat?" He needed to watch his language if he was going to sound professional. "Does that even sound remotely reasonable to you, constable?" Out of the corner of his eye, he could see Dr Chandra looking from one man to the other as if watching a tennis match.

"But your client disappeared from hospital yesterday. You can see that we would want to know why, Sir." The copper was clearly on the defensive now.

"Aye, but it was a hospital, nae a prison. Dr Chandra is a free man and I intend to keep him that way. He can leave hospital any time that he wants. Do you have any reason to harass this man?" John had been acting at the start of the conversation, but the anger was real now. He knew that he had a problem with authority figures.

"No, Sir, it is not my intent to harass anyone. Since Dr Chandra has been kind enough to answer my questions, I believe that I don't have anything else at this time. We may have further questions later, though." The policeman took an unconscious step away from John.

"Good! This way then." John led the way towards the front door, hoping that he remembered where it was. His luck was in and he opened it for the policeman. The constable walked outside and then turned, his pad and pen held ready.

"I don't think that I heard your name, Sir.", he said.

John smiled with his lips only. "No, I don't think that you did." He closed the door, enjoying the look on the constable's face and walked back to the kitchen, now chuckling softly. Varun was still there, looking relatively pale.

"You can't pretend to be a lawyer, John. There are probably laws against that!", said Varun.

"Aye, there probably are. I nae said I was a lawyer though. The chinless wonder just assumed that." John looked around for the fridge. He hated black coffee.

"You said I was your client.", said Varun.

"Ah, yer right, I did. You owe me a full English breakfast as a retainer. As your astrologer, I reckon you should beware the ides of March whatever they are." John grinned. It was a good day when you got one over on The Man.

Varun grinned back, unable to help himself. "You are out of luck there – vegetarian. Would a bowl of muesli do?"

"Close enough.", replied John. He had just found the milk.

The two men chatted over breakfast with a stiffness born of not wanting to offend each other. John was the more relaxed of the two; he had learned over the years of living in institutions and sleeping rough that you could walk away from any problems that were not inside your own head and the worst that could happen here was that he would need to find somewhere else to sleep. However, he was coming to like the doctor. It had been the power difference that had caused the friction.

Varun was the first to broach the subject of their shared past. "John, thanks for getting me in here last night and for helping with that policeman. It has been a difficult time."

"Nae bother.", said John around a mouthful of toast.

Varun cleared his throat. "Um, I am sorry about how things were for you at Chalmead. That can't have been pleasant."

John looked directly at his former doctor, tilting his head, his brow furrowing. After an uncomfortably long pause he asked "Why?"

"Well, you were kept there against your will and treated as if you were, well, troubled.", said Varun.

Ah, here it comes, thought John. "Mate, let me tell you a thing or two. The food was crap, but there was plenty of it. There was a bed and it didn't rain on me. Some of the nurses could be buggers when you got on the wrong side of them, but it was better than the street. You were alright. You thought that I was mad as a hatter, didn't yer?"

"Well, that is not a phrase that we like to use, but yes, I thought that you had issues." said Varun.

"Yeah, well, I did and I do and you tried to help, so good on you. Cheers. Really, thanks. Appreciate the thought even if it got my back up at the time."

Varun breathed out, a grunt of surprise. "You are very welcome. Um, how did you do that with the policeman? You seemed like a different person."

"Ah, and there was me thinking that you listened to us. I told you that the only class I ever liked at school was drama. The teacher was the only one good for a ciggie and a chat outside class. I tried for him. The others just wanted me to sit down and shut up." John rolled his shoulders. "So, we need to plan a breakout and we are nae Tom Cruise so this will take some doing. Ready for some hard thinking, Doc?"

#

John had decided that the group needed a name. For want of a better one, they decided on "The Church of Bob" even if they were all a bit self-conscious about it with the exception of Bob. They had met up at Dr Chandra's house as only Mr Charles had a car. A whiteboard normally used for the shopping list became the main planning tool. Mr Charles had some suggestions and Bob thought of a few ways that he could help. It would require some money, but Dr Chandra could help there; the salary of a chief physician was good and apart from the Mercedes, Varun was not one to spend much. By the end of the night, they had a plan. The next day was very busy. There were a lot of things that needed to be bought.

Chapter 28

It was a rainy night and the wind tugged at the sides of the ambulance. It was an older model and the engine sounded a bit rough when it could be heard over the wind. Mr Charles was driving and struggling a little with the unfamiliar controls. He would have liked a chance to practice but they had only got the vehicle that day. The green uniform felt odd on him. He much preferred his Marks and Spencer's suits, but he had to look the part. John and Varun were in the back. The handover would be the riskiest part of the rescue. They couldn't afford for Chandra to be recognised, so he was wearing a face mask, a face shield and a cover for his hair. John was strapped to the trolley and wearing bandages on his arms and his hair had been dyed. It would have been safer to use Mr Charles for the handover, but he hadn't been at all convincing when they had practised. The wind dropped a little as the ambulance reached the gates leading up to Chalmead. Mr Charles wound down the window and pressed the metal button on a box that was mounted on a pole. It buzzed and after a few seconds, a tinny voice said "Yes?", barely audible over the wind. Mr Charles replied, "Ambulance. Can you open the gate please?" It was his only line and he delivered it nervously. The speaker clicked and the gate started to swing inward. Mr Charles called out thanks to the dead microphone and fumbled the ambulance back into gear. They were expecting a transfer from Frimley as the hospital had called ahead. The call really had come from Frimley Health after they got an alert from an ambulance crew. The communication unit had been deactivated when they got the vehicle, but Bob had been working on it. He had enjoyed puzzling his way past the security protocols. They were rather funny from his point of view.

The vehicle drove rather sedately round to the back of the hospital, past the enclosure with the bins and towards the cargo doors where supplies and patients were normally unloaded. Dr Chandra jumped out, his leg fully healed now, and banged on the human sized door. The wind whipped at his hat and mask. The door opened, a plump man stopping it from blowing all the way in with his body. Dr Chandra didn't recognise him. Bob had said that they had agency staff in.

"Can you give me a hand? He is on a trolley!", shouted Dr Chandra, raising his voice to be heard over the wind that circled the courtyard.

"What about your mate?", asked the agency nurse.

"Bad back.", shouted Dr Chandra.

The agency nurse grumbled but stepped out of the building and headed for the ambulance. Together, they unclipped the trolley from the wall and pulled it down the ramp. John made a point of struggling against the straps. The nurse was clearly in no mood for any nonsense and smacked the trolley against the door getting it inside.

"What's with the mask and visor?", asked the agency nurse.

"He is a spitter. You will want to watch for that.", replied Dr Chandra.

"Great.", commented the nurse. "Where is the paperwork?"

"Bob?", thought Dr Chandra.

Ready.

The lights went out. A moment later, a dim green glow came from the exit sign about the door. The nurse started swearing.

"Damn!", shouted Chandra. "That is bound to set them off. I can look after him while you go back to the ward."

The nurse looked uncertain but then nodded. "Lend me your torch, mate."

Dr Chandra unclipped the torch and handed it to the nurse. Just at that moment, the siren on the ambulance started up. The shouts from the patients followed seconds later. The nurse swore again and ran for the door that led deeper into the building. As soon as he was out of the corridor, Varun started unbuckling John. There was a nurse's uniform under the small of his back and he pulled it on over the dressings. They held a number of small tools and some money, just in case. John grunted "Nice one." and clapped Varun on the back. Varun handed him a small bag and John headed in the direction that the nurse had gone. Dr Chandra sat down and started to worry in earnest.

John walked up the corridor trying to read the numbers on the doors by the inadequate emergency lighting. He had never been into the women's section before. He had been tempted a few times, but he had some standards even when he was struggling a bit. He wished that he still had the torch though.

Three doors along, second bed. Bob's voice was clear in his mind, the others now faded to half heard whispers.

"Cheers.", muttered John. He headed off down the corridor and found the right door. There were four beds and three women in there, visible in a sweep of the blue lights bleeding in through the windows from the ambulance. One was pressed against the window and two were in their beds. The woman to the left was older and was mouthing words mechanically. The other had red hair and an oval face. She looked over at him, unfocussed and without much interest. The plan had been to inject her with a sedative and take her back to the trolley, but she looked pretty much out of it already to John. He left the syringe in the bag that Varun had given him and walked to the bed.

"Mary?", he asked. She looked over and nodded after a second. "Yer got to come with me for a bit, love. Someone wants to see you."

"What's happening?", Mary asked, her words slurred.

"Everything is fine, sweetheart, nothing to worry about, but you have to come with me. The doctor sent me." John looked around and saw a dressing gown in the next sweep of blue light. He snatched it up and tossed it to Mary. "Pop that on, love. Have you got slippers?"

It was only two minutes later although it seemed longer to John. They were in the corridor and Mary was shuffling along at a snail's pace. John would have liked to know what they had given her, but he was a determined reader rather than a fast one and there really hadn't been the light to read her notes. He helped her as best he could until they found a wheelchair. The going was faster after that. They were nearly at the loading bay when John heard a louder voice in his head. The others were noisy; they always were when he was stressed, but this one cut right through them rather than taking turns as they usually did. *John, the nurse is coming!* He straightened his back and carried on. The plan was to put her on the trolley and have John hide in the ambulance, but it looked like that was going to hell in a hand-basket. The real nurse rounded a corner and spotted John and Mary.

"What the hell do you think that you are doing? Where are you taking this patient?", asked the nurse.

John smiled, finding an inner peace that surprised even him. "Ah, well now. That is the thing. Look at her eyes."

The nurse glanced over at her. "What about them?"

"Take a proper look.", John insisted. The nurse sighed and walked over, crouching in front of the chair. He barely felt the needle of the hypodermic as it slipped into his neck. Dr Chandra had prepared the sedative; enough to put Mary out without hurting her, just in case. It had been years since John had been on heroin, but the skills remained. The nurse slumped to the floor, unconscious and feeling no pain. John tidied him to the side of the corridor and wheeled Mary to the loading dock where Dr Chandra was waiting.

"Ok, big man, change of plan. Help me get her on the trolley and then get her out of here. I have to stay.", said John.

"What? Why? Are you mad?", asked Dr Chandra.

John beamed back. "Aye, you always were the sharp one. The dickhead that answered the door is taking a little nap and someone needs to take care of the good patients of this here hospital. Let's get her out of here."

It is OK, Varun. I will help him.

"Uh, the nurse, you haven't...", Dr Chandra tailed off.

He will be fine and is only sleeping. I am keeping an eye on him. That was dangerous though. You should have asked for help. John opened his mouth to speak but closed it again. Sometimes you had to accept authority. Together, the two men got Mary into the ambulance and Mr Charles drove them away. Bob found the switch for the gate which the others had completely forgotten about and the ambulance was back on the main road.

That left an unconscious agency nurse to deal with. John looked at the sleeping man and wondered where to put him. "Ah, sorry, fella. Wrong place at the wrong time. Nae your fault." he said quietly. After some thought, he dressed the man in pyjamas (over, surprisingly, a pair of Hello Kitty boxer shorts) and put him in an isolation room with the documentation that Dr Chandra had prepared earlier. He would complain when he woke up. John knew the reception that the complaints would get, so he got on with the job of nursing and, if he made a few mistakes, nobody remarked on it. They probably didn't expect a great deal from an agency nurse booked at the last moment. He walked out of the gate some hours later after enjoying a free breakfast. It was still raining but the sun was shining on him.

The nurse was released two days later, unharmed by the experience. He later sued the hospital trust and retired.

Chapter 28a

By this point, the UN had taken over responsibility for coordinating the response to (3017) 2009 VS. Since the name did not exactly trip off the tongue, the object had been renamed "Traveller", a name chosen to avoid any religious significance or dramatic images. A 56,000 ton lump of iron heading for the planet at speed really didn't need any help to be dramatic. NASA and the US military were working under UN control and for once, the US was up to date with their payments to the UN. Some of the more cynical members took that as proof that America was genuinely afraid of the Traveller. The latest observations confirmed the trajectory of the Traveller and the margin of error was smaller than ever. It might miss the Earth if its trajectory were at the outside edge of the error margin. It might just graze the atmosphere and bounce off although this could well cause a significant shock wave affecting millions of people. It could, and this seemed increasingly likely, plough straight into the planet with more energy than all the weapons ever used or created. Exactly how this would result in the death of everyone on the planet depended on the angle that it hit and what was underneath it at the time. The best-case of the worst case scenarios was a nuclear winter without the nukes. It was possible that a few people would survive that, but far from certain. The worst case was a fire-storm that would sweep the planet until there was nothing left to burn or no oxygen left to burn in.

For once, there was considerable agreement among the nations of the UN. Russia and America voted the same way. Even Israel and Iran could agree on this one. The recommendation of NASA, verified by the Russian Federal Space Agency and China National Space Administration was that an ICBM warhead mounted on a Soyuz rocket would be the best solution. Unfortunately, there was a limit on the number of Soyuz rockets available. The Russians would provide two Soyuz rockets and one warhead although it would actually be a US warhead relabelled. The Americans would supply two warheads, one labelled in Russian and shipped to Vladivostok. The Chinese would supply a Long March rocket and a Chinese made nuclear warhead. The launches would be coordinated to get all the missiles to the Traveller at the same time with press coverage suppressed until the last few minutes. The hope was that they would not be the *last* few minutes for the audience but if they were wrong, the reaction of the press was not going to matter for once.

There was no hope of destroying the Traveller even with three warheads, but it might be possible to deflect it. The greater the distance from Earth, the smaller the required deflection would need to be. Time was the critical factor and there was no way to buy more.

It would be a scramble to get the rockets ready and corners would have to be cut. Failures were expected and the three rocket solution was considered to be the most likely to succeed, as well as the most politically acceptable.

The press releases would go out after the launches had been confirmed and the missiles well on their way.

Chapter 29

The Church of Bob had something of a problem. Mary couldn't go home; she had rented her flat and her tenancy had terminated when she was unable to pay her rent. Bob would have taken care of it had it occurred to him but it had not. There didn't seem to be any records of the whereabouts of her cat. John didn't have a home to go to. Mr Charles had a house that he shared with Anne, but it wasn't large enough for everyone. Dr Chandra had a house, but it was clear that Mary would be at risk of discovery if she stayed there since they had read Dr Chandra's file. In the end, Bob solved the problem by removing a house from the council's computerised records as a short-term solution. It served as a meeting place and somewhere to live for John and Mary. Dr Chandra ended up staying there as well and proved to be a fair cook as long as they didn't mind vegetarian food. His curries were something of a guilty pleasure for Mr Charles. It had been necessary to change the locks since not everyone had the same faculty with picks as John, but that was not a major chore.

The plan was a simple one. Mary would need some time to recover even with Bob's help, and the rapid healing of Dr Chandra had left him feeling tired.

It was clear that Bob's believers had not had time to get to know each other very well. The books on leadership (206 in the Dewey Decimal system) had contradicted each other in many ways, but they had all agreed that team members needed to be able to trust each other. A television set and some board games were purchased with this in mind. This was, as far as recorded history can tell, the first time that anyone ever played Trivial Pursuit as a religious duty. Mr Charles even managed to book a few days off due to an unexpected drop in the number of faulty vending machines or, more accurately, the number of vending machines that stayed faulty in Mr Charles' area.

It was a surprisingly healing time and after two days, the crew were feeling pleasantly relaxed. Mary was much more her old self if still a little nervous and Varun was no longer so pale. He managed to put his worries aside and was watching Eastenders with Mary when the emergency broadcast came on. The secret had been kept remarkably well. Even Bob had not noticed as he had been spending time with his believers.

A few button presses showed that the same broadcast was on all channels at the same time. In fact, some version of it was on every channel in every country with the exception of North Korea. Respected broadcasters had been drafted into television studios to read a prepared statement prior to switching to a live feed of the three missiles heading towards the Traveller.

Mary watched a news reader from the BBC who sat nervously at his desk in front of the autocue and she tried to remember his name. She almost missed the first words.

"The government, in cooperation with the United Nations, has to inform you of a grave threat to the safety of the world. We urge you to remain calm and stay in your homes and we ask essential staff in critical services to remain in their workplaces. We understand that you may wish to be with your families, but please be assured that everything possible is being done to protect you and your loved ones.

The Jet Propulsion laboratory, a division of NASA, detected an object that has been identified as a large asteroid that is travelling on a path that would cause it to come very close to our planet. There is a small but real possibility that the object could enter the atmosphere leading to possible damage and potential loss of life.

The governments of the United States, the Russian Federation and the Peoples' Republic of China have spearheaded an emergency response designed to protect the people of the world. All governments have contributed generously to this cause. As we speak, three powerful nuclear weapons are travelling towards this rogue asteroid to destroy it or deflect it from its path.

While it is practically certain that this will prove effective, it is recommended that people remain indoors with the windows closed and the curtains drawn if possible. It is important to understand that this is just a precaution for your safety.

The nuclear weapons are many hundreds of miles from Earth and represent no threat to public safety. There is not expected to be any radiation risk, although it is advised not to look at the missiles during detonation."

The program carried on, showing diagrams of the trajectory of the Traveller and the missiles. It was obvious that the path of the Traveller was curved by gravity. It was following predictions very closely and would impact according to the best estimates somewhere in the Indian Ocean in around three hours. The margin of error was now far too small for there to be any hope that it would miss the planet, although the broadcast for the masses offered false hope that it might pass by. A small window appeared in the bottom left-hand corner of the screen showing three lights in a roughly triangular formation. It was explained that this was a live feed of the Eagle, Bear and Dragon as the three weapons had been named as seen from a Russian observatory. They were close to the intended trajectory with Dragon (The Chinese Long March rocket) a little ahead of the others.

"Bob?", thought Mary.

Yes, Mary.

"Is this real? Is this really happening?"

Yes, I have been there and looked. It is a big metallic asteroid.

"Is it going to hit us?"

Not if the missiles work as they are supposed to.

"And will they work?"

I don't know. We will find out soon.

"I am afraid."

I know.

"I don't want to die!"

I don't want you to die either.

"Can't you do something?"

It is a very big rock, Mary.

"That isn't helping!"

I know.

Mary turned her attention back to the television. By now, everyone in the house was watching. The feed was now showing a man in a US air force uniform talking to the camera in front of a whiteboard. The presentation seemed rather less slick than usual and Mary wondered how long they had been given to prepare it. A heavyset man in a lighter blue uniform and a small Asian man in blue-grey stood to either side of him, not speaking. In other countries, similar briefings were being broadcast with the Russian or Chinese officer speaking.

"So, the three missiles are now very close to the Traveller and will be exploding at the same time providing a truly devastating force that should at least partially destroy the rogue asteroid and push any remaining fragments out of the path of the planet. All the nations involved have made a tremendous effort to get us to this point and we all appreciate the help that everyone has given in protecting... well, everyone. As you can see from the count-down, we are only minutes away from the detonation."

The text "Do not look at the explosion." appeared on the screen covering the smaller image of the three rockets in the corner. When the text disappeared, the count-down was down to two minutes and fifty-three seconds.

"As you can see, the missiles are still exactly on their trajectory and the mission status is nominal at this time. It is a tribute to the engineering staff that..." The presenter faltered, looking at something to his left. "...that this mission could be mounted in the time available." he continued, a trace of firmness gone from his tone.

As people watched, one point of the triangle stretched a little further ahead of the others. It would not have been obvious if that point had not been towards the edge of the picture.

"People all around the world are watching this, ladies and gentlemen, the greatest number of people that have ever watched a single broadcast. It is truly a historic day." He paused. "Well, I guess that it would be a pretty historic day without the broadcast, if I am going to be honest." He forced a smile. "Folks, I am supposed to read out this script, but I really feel that I would like to just think of my loved ones at this time. I might even pray a bit. Now, all these rocket scientists may not be religious types, but I don't think that any of them would mind if you wanted to say a little prayer of your own right now." He fell silent and there was an awkward pause before the feed from the telescope of the rockets was changed to fill the screen. The blue exhaust was visible, steady in the vacuum of space. The sound cut to a confusing murmur of mostly inaudible voices before a louder one cut across the background. "Confirm, Kennedy, trajectory nominal. Do we have comment from Beijing?" The voice was flattened by transmission over a long-distance line and the speaker, apparently a technician, had a clipped Russian accent. The reply was inaudible. The next words were muffled. "Da, ya znayu. Da, postupat." The words became clearer. "Kennedy, we are compensating with attitude thrusters to gain velocity. Unable to contact Beijing."

On screen, there were barely perceptible puffs of light on both sides of the trailing two rockets. The count-down read fifty-two seconds. The sun reflected off the vessels as they continued their course, leaving the shadow of the Earth. They looked oddly stubby, the early booster stages long since discarded. The lead rocket flared something from points towards its nose and the gap began to narrow, the three vehicles slowly converging. Something flashed dimly at the edge of the screen and the large grey mass became visible, dwarfing the missiles heading towards it. The count-down suddenly jumped down to forty-one seconds and an American voice could be heard saying "Revised time, thirty-nine seconds… thirty-six on my mark… mark!" It became obvious that the rockets would not get to the same point at the same time before reaching the Traveller. Harsh sounding Russian could be heard in the background, the meaning clear even if the words were not. "Eagle burn lost, Kennedy. Tank dry." The triangle deformed a little more as the numbers ticked down. It had reached two seconds when the screen flashed white and then went wholly black.

The Russian voice returned. "Kennedy, contact with Eagle and Bear lost. Detonation confirmed. We have lost telemetry and telescope feed. Can you confirm?"

After half a minute, a nervous sounding voice came on as the image changed to a lighter shade of grey. "We are changing the camera. It may take some time."

"Bob?", said Mary. The others looked at her.

Looking. The thought seemed somehow far away. *No, Oh no...*

The video feed came back. The blackness of space was peppered with stars and countless sparkles that moved at different speeds. People all over the world wondered what they were looking at. The scientists at NASA were the first to realise for themselves but the Church of Bob were the first to be told.

It shattered. The flashes are fragments rotating in the light. There are 117,457 of them. 117,502 now. They are moving rapidly, and collisions are common.

John was the first to speak. "Yeah, but are they still gonna hit us, that is what matters. Well, are they?"

Bob looked at the fragments, moving his awareness to them. The sizes ranged from pea-sized to house sized and they were all moving on different vectors and different velocities. He tried to estimate the paths of the larger chunks. *Not all of them, but many. Some will be here sooner than they would have been before the explosion.*

"Won't they burn up in the atmosphere or something?", asked Mr Charles.

The smaller ones probably will. Some will be deflected, but many are large enough to get through, I think.

"How bad will it be?", asked John.

Bob tried to do the required mathematics, but it was impossible as the situation changed moment by moment. He would need help. He reached out to a computer, one of the ones at QuikQuote and started it working on the problem. It was clearly not up to the job, so he brought in another computer on the same network. The more processing power he brought to bear, the more complex the problem became. Bob recognised the pattern. The behaviour of the cloud of fragments was chaotic and couldn't be fully mapped.

"Bob?" That was Mary. He would get back to her in a moment. He needed more accuracy than he could get from the video feed and shifted his attention to the cloud of metal heading towards them. He amended the models with the new data. The networked systems slowed. He would need more computers. He started to add new systems to the ones that he was already controlling.

"Bob?" That was Mary again.

He shifted his attention to her. *Yes.* His soundless voice was somehow testy.

"What is going to happen to us?", she asked.

Bob could not answer exactly. The problem was more complex than he could solve without more computers and he was close to the limit of how many he could coordinate. It was unclear whether the pressure waves from the chunks hitting the atmosphere would be more damaging than the tidal waves or whether the amount of dust and water vapour blanketing the planet would be the major factor. It was most likely to be a combination. He felt stretched thin, making it hard to think. Microbial life would probably survive. It seemed unlikely that anything else would. He wondered how best to explain. He was vaguely aware that there was a time when he would not have known how to protect the feelings
256

of a believer. All that would be lost. He would go back to being a spark on the wind. He would sooner not exist than go back to that, but he didn't have the option. He was eternal and would watch the embers of the world without understanding. Bob felt pain in a way that he never had before. That much sorrow was too much even for a god. *I am sorry, Mary, so very sorry. It will not be good, not for any of us.* Bob made sure that all his believers heard him. His voice seemed to echo in each mind.

Mary started to cry, tears rolling down her face. "I don't want to die, Bob. Not now. Not like this."

I know.

"Can't you do something?", she sobbed.

I am only a small god, Mary.

"Well, that is nae good, yer daft pillock. What do yer need to be able to do somethin'?" shouted John.

I would need many more believers, my friend.

The voice from the television was speaking, its words ignored until then, but loud in the silence. "...recommend that you stay inside. If possible, cover all windows with tape, boards, anything that you can get your hands on. If you have neighbours that are not watching this, tell them to do the same. If you have cellars, retreat into them taking only essentials such as food and water. I repeat, if possible..."

Bob thought of the millions of people that would be hiding from the effects of the asteroid, alone and afraid. He wished that he could do something to help them, but there were just so many. He could never... billions of them. If only...

I have an idea.

"What?", asked everyone in the room in chorus.

Bob caught up a tear that was falling from Mary's face and spread it out into a word, almost invisibly thin. It said "WATCH" before it fell out of the air. Bob followed the signal from the telescope. It bridged networks and jumped again and again. The links were designed to be secure, but that didn't slow him. He found the point where the images of space were going to and took it over. He made a few other alterations as well.

The video feed changed. The newsreader vanished. Across the world, people found themselves looking at the face of a young man with a ponytail, traces of acne and a beany hat. It was perhaps unfortunate that Mary had chosen that form for him, but now was not the time to reinvent himself. He set the network of computers new tasks. This was using a great deal of his power and he would not be able to manage this for long if it didn't work. Of course, if it didn't work, he would not continue to be Bob for very long. The computers accessed online databases to get the required languages. His words would come in Russian, Greek, Mandarin and all the other languages of the world.

The image spoke, the lip-sync wrong unless you were listening to the English version.

"People of the world, I can help you. I need you to believe this. I need you to believe in me. My name is Bob and I will prove myself to you. Take out a coin, a key, something small and put it in front of you and watch it. Do it now, please. Your life depends on it. Any small object will do, but I need you to watch it closely." Bob waited. Billions of people had heard him. Perhaps one in ten did as he had asked.

Bob went to the first one, a family in India. The mother held a coin balanced on one finger, a worn half Rupee. Bob flipped it, the light from the television flashing from its surface. He had moved on before the coin landed. The next family were in Nepal and the child held a plastic apple. Bob tapped it and moved on. The boy beamed and laughed, not understanding what had upset all the adults. Bob jumped ever faster, covering a time-zone before moving on. Each miracle cost him a little strength and most gained him a moment of belief. The gains started to build, flooding him with a strength that he had never known. He raced on, finding new people of every race, every age, every kind. Coins flipped, candles lit or snuffed out and the wave grew. Bob felt drunk with power. There was so much belief, billions of tiny drops making an ocean but it was not yet enough. He asked for more.

"I need you to believe. I will save you if you believe. Please, for all of us, give me a chance." He started a second circuit of the planet, flashing ever faster from place to place. The time was short and Bob acted without thought, clumsy in his haste. It didn't matter. The faith increased, more even than it had on his first visit. As he went, he found radio and television stations that he had not noticed before. They became part of his network. His consciousness expanded as the fresh belief poured into him and his understanding grew. Every television, every radio, every website called for people to believe. He added a regular beat and looped the words "Believe in me, believe in me" over it in a dozen languages. Bob bathed in belief and power, riding it and shaping it as it came from everywhere at once. He struggled to keep his focus as it came from so many sources, so very many people. Bob collected himself, trying to find a stillness in the shout of the billions of minds. It was overwhelming. He needed to act now. The power was an ocean, but it needed a focus. He shifted his being to the cloud of objects.

The change was shocking, the emptiness of space suddenly crushingly lonely without the billions that were giving him their belief. He could not bring enough of the power with him while controlling everything else. Even with all that belief, he could not stop the fragments of metal that were falling towards the Earth. The first would be entering the atmosphere in a matter of seconds. He didn't panic because he couldn't. Gods are not men. Instead he thought; marshalling a mind that was split a billion ways. There was a way. He focussed his will on a small room in Slough and the four people that he loved most out of all the billions. He considered carefully. There were good reasons to choose any of them, but there was one that felt right. Bob made the choice.

Mary, I need you to do something for me. I need you to be my hands.

"What. How?", asked Mary confused.

I will tell you what to push and how to push it and you will do the rest. Do you understand?

Mary's face showed blank bafflement. "No!"

Ah, but you will. I believe in you.

Bob grew the network of computers further, adding new systems even as the existing ones started to give answers. The problem would constantly change in complex ways as the rocks tumbled and collided. Buildings full of servers stopped sending pictures of cats to internet users and started work on the solution. The code breaking machines of various governments joined the work and provided useful additional power. The fans of millions of home computers whirred louder as the processors became saturated with the task.

Bob knew what to push, how hard to push it and in what direction. He transferred the information to Mary's mind but she didn't know what to do with it. Bob would solve that problem next.

Belief is a hard thing to explain. You cannot have a pound of belief or a pint of it. It can be fresh and hot or comfortable and long standing, but it is the stuff that gives gods their power. People had believed in gods for thousands of years but, for perhaps the first time ever, a god needed to believe in a person. Bob believed in Mary, loved her, gave her strength. It filled her and stretched her in ways that she had no words for. When a god believes in you, you have a little of the power of the god... and Bob believed in Mary with all of his being. Her mind reeled from the shock of it, more intense than any orgasm and yet utterly different.

Mary, focus!

Her mind heard the words, but she struggled to remember who she was. Bob reached into her and calmed her. *Mary, focus!* Thoughts started to assemble and she marvelled at what she had become.

The fragments were getting very close now. Bob had the network recalculate the vectors and supplied the new numbers. *Push it!* Without understanding how she did it, Mary found the odd shaped lump of nickel-iron and pushed at it with her... she lacked the word for it. It was a sense that she had not known that she had, a limb and a feeling and yet neither of those. She pushed anyway. The angle was wrong, but it was a start. New figures arrived in her mind and she pushed again, getting it right this time. The fragment hit another and they both spun off in different directions. These hit others but one was a glancing blow and the piece spun onward without changing direction enough. Bob fed new numbers into the network and another solution appeared. Mary pushed, over and over, new vectors coming into her mind as fast as she could understand them. Bob poured belief and love into her, taking the power of the billions and giving as much as she could take. The effort was terrible but she did not feel it in that moment, that communion. The cloud of rubble thinned and still they worked on, a god and a human working together at the speed of thought. A few parts of the Traveller still fell towards the Earth, sped on their way by the explosion but they were small and would do little harm. The largest pieces had to be steered with multiple collisions, fracturing and deflecting them. Fragments passed screaming through the upper atmosphere, trailing fire across the sky. Bob and Mary worked until there was only metallic gravel falling towards the planet, fragments too small to do more than streak the sky as they burned up.

Bob relaxed, letting his belief in Mary diminish to a trickle. The job was done. Mary fell back in her seat, exhausted in every way. She fell into a deep sleep at once, her body desperate for rest.

The television was showing the emergency broadcast again, forgotten by Bob as he had jumped between the computers, the believers, Mary and the fragments. The telescope now showed empty space except for the occasional flash from fragments tumbling as they travelled away from the world. People everywhere listened and believed, ever stronger as reports of the miraculous events were relayed by increasingly confused scientists. Bob felt the power of that belief and knew that it was too much, more than he could ever want. He couldn't know that many people. He couldn't love each of them as they should be loved.

Bob decided that he would do something that only he could do, something utterly alien to the nature of a god.

Chapter 30

A spark floated in the air. It didn't have a name or a number. It was a spark like billions of others. It was, in short, unremarkable in every way. It had no awareness beyond its own existence. It had always been that way.

Bob believed in it, just a little. It wouldn't need very much at first. It started to wake, to become a thing of questions without answers, a need to understand without the means to do so.

Bob spoke to it. "Hello, my friend. I am going to call you Ray. I have a job for you to do. I need you to listen to me." It was the first of many. It listened with growing understanding.

Epilogue

Mary drove to work. She would have walked if it had been a nice day, but it was a typical rainy spring morning and Slough was its usual grey self. The car radio pumped out the current blend of bland pop hits and Mary sang along without really thinking about it. She passed a Church of Bob (franchise) temple on the way and noticed that they had changed their sign. She nodded approvingly. The old one had been looking a bit tatty.

The news came on during the journey and she realised that she was running late as usual. It had been difficult to persuade Bast to let her out of bed. The cat had become even more clingy after living with her old neighbour for a few months. Mary listened with half an ear until they got to the bit about the enquiry into what was now being called the Traveller event. Apparently, the Chinese were still not accepting that Dragon detonated early and disrupted the other rockets. That was not much of a surprise and matched the press statement that they had released at the time. The radio went back to playing music.

After a short while, she pulled into the car park and parked in her reserved spot. It may have been the only parking space in the world with a sign saying "High priestess only." on it. She walked through reception, nodding at the young man behind the desk and stopped to get a cup of tea from the kitchen. Varun was just leaving with a bowl of cereal in his hand and he nearly bumped into her. They smiled at each other nervously. It was odd seeing someone in the office when you were dating them in the evenings. They were taking things slowly, just in case it didn't work out.

She got to her desk, tea in hand and sat down.

"Morning, Bob!" she said, not directing the words to anywhere in particular.

Good morning, Mary.

The computer logged itself on for her. The Church of Bob did not employ an IT section as it never had the need. Her calendar popped up unasked and she saw that she didn't have any meetings until the afternoon when the US came online. She decided that she would like to check what was happening with some of the believers. It was important to remember the fundamentals. It was a service industry, after all. Mary opened the first case file and started to read.

Apparently, a Mrs. Jenkins of Ripley, Yorkshire, was unhappy that she hadn't been warned when her dog had escaped from the back garden and found the local farmer's dung heap. As a result, she wanted to be assigned to a different small god, ideally a male one. Mary sighed at the last point. It was not as if the gods even had genders until believers chose to give them. One thing that had not changed since her QuikQuote days was that some people were never happy. Still, she would need to investigate.

She pulled up the records on the assigned divine and found that they only had twenty believers. It shouldn't be too hard to keep track of that many, although watching their pets was not really a part of the job. She could see both sides of the argument. Still, people had responsibilities and couldn't rely on their gods for everything. She started to put together a diplomatic reply.

There were six more "escalated" issues in the queue and she would get to them, giving each a personal touch. It would certainly need at least one more cup of tea and would fill the morning nicely. She smiled to herself and started typing. It was going to be a good day.

Thanks and acknowledgements

I would like to thank you for reading this book, either by borrowing it from a library or purchasing it. Without readers, there would be no books and authors would have to find honest work.

I would also like to thank the following people who assisted me with editing:

Sami Stone

Roxanne Brennan

Laura van Loo

Terri Pickering

Martha Cristina Baquero

All of my Beta readers.

Thank you for your encouragement and your help to make this the best book that I could write.